# ZERO DAY GHOST

## Scott Olson

# THE CAR

THE COLLECTIVE'S counterattack is a gut punch. Their botnet swats Emily's viruses like so many flies and then crashes her servers in retaliation. When it's over, she stares at her laptop screen, unable to accept the totality of her defeat. How did her old hacker comrades detect her presence? And now that they've beaten her, what will she tell NSA senior management?

She places the laptop on her mother's nightstand and puts her head in her hands, struggling to hold back the tears.

"Having work troubles, spy girl?" says a tremulous voice.

Emily looks up. Her mother, Audrey, is awake, her bald head propped on a stack of pillows.

"I lost a fight with a botnet," Emily admits.

"You were fighting robots?" Audrey says, her wispy eyebrows furling with confusion. "Were you playing computer games? I thought you were doing real work."

It is a game of sorts. Except losing means being fired. Or worse.

"Remember when your computer got that virus last Christmas?" Emily asks.

Audrey nods, her expression darkening.

"They stole my credit card number," she says, "and forced me to open a new checking account."

"Imagine if a million computers got infected," Emily continues. "Only, instead of attacking their hosts, these viruses just lived in the computers and stole some of their processing power."

"Like parasites?" Audrey asks.

"Exactly. And imagine those parasites worked together, like a little virus army, to attack Amazon or some other big website and bring it down. That army of cooperating parasites would be called a botnet."

"They'd be doing the Lord's work," her mother replies, "taking down the Amazon capitalist empire."

An extremely Audrey point of view—annoyingly simplistic and ideological.

"The botnet I'm fighting is attacking the government," Emily says. "It's trying to break into the Department of Defense."

"An even more righteous cause," her mother says, folding her arms.

"Except I work for the government now," Emily retorts, "and they specifically asked me to stop this attack. But I failed, and now I'm in trouble."

"Your heart isn't in it," Audrey says. "You're fighting for the wrong side."

Emily sighs. She didn't move here to argue politics; she's here to care for her ailing mother. She has to remember that. She puts her hand on Audrey's papery forehead and recoils in surprise. It's far too hot.

"You're supposed to be asleep right now," she says quietly, "and gaining some strength."

"The pain's worse," her mother admits.

Emily grabs the oxycodone and twists the cap, preparing to give Audrey another dose. Her mother places a bony hand on Emily's arm.

"No more dope."

"You need sleep."

"When I was practicing medicine," Audrey says, her dark eyes growing hard and earnest, "The patients would ask me for opioids. But I didn't want them to become victims of the pharmaceutical industry or get addicted to their evil poison. Handing out dope like oxycodone felt like a betrayal of the Hippocratic oath."

That's Audrey. Principled, even when it doesn't matter anymore.

"How about some tea then?" Emily suggests. "I have North Star oolong, and it's–"

"That overpriced stuff you got from Chinatown?" Audrey interjects, a little color returning to her cheeks. "Did my brother give you a taste for fancy tea?"

The honest answer is yes; she gained an appreciation for good tea during the lost years—when Audrey was in prison and Emily lived with Uncle Ip in Hong Kong. But as far as Audrey is concerned, any knowledge gained from Ip is worse than useless.

"North Star tastes better," Emily says, standing her ground, "and it doesn't cost much more."

"Just bring a tea bag," her mother says, "and quit putting on airs."

Audrey's frown signals that the matter is settled, so Emily ascends to the kitchen and obediently fills the teakettle. But her chest hardens like she's swallowed a boulder. Moving to San Francisco hasn't improved her relationship with her mother, but being far from the NSA has dramatically worsened her job prospects. The whole idea of coming back here, of working remotely and staying with Audrey during her final months, was a huge mistake.

*I'm on the fast track to unemployment*, she thinks, *which is the fast track back to prison.*

She takes a few deep breaths, places the teacups and teabags on the tray, then carries them toward the stairway.

Perhaps she can attempt one more cyber attack against The Collective before her probation ends. Perhaps she can still save her job. Perhaps the NSA won't claim she's violating her parole.

Before she can give her failing career any more thought, the floor lurches. Not a small tremor, like when a streetcar passes, nor an everyday shudder from an ocean breeze. The entire room shifts as if the house is on wheels, and an enormous thunderclap shakes every board and rafter, making the tray fly from her hands and sending her tumbling down the stairs, along with pill bottles and teacup shards.

*An earthquake!* she realizes. *A huge one!*

She struggles to her feet and dashes toward Audrey's door. Her poor mother is probably terrified by the upheaval, and Emily should let her know what's happening. But a dust cloud obscures her vision, and she stumbles over the buckled floor.

*Was the quake nearby? Is that why the damage is so bad?*

Audrey's door is twisted from its hinges; floating dust obscures the space beyond. Emily steps inside.

"Audrey?" she calls.

An inhuman growl rises from the void. She takes another step, and her spinning mind struggles to understand what she's seeing: a gleaming monster squats exactly where Audrey's bed used to be, stinking of ozone and an earthier scent she's afraid to identify. It's a car...with a chrome-colored body and opaque windows, and it's parked in her mother's bedroom, emitting a faint ticking sound like an overheated skillet. Its crumpled nose presses Audrey's headboard into the far wall, though the bed itself isn't visible. A puddle of dark liquid pools around the front tire.

"M-mom?" she calls again, peering below the car. The

space underneath is dark. Is her mother wedged into that gap? Could she still be alive?

The tires give an ear-piercing screech, and the car jumps backward. Emily recoils, her cold fear turning to boiling rage.

"You've pinned my mom under your car," she shouts. "Keep still until help arrives!"

As if in answer, all four tires spin in unison, and the car lurches again. An awful realization grips her: The driver is fleeing!

She pounds the charcoal-colored window with her fists.

"Stop moving!" she screams. "Hold still!"

*The cops*, she thinks. *I've got to call them!*

She digs through her pockets, searching for her phone. But it's on the nightstand by Audrey's bed. Or it was.

The car lunges again, leaping toward the chasm that, five minutes ago, was a smooth wall.

"Police!" she screams to nobody in particular.

A shard of wood, kicked by spinning tires, strikes her forehead. She raises her arms as more debris pummels her face and chest. The car howls as it forces its way through the jagged opening, bumps over the curb, and races down the street in a cloud of smoke.

Emily searches the obliterated space. Could Audrey be alive? Could she have survived those brutal tires and that gleaming bumper?

She reaches the far corner and gasps. Audrey is on the floor, wrapped in a red-stained sheet.

"Mom!" she says, cradling Audrey's limp body in her arms. She removes the sheet from her mother's head. Audrey's eyes are wide, and her mouth is open like she's about to scream. But there's no sound, no breath. Emily feels for a pulse. Her mother's heart is still.

Emily embraces the body as tears of confusion pour from her eyes. Did the driver lose control, or was this intentional?

An electric hum rises from outside. Beams of light play

along the wall. Shadows shift and intensify. The car is returning.

She struggles to her feet and drags Audrey's body toward the doorway. The car bursts into the room and rumbles over Audrey's splayed legs with a sickening crunch. It misses Emily's feet by mere inches, then slams into the far wall amid an avalanche of plaster. It reverses itself, races backward, then plunges through the hole and onto the street. It circles and then accelerates away, its tires screeching. Emily drags Audrey further from the destroyed bedroom and into the hallway as the sound of chirping tires fades into the distance. Soon the only noise is wind whistling through the hole in her mother's demolished wall. The car is gone before the cops, or anybody else, can stop it.

She looks at her mother's crumpled figure, then through the opening in the wall, trying to see past the fog. Why did this happen? And how? Hot tears trickle down her face. She gives her mother's doll-like body a final embrace, then lays it on the floor. Police sirens crescendo and go silent. Car doors slam. Footsteps approach.

Emily came back to San Francisco to care for Audrey and ensure she had a dignified ending to an otherwise chaotic life. Somehow, she failed to accomplish even that simple task. Can she put this right? How would that be possible?

# THE COPS

EMILY TAKES the seat in front of Lieutenant Navarro, whose coffee-colored eyes fix her with an inscrutable gaze. Behind the Lieutenant, a pink-faced man in a rumpled suit wedges himself into his chair. The Lieutenant doesn't introduce the man. She acts like he isn't there.

"There are a few details we need to clear up, Ms. Hernandez," the lady cop says in a nasal voice.

In the week since her mother's death, every encounter with the police has been relatively positive. They've been solicitous, even sympathetic. But this Navarro feels more like the cops of Emily's youth: haughty and not to be trusted.

*I'm cooperating,* she reminds herself, *because the Lieutenant is here to help me.*

"From your statement," the policewoman continues, "I couldn't determine where you were during the crash."

"It wasn't a crash," Emily blurts, her face tingling.

Less than sixty seconds into the meeting and she's picking a fight.

"What would you call it?" the woman asks coolly.

"A deliberate act," Emily replies. "The intention to harm."

The lieutenant's face is stony, but her birdlike eyes are quick and flitting.

"Fair enough," Navarro agrees. "Where were you during this deliberate act?"

"Walking down the stairs. The whole house shook, and I was knocked off my feet."

The policewoman jots another note and folds her hands."

"Did you proceed to the ground floor?"

Emily's arms tingle. She's been through this with at least four sets of cops.

"I l-looked into Mom's bedroom," she stammers. "The car filled the whole space."

"You approached it?"

Wasn't that the natural thing to do? It drove over her mother, after all. She swallows, forcing down the rising anger.

"The windows were dark," she says. "I couldn't see the driver."

"You tried the door?"

"There were no latches."

The pink man shifts in his chair, and the lieutenant frowns, jotting another note.

"Eyewitnesses report that the car was a Volkswagen Beetle. Are you saying it had no door handles? No way to open it?"

"It wasn't a Beetle," Emily replies, her cheeks warming, "nothing like you'd find at a dealership."

The big man looks up, meeting Emily's eyes for the first time. His irises are strangely washed out, an almost colorless gray.

"Multiple witnesses," he says in a rumbling voice, "identified the car as a late model Volkswagen. You're saying they're wrong?"

She looks between the two cops, uncertainty growing in her overstimulated brain.

"My neighbors have doorbell cams," she says. "Have you retrieved their surveillance video?"

The big man folds his arms and gives her an appraising look.

"We issued subpoenas," he mutters. "The data's missing."

For every neighbor? From every camera?

"Your neighbor lady," Navarro adds, consulting her notes. "Ms, uh, Chin, I believe, took video with her phone. That's gone too."

Emily glances between the two in disbelief. Did lightning fry every camera on the street? Did the car somehow wreck the local network cables?

"Were there people who had reason to harm your mother?" Navarro asks.

Emily stares, stunned. What do they know about Audrey?

"Everybody loved my mother," she lies.

*Except for me.*

The pink man leans forward, and the chair creaks under his shifting bulk.

"She was a member of the Oppressed People's Army of Liberation," he says. "Not exactly Mother Teresa."

"She was a doctor," Emily says firmly. "And, yes, some of her patients were fugitives or even terrorists, but…"

Her voice trails off. She sees her mother as she'd been in her prime, confident, defiant, and mercurial. Her eyes fill with tears.

"Where's your restroom?" she asks, rising from the chair.

"To the right, end of the hall."

Emily follows the lieutenant's directions, then stands at the sink, splashing water on her forehead and cheeks. She examines her reflection in the mirror. Her eyes are puffy, and her hair is disheveled. These cop questions make no sense. Would some geriatric enemy of the nearly defunct OPAL hold a grudge after all these years? Even if there was such a person, why would they hate Audrey? She wasn't a conventional OPAL soldier; she didn't participate in bombings or direct actions. She was a healer, a caregiver.

Emily retrieves a brush from her purse and pulls it through the knots and tangles in her hair, then applies a little lipstick, restoring her appearance to a semblance of normal. She retakes her seat in front of Lieutenant Navarro, keeping her features as neutral as possible. The policewoman's face seems, if anything, even stonier.

"You've been arrested twice," Navarro begins without preamble. "First, when you were a minor."

"I don't understand–" Emily begins, but Navarro interrupts.

"The arrest reports say you seriously injured a young man named Edward Wang."

Emily blinks, trying to collect her thoughts. What sort of interview is this?

"Eddie Wang tried to rape me," she says cautiously.

"You beat him with a baseball bat," the pink man says, a slight smile twisting the corner of his mouth. "You damaged his brain so bad that he had to go to special school."

Navarro glares at the man, who meets her gaze for a moment, then looks down at his notepad. The Lieutenant exhales, then continues.

"At the time of the incident," she says, "you were living alone, even though you were a minor. Is that true?"

Her mother was in Nepal, giving medical aid to the communist insurgency. Audrey was so wrapped up in her righteous cause that she didn't weigh the real-world risk of leaving a thirteen-year-old alone for six months. It's a sad story—part of the whole tragic history of her troublesome mother.

"I don't understand how that's relevant," Emily says, her mind buzzing with rising alarm.

"Your mother was ultimately convicted of child endangerment," Navarro says. "In the eyes of the government, she was responsible for what happened to Eddie Wang. So we're wondering whether he might hold a grudge."

"Ask him yourself," Emily says, folding her arms, "or his mother if you can find her."

The lieutenant's brown eyes, and the big man's gray ones, rest on her like two hyenas sizing up their prey. Navarro opens a folder. Emily grips the arms of her chair with sweaty palms.

"Your second arrest," the lieutenant continues, "was for computer fraud and abuse, a federal charge. You were convicted and sentenced to ten years but served only a few months. Your settlement with the DOJ is sealed. Can you tell us anything about that?"

Emily resists the urge to bolt for the door. She shouldn't have come without a lawyer.

"Why am I here?" she asks.

"To help us find the driver of that car," Navarro says with a shrug.

"And you think I know them?"

The policewoman fixes Emily with her sparrow's eyes, and her petite hands ball into fists.

"We know," Navarro says slowly, "that some kind of car, perhaps a Beetle, smashed into your mother's bedroom. On the way to that crime, it passed multiple surveillance cameras, but none recorded anything. It fled your block, evading all contact and observation by law enforcement. Then it just vanished."

"And nobody got the plates," the pink man adds unhelpfully.

The Lieutenant's face reddens, but she keeps her eyes locked on Emily.

"Forensics found paint fragments, tire tracks, and a piece of tail light," she continues. "Every scrap was aftermarket, nothing gave us a specific make or model. It was like somebody built a homemade car with a cloaking device."

The woman cop pauses, taking a trembling breath as if the facts are taunting her.

"The most bizarre cases usually leave a wide wake of evidence," she continues. "We get a crowd of witnesses and a station full of suspects. But here we have a brazen hit-and-run and barely a ripple."

"There is Ben Katz," the big man mutters.

"Yes," Navarro says with a sigh, "there is Katz."

Emily flinches, unable to hide her surprise at the incongruity of that name. Ben Katz? Her *co-worker?* The portly guy who lives 3000 miles from here?

"What does Ben have to do with this investigation?" she asks.

The big man stands, head rising until it nearly touches the ceiling—until his bulk fills the cramped office like an elephant in a phone booth. He strolls past Navarro's desk, stopping only when his tree-like legs are inches from Emily's shoulder. He peers down at her with a pained expression. Her arms crawl with discomfort.

"You and Katz are both employed by the NSA," he says. "That right?"

She meets the pale eyes, FBI eyes, she realizes.

"Yes," she says quietly.

"He your boyfriend?" he says in his rumbling voice.

She suppresses a shudder. Ben is a close friend, her best friend from work. But a lover? Yuk.

"We're assigned to the same project," she says, "and talk every day. But we're just friends, that's all."

The agent leans so close that his aftershave fills her nostrils with a medicinal scent.

"Do you know where Mr. Katz is now?

"How is this related to my mother?" she says, her pulse accelerating.

"He didn't show up for work the morning after her death," the pink man says. "Two days later, cops found his abandoned car near the Elizabeth marine terminal in New

Jersey. We sent people to his apartment. The place was ransacked."

Her heart vibrates in her ribcage. She takes a long breath, trying to calm it. Ben must be sick or traveling or something. Her boss, Mac, will know what's going on. She'll ask him tomorrow."

"I can't help you," she says weakly.

Navarro stands abruptly and holds out a business card. Apparently, the interview is over.

"If you do remember something," she says, "or if Mr. Katz contacts you, will you please call me?"

Emily takes the card hesitantly, unsure of what sort of commitment is attached to it.

"You don't believe my mother's death was a sideshow gone wrong?" she asks. "Or some drunken clown with a homemade sports car?"

Navarro's sparrow eyes peer deep into hers as if trying to extract a confession. The clock ticks on the wall. A drop of sweat trickles down Emily's back.

"There was nothing ordinary about your mother's death," the lady cop says finally. "Nothing at all."

# TWO WEEKS AGO

EMILY TOOK a seat at her kitchen workstation while the music of Tame Impala wafted from the Bluetooth speaker she placed next to Audrey's door. The sound was probably enough to stop her mother from eavesdropping, which was important because she couldn't take many more lectures about the NSA and its evil influence on humanity.

She donned her headset and queued the video. Her co-worker Ben Katz's crooked-toothed grin filled the glowing screen.

"Fellow human!" he boomed. "Are we resuming our inter-minable and redundant testing discussion?"

"Not you, too," she said wearily.

His bushy eyebrows rose in mock surprise.

"Are you implying I don't love testing?"

"I just got off the phone with Mac," she said.

Her boss had been more than a little unhappy with the pace of her progress. He'd even started mentioning the terms of her parole and other unsubtle hints.

"I have three weeks to get my attack working, or I'm fired."

"Ah," Ben said thoughtfully, "so it's true then."

"You knew?" she asked, a pang of hurt stabbing her chest.

Ben was her coworker, after all. Shouldn't he have warned her if her job was on the line?

"A few hours ago," he admitted, "I got this weird email from Amit Pradhan. It was sort of an ultimatum. He wanted a data dump about your project. I fed him some BS and got rid of him, but the whole interaction was creepy. And after those recent attacks on the defense department, I knew the higher-ups were impatient. I mean, your work finding Zahra *has* been a little slow of late, even by the NSA's bureaucratic standards."

Amit Pradhan: corporate climber and butt-kisser extraordinaire. Had he promised the higher-ups some magical solution? As if he knew the first thing about The Collective or the APRIL botnet? *Her* botnet?

"We only get one shot at this," she said, "and bumblers like Amit might cause more harm than doing nothing."

Ben smiled knowingly.

"Harm for the NSA?" he said. "Harm for your career? Or harm for Zahra?"

"Zahra betrayed me," Emily said hotly. "She's the reason I went to jail."

"May I ask a rather direct question?" Ben asked calmly, apparently unphased by her minor outburst.

Emily took a deep breath, slowing her spinning mind. What was Ben after today? What were they even talking about?

"Do you ask any other kind?" she said.

"What deal did you strike with the NSA?"

It was an odd and unusually probing question. Ben usually avoided questions about her criminal past or the way she'd come to the agency.

"Like, what kind of salary I negotiated?" she asked sarcastically. "Or how many vacation days I asked for?"

"I mean no disrespect," he said, "but the NSA leadership didn't pull crazy strings just to spring a former hacker from

jail, however cool and funny you might have been. They
wanted something in exchange for your freedom."

Why had he chosen now to discuss her sordid past? What
was his point?

"The Collective," she said, choosing her words carefully,
"was supremely skilled at eliminating competitors. As a
comrade in that group, I sabotaged, outed, or otherwise
harassed competing organizations whenever they threatened
to steal from the same fat target we were robbing, like when
the Russian Fancy Bears raided the Bank of Wisconsin, for
example. I doxxed their top hackers, they got sent to Russian
jail, and we kept 100% of the Wisconsin take. That was my
role for The Collective."

"Which explains why you're so knowledgeable about the
NSA's many enemies," he replied, "and why you've been
extremely effective in going after those smaller groups. But
Mac must have wanted more than the heads of a few Russian
hackers."

He'd wanted plenty: her cousin Kaylin's bank accounts,
for one, and proof of her ex-boyfriend Seymour's involvement, for another. But she'd bargained the NSA down to a
single, enormous act of betrayal.

"I promised Zahra," she admitted with a sigh.

Ben nodded, obviously unsurprised.

"This virus of yours," he continued softly, "is an indiscriminate weapon and potentially very damaging to Zahra.
And I assume it would also be damaging to other hackers in
her empire as well. You might wind up hurting lots of your
old friends."

Emily shrugged—the problem in a nutshell.

Her acknowledgment seemed to satisfy him. He smiled
brightly, amplifying his already uncanny resemblance to Jerry
Garcia.

"Does Mac understand your quandary?"

"He suspects."

Ben stroked his beard thoughtfully.

"Every talented hacker comes to the NSA with baggage. You can't learn the trade unless you dabble in the dark arts. And when we turn toward the light, we choose which facts to reveal about ourselves and which to leave buried. Is that a fair description of your conundrum?"

She nodded, surprised. He seemed to understand her situation *too* well. What kind of skeletons were in Ben's closet? Who was he hoping to protect from the NSA's probing spotlight?

"Given your family history," he continued, "as well as your former role in Zahra's collective, you probably have more baggage than most of us."

Again she nodded, holding back the tears. Nobody had ever summarized her quandary so clearly and with such empathy.

"So I'm guessing all your special tests have to do with letting those sleeping dogs lie," he said. "And your struggle is really about betraying only Zahra and nobody else. Is that right?"

She suppressed the urge to hug the screen. Ben always came through for her, even when she didn't ask him to.

"It's so hard to make sure my attack won't hurt the people who… who don't deserve Zahra's fate," she admitted.

"Have you considered a live trial?"

"The NSA network is monitored; the data will be there for anybody to see."

"And running your tests outside the sanctioned network is against the rules…" he said, letting his voice trail off.

She smiled. He was telling her that he would turn a blind eye to any private tests she might want to run. And he was right. Running those tests outside of the NSA network would be the quickest way to learn whether she could harvest Zahra's secrets while keeping her old friends out of harm's way.

"Do you think it's too obvious?" she said with renewed energy. "Will Mac or Director Chip realize I'm holding out on them? Will they be angry?"

"*Please*," Ben said scornfully. "Mac stole you away for the same reason that Zahra kept you close: because you're so damn useful. If anything, he should worry less about squeezing you for golden eggs and more about keeping you happy, healthy, and working for the good guys."

She nodded appreciatively but couldn't help wondering–why all this frankness? Was Ben giving her his trust? Or was this a debt to be repaid? Did it matter? If she wanted to disentangle herself from her criminal past while also protecting semi-innocent people like Kaylin and Seymour, then running a private test might be her only hope.

"Mac and Chip don't have as many options as they pretend," Ben continued. "So throw them a few bones and stay out of trouble. You'll be the analyst of the year."

Emily smiled and nodded her agreement. She hoped that Ben was right.

# CAN WE TALK?

MAC PARKS his car by the Severn River Marina and cuts the engine. The gravel lot is empty at this late hour, and the little pleasure boats are tied up and quiet. All this sneaking around may be a waste of time, but he'll be damned if he lets Director Chip or anybody else listen to his calls.

The encrypted VoIP application chirps. Emily joins him.

"Can we finally really talk?" she says, voice strained with emotion.

"I'm secure," he says softly.

Her breathing is audible and heavy as if she's finished a long run.

"It's been…" she pauses, then stifles a sob, "…a difficult week."

Needles of pain jab his heart. She's 3,000 miles away, and there's little he can do to help. This call will make things worse.

"The cops brought me in," she continues. "They had an FBI agent with them."

He's seen the report. The bureau assigned that lumbering ox Alfred Nelson, a man with no tact and even fewer brains.

"I'm a suspect," she adds.

Agent Nelson probably made that crystal clear through his bullying and belligerence.

"They're throwing darts," he says, "just seeing what sticks."

"He told me Ben disappeared," she continues, a note of accusation creeping into her voice. "I felt stupid not knowing."

"I wasn't allowed to talk about it," Mac replies pathetically.

"Wasn't… allowed?"

The lies are harder than he thought they'd be.

*It's for a good cause*, he tells himself, though he doubts that's true.

"Blockchain forensics show that Zahra moved five million worth of Ethereum the morning after your mom died," he says. "An hour later, security cameras recorded Ben leaving his apartment. Nobody's seen him since."

The security camera part is true; the crypto story is bull-shit. But since there are no coincidences in spycraft, Emily will draw the obvious, false conclusion.

"Ben has never been within a thousand miles of Zahra," she stammers. "He hated her, hated what she stood for."

Mac imagines Emily's intense hazel eyes burning with righteous anger.

"If Ben *does* work for Zahra," Mac continues, pressing the point, "then he certainly told her about your upcoming attack on her botnet. That car in your mother's bedroom was Zahra's payback."

Whether or not that's true, it's the story Director Chip wants Emily to believe. The one most likely to motivate her toward the desired action.

"We've got to find her before she strikes again," he continues. "Because next time, she might succeed."

"How can we find her?" Emily asks, her voice hushed, vulnerable.

They've arrived at the big ask. The request Chip has been pushing him to make ever since Emily joined the NSA three years ago.

"You've always maintained," Mac says slowly, "that you severed all contact with Zahra and The Collective."

"I have," she says softly.

"I've given you space to transition from criminal to legitimate government employee," he continues. "I've believed in you, and I still do. But people have questions about where your loyalties lie."

"They think I killed my mother?"

"Our leaders are imaginative when it comes to conspiracy. They believe you might still be working for Zahra and suspect the attack was a punishment to keep you in line. We've got to prove they're wrong."

"I'm trying!" she says, her voice rising in fear and desperation.

He sighs, pushing the self-loathing as far down as it will go, steeling himself to become an even bigger asshole.

"I'm not talking about hacking anymore, I'm talking about about human contact. We need your friends to help. We need them to lead us to Zahra."

"People… could get hurt," she says quietly. "People I love."

"Zahra forced you to choose," he says. "It's either the NSA or The Collective."

He might even believe that last part. After all, who besides Zahra would use such a brazen show of force? Who else would want Emily dead?

She says nothing for almost a minute. Her soft breathing is the only sign of her presence on the call.

"When it's done," she says finally, "can I come back to Fort Meade?"

He squeezes his eyes shut. If there's a place in hell for the weak-willed, self-serving, and manipulative, they're warming it up for him.

"We have to prove," he says, struggling to keep his voice calm and authoritative, "that you're part of the solution. That's how we salvage your career, Emily. And it's how we make space for you back here... with me."

# EVADING SURVEILLANCE

EMILY ENTERS the house and stops in front of her mother's bedroom door, now sealed under plastic sheeting. She pulls off a strip of duct tape and peels back the barrier. Cool air, smelling of motor oil, disinfectant, and death, wafts through the opening.

*I triggered this somehow,* she thinks, *through hubris, carelessness, or plain old incompetence, I brought death to my mother's house.*

"I'm sorry, Audrey," she whispers aloud.

The wind whistles through gaps in the damaged walls as if in answer. "You're always sorry," it says. "You're always sorry."

As she steps into Audrey's room, the stink of decay and disinfectant threatens to overwhelm her. She slows her breathing, keeps the bile down, and glances around the ruined space. Her mother's bed is shattered into matchsticks, and the headboard is buried in the plaster wall as if fired from a cannon. She closes her eyes, trying to block out the enormity of her failure. The memories rush in anyway.

She had followed her cousin Kaylin into Zahra's Collective, seduced by money and the chance to be part of an elite group. Their utopian vision and vast technical accomplishments made her feel powerful, even unstoppable. Yet her involvement with Zahra's gang ended in prison. Then she joined the NSA, and her hubris only grew. She rose through the ranks and became the youngest analyst ever to penetrate a foreign military's defenses. At the NSA, she was seen as a hardened cyber-criminal turned super-spy, the best example of the agency's new breed of hacker. Yet her desperation to cling to that success led her to make the dumbest mistake of her life: She listened to Ben and launched an attack from her mother's unsecured network. Her laptop became a homing beacon for whoever Zahra hired to kill her. Audrey paid the price.

She walks upstairs to the kitchen and looks out the window. A van crouches on the far side of the street, its plain white sides and tinted windows screaming "FBI surveillance." She should welcome their vigilance; they're probably protecting her from more attacks. Yet the sight of that stupid government vehicle makes her chest tighten, and her stomach churn. Is that big pink FBI agent out there right now? Is he peeping at her through his government-issued binoculars? Has he hidden listening devices in her home?

The old kitchen smells of cooking oil and boiled cabbage. It evokes memories of Audrey's terrible cooking, along with her numerous other failings as a mother—Emily's vision clouds with tears. Audrey didn't deserve to die, not like that.

She turns from the window and regards her shiny new laptop. Is Mac right? Was Zahra behind that attack? If so, why choose such a bizarre form of assassination? Why can't the cops find any evidence or suspects?

She opens the laptop, puts her hands on the keyboard, then visualizes the murderous car. It was sleeker than a Beetle. Its sides were smooth. It looked a bit like an egg or a small zeppelin. She types in some web searches: "Egg car," "Classic European car," and "Similar to Beetle."

Dozens of photos come back with captions like "Fiat 500,"

"Renault Dauphine," and "BMW Isetta." None look like the machine she saw three nights ago. She needs a rough sketch, like those facial composites that cops use. She downloads photos that resemble the car she saw, then imports them into a photo editor and uses a combination of layer masks and AI tools to merge them together. She submits her franken-photo to an image search. The results are even more disappointing: old Chevys, Volkswagens, and Citroens. Nothing like the futuristic machine she saw that night.

She sighs, examining her hand-crafted image. The proportions are right, and the body color matches her recollection, but the windows are wrong. The actual car had charcoal-colored glass. She employs the paint tool and colors her car's windows dark gray. Then she runs the search again. Old Studebakers, Toyotas, and a Burning Man mutant vehicle roll down the screen. But on the second page, a blurry photo catches her eye: an egg-shaped vehicle, smooth, silver-bodied, with narrow, dark windows. The caption reads: "WayGo prototype, Nov 2024".

Her heart races. The photo quality is poor, just a paparazzi shot, but there's no mistaking the lines and paint color. That's the machine that crushed her mother to death.

She stares at the caption: "WayGo."

A shiver runs up her back. Ben always says coincidences don't exist in Spycraft, that they're only relationships people don't yet understand.

"Seymour," she mutters quietly.

Her ex-boyfriend had supposedly left The Collective and found honest work. He'd taken a job with WayGo Self-Driving Vehicles in Mountain View. It seemed an odd choice at the time; Seymour was always more comfortable outside the conventional world. Was it just a cover? Had Zahra embedded him in WayGo for some purpose? And would Seymour have gotten mixed up in anything as heinous as using one of his cars as a murder weapon?

Her agreement with Mac, a condition of her release from prison, was to divulge any and all secrets about The Collective that would lead them to Zahra. And she's been as faithful to that promise as she could stand to be, violating it only to protect Kaylin, Seymour, and a few others. But telling Mac that a WayGo car killed Audrey would be like throwing Seymour to the dogs. The FBI would harass him, spy on him, and maybe finally link him to The Collective, something they've tried and failed to do for years. Or perhaps they would dig up his exploits with Antifa and Anonymous. And unlike her, Seymour would never cut any deals to save his skin. He'd just rot in prison.

She sighs. She won't betray Seymour to that fate. Not yet, anyway. But she needs some answers: Why did he join WayGo? What connections does he maintain with The Collective? And does he realize that one of his self-driving cars went missing?

She shudders at the thought of contacting him. Things ended messily, and his opinion of her only worsened after she betrayed The Collective. He won't agree to see her willingly.

She parts the curtains. The FBI van is still there. She has to escape their surveillance, has to ensure those gumshoes don't hear her conversation with Seymour. She sighs. Half a lifetime ago, she evaded children's services by slipping through the rotting fence between her mother's backyard and Ms. Liu's yard. Could that work again? How closely is that big pink FBI agent watching?

She packs a few belongings and creeps out the back. The weeds in her mother's yard are tall from neglect, and the air is damp and dense with fog. She dislodges a dry-rotted board from Ms. Liu's fence and slips into the old woman's yard. She eyes the darkened house for signs of life, then stumbles into a neglected rose bush that viciously scratches her face and arms before she's able to disentangle herself. Once free, she passes through Ms. Liu's rusted gate and manages to hop aboard one of the last streetcars of the evening. As she watches the darkened shops and restaurants roll by, she collects her thoughts. Seymour is many things, but a good liar isn't one of them. If she confronts him with facts, he won't hide what he knows. Yet she prays that he knows absolutely nothing. It would be heartbreaking to learn that he helped Zahra, even indirectly, to murder Audrey.

The streetcar rumbles and bumps on its way downtown. She'll catch the interurban Caltrain to Mountain View, then walk to Seymour's house. It's a bit of a crazy plan, yet it's also the plan Mac asked her to follow: she's exploiting her old criminal contacts to get intel she can't gather through any other means. She just hopes this desperate move won't snare Seymour in her mess as well.

# MOUNTAIN VIEW

EMILY DISEMBARKS at the Mountain View CalTrain station, which is little more than a forlorn slab of concrete. Five other passengers get off with her, then quickly disperse, leaving her alone on the platform. What will Mac do when he realizes she evaded FBI surveillance? Will the intel she gathers make up for the trouble she's causing?

She strides down the darkened street, past closed shops, and toward the quiet neighborhoods beyond. She reflexively reaches for her phone, planning to consult the map, then stops cold…she left it at home in case the feds were tracking it. She wanted them to believe she was being a good little suspect but forgot that she might need the phone for navigation.

A cool breeze blows from the west, and the scratches on her face sting in protest. She probes the oozing surface of the deepest cut and winces. Ms. Liu's rose bushes were nasty, and she must look like the Bride of Frankenstein. But the streets are dead quiet; there's nobody for her to scare. She peers into the shadows of the suburban maze that stretches before her. Although it's been a few years, she knows where Seymour lives. She'll find him without electronic help.

She makes a few wrong turns but manages to locate

Eichler Lane, Seymour's street. It's lined with mid-century homes, each sporting a manicured lawn as well as an Aston Martin or BMW in the carport. The houses are so uniform and perfect that she imagines every driveway has its own boy or girl bouncing an identical red rubber ball, like the children on the planet Camazotz.

Seymour's house is precisely as conformist as all the rest, except for the decrepit VW bus parked or perhaps abandoned, in his driveway. This wreck, which he nicknamed "Nemo," is covered with rust and surrounded by a prodigious oil slick. The bus symbolizes Seymour's superficial rebellion, his attempt to distinguish himself from the tech elite surrounding him. As she approaches it, the familiar scent of gasoline and mouse droppings takes her back to their road trips together. They visited Santa Cruz, Death Valley, and the Sierra Nevadas. At night they snuggled in the back, warm and safe under a mountain of blankets, unaware of how fleeting the good times would be.

She approaches his teal front door, which is illuminated by soft ground lighting. But as she presses the doorbell, foreboding takes hold. Is the FBI following her? Did she lead them here?

The latch gives a clack, the door swings back a few inches, and a chestnut face peeks out. Seymour's curly hair is disheveled and somewhat longer than she remembers.

"May I help you?" he asks.

When she steps into the light, his eyes first widen, then narrow as they settle on her scratched face.

"Have you been skateboarding again?" he says.

A car rumbles past, making her start with fear. Is it the cops?

"Can I come in?" she blurts.

He stares, his expression unreadable in the dim light.

"Not necessarily."

Why did she think this would be easy?

"We need to talk," she continues, shifting her weight from one foot to the other.

He frowns.

"About?"

A second car glides past, its electric motor whirring in the night air. Why are so many vehicles cruising around right now? Are government agents circling the block? Are they closing in?

"About what a jerk you are!" she shouts and throws herself through the partly closed door. She topples him backward and lands on him, staring into his wide eyes.

"And about WayGo," she adds.

His brow furrows with apparent confusion.

"We aren't hiring."

"I want to talk about *problems* at WayGo," she clarifies.

"Then, by all means, come in," he says, pushing her off him.

They scramble to their feet, and he leads her to a vast living room furnished with a ratty couch, a battered coffee table, and a low bookshelf. The far wall is adorned with two tall flags: one red and the other black—the symbols of Antifa.

"You haven't remodeled," she observes.

"Your face looks like you wrestled a porcupine," he says in reply.

She reflexively touches the deepest scratch, which stings in protest.

"It's been a bad week."

"Water?" he asks, motioning toward the kitchen, "or a cup of tea? You always liked tea when you were upset."

"Water's fine."

He returns with two glasses and takes a seat on the couch. She accepts the offered glass and sits next to him.

"What's it like working for an over-capitalized startup?" she asks. "Are you still solving the world's most boring task?"

"I mentioned that we don't have any job openings," he says, his dark eyes wary.

She sighs. Small talk is useless in this situation. She'd better cut to the chase.

"My mom's dead."

The words rest on her heart like lead weights. She hasn't said them aloud before.

"I'm so sorry," he says softly.

An oversized black and white clock shows that it's nearly one in the morning. How did it get so late?

"A car drove through the wall," she says, struggling to push through the words, "and crushed her."

"Did they arrest the driver?"

"No driver," she says, looking at him intently.

Confusion, then recognition, plays across his face.

"A driverless car?"

She pulls her laptop from her backpack and opens the photo she found.

"Ever seen one of these?"

He stares at the glowing image, and his expression darkens.

"A WayGo M64."

"Do you know how it ended up in my mom's bedroom?"

His eyes dart briefly around the room, then he jumps to his feet, switches off the lights, and peers out the window.

"Are your agents here?" he asks. "Is this a bust?"

She breathes deeply, quieting her churning stomach.

"I'm not here in an official capacity."

He stalks along the wall like a cornered cat.

"Did the NSA hack one of our cars?"

"I pissed The Collective off, and they sent a WayGo in retaliation," she says.

"The Collective?" he repeats in disbelief.

"I infected APRIL with a virus," she adds softly.

"You pwned their botnet?"

"Tried to."

"Even if that's true," he says, massaging his temples, "they wouldn't –"

"One of your cars appeared less than two hours later," she says, interrupting him. "They used my laptop as a homing beacon. I stupidly left it next to Mom's bed."

"The Collective may have noticed you messing with them," he says, his voice rising, "but they did *not* send one of my cars to your house. Zahra would not physically harm anybody."

Emily's face burns. Now she's on her feet as well.

"She took ten times the cut of any other comrade. And when she thought I was challenging her, she sold me out to the FBI."

"That makes her a murderer?"

"If she didn't send that WayGo, then who did? You?"

"You're forgetting the whole story," he says, folding his arms. "Like when she bailed you out of your financial troubles. Your mom wouldn't even have a house if Zahra hadn't rescued you."

"And you're forgetting how she lied, cheated, and stole. Not just from our enemies but from the rest of us too."

"Do you know what it's like to risk everything for a cause you believe in?" he says, his voice rising.

He's just baiting her now, restarting old fights.

"Because she loved us, Emily," he continues, "and she risked everything for us."

"She was greedy, self-serving, and double-dealing. She exploited our minds to enrich herself."

He stares with those hard, brown eyes.

"I won't help the NSA, and I won't destroy Zahra."

How easily they fall into these familiar patterns. It's why Seymour wasn't compatible with her new life, why they had to split.

"I'm not here as an NSA employee," she repeats—though that's not strictly true.

"But based on your flimsy story," he says, "I'm supposed to help you find Zahra? Should I sell out your cousin Kaylin while I'm at it? Because if Zahra's involved, then Kay is too."

"I'm asking you to prove whether I'm crazy or sane. If I'm crazy, you'll have wasted just a few hours of your time. If I'm sane, you'll save your company from whatever trouble The Collective is bringing you."

He shakes his head.

"Even if I accept that international hackers compromised my company, there would be the little matter of the car itself. The M64 prototypes were built like tanks, but they can't just stray fifty miles north, trash your house, and come home without anybody noticing."

She pulls a scrap of paper from her bag, scribbles her secure messaging ID, and holds it out to him.

"That's exactly what happened," she says. "So figure out how and why, then let me know."

He puts his hands in his pockets.

"Not interested."

She balls up the paper and throws it at his feet. His scowl deepens.

"You've never called or texted," he says, voice quivering. "Not once in three years. I didn't know if you were okay, or how life was treating you, or what you were doing in your self-imposed exile."

"It was the life I wanted."

"And now you show up on my doorstep," he continues, "and accuse me of being an accessory to murder. Then you demand that I help you betray Kay and Zahra!"

There's too much scar tissue here, too many hard feelings to overcome. She'll have to face this disaster alone… somehow.

She grabs her backpack and walks to the door, pausing at the threshold.

"Either Zahra's a murderer," she says, "or she's in deep shit. And it has something to do with WayGo. I just thought you should know."

She steps outside and slams the door behind her. Nemo stares at her with its doleful chrome-rimmed headlights.

"I needed to make a clean break," she says to the car, "I was being fair to both of us."

Nemo doesn't honor this excuse with an answer. She stomps past it and into the night.

She shouldn't have come here. Shouldn't have assumed Seymour would listen to anything she had to say. The whole interaction was overwhelmed by their history and by how much he hates her life choices. She'll have to find another way to reach Zahra. She'll have to do this on her own.

# COFFEE SHOP

EMILY RUBS her sleep-deprived eyes and looks through the coffee shop window. The orange glow of the rising sun encroaches on a sapphire sky. The trains are running by now; she can go home if she wants. She touches the scratch on her face and shudders. Was yesterday just a bad dream?

She orders another latte, dreading her next visit to the shop's disgusting restroom. As she sips it, a young man in chocolate-colored slacks and orange sneakers plops down next to her. His hair is impeccable, extensive, and stylish. He can't be an engineer... probably not even a founder. A sales drone, maybe? A marketing man? She risks a second glance. He's studying his laptop, eyes intent, handsome olive skin shining in the morning sun. He's the sort of polished Harvard or Stanford grad who circles the valley like a shark, scenting fresh money. She could have been like Seymour, chosen to swim with these venture-backed gold diggers. It wouldn't have been so very different from living inside Zahra's reality distortion field. Yet the tech titan's world is just as utopian, just as impractical, and just as intellectually dishonest as Zahra's, or her mother's for that matter.

She tears her eyes away from the man and focuses, once

again, on her active hack into the WayGo email servers. Thanks to the APRIL virus's widespread dominance and all the backdoors it has created for The Collective, getting access to WayGo was simplicity itself. She just leveraged one of their backdoors into the Microsoft Exchange email server and was soon perusing the entirety of the company's sensitive communication.

"You work for WayGo," a smooth voice says, interrupting her concentration.

She turns, startled. The venture-funded hipster is smiling at her, his whitened teeth iridescent in the dark shop. He nods toward her screen.

"Noticed the logo. We're looking to partner with you guys."

She gently closes her laptop, forcing a smile.

"I'm just a contractor. No stock options."

His smile fades.

"Such a great company," he says, picking up his cup, "they'll change how we think about mobility."

Or homicide, she thinks.

She moves to a corner booth and positions her laptop so the screen is hidden from the rest of the cafe. Four hours, six cups of coffee, and multiple restroom breaks later, sleep deprivation is causing her to flinch and see spots. But she's also learned something: Don't buy WayGo stock. Their cars have frequent fender benders, often stall in traffic, and sometimes deliver life-threatening shocks to the technicians. The sheer volume of communication about vehicle failures could take weeks to organize. And without Seymour's inside knowledge, it could take months to make sense of it all.

She rubs her sore eyes with the heels of her hands. The efforts of a lone wolf won't overtake Zahra or her legion of hackers. Only the NSA, utilizing its huge array of resources, stands a chance against this foe. The thought brings Ben to mind, his scraggly beard and glittering eyes lighthearted as always. Is he part of all this? Assuming she can somehow save her job, will he be there when she returns? If he doesn't come back, then who will be her sounding board? Who will tell the bad jokes?

She slams the laptop shut and heads out into the bright afternoon, sweating under the Silicon Valley sunshine, gathering her thoughts. The WayGo correspondence she's read is distressingly routine, even banal. And from what she's seen, Seymour's point seems true: Nobody, not even an insider, could realistically take a WayGo for a joy ride. The cars are tracked too carefully and in multiple redundant ways. Even The Collective, with all their technical prowess, couldn't realistically sneak one out without raising alarms.

She walks until she reaches the edge of the San Francisco Bay, folding her arms as she looks out over the brackish water that sparkles in the late afternoon sun. She knows what she saw. A WayGo prototype found its own way to San Francisco, smashed into her mother's house, crushed the poor woman to death, and escaped into the night. Zahra, or another comrade in The Collective, converted an ordinary driverless car into a deadly weapon. But it will take months to navigate the labyrinth of WayGo systems and correspondence to reconstruct how they accomplished that deadly feat.

She sits on a park bench and opens her laptop. Her stomach is acidic, queasy from too much coffee, and her caffeine-encumbered hands tremble as she composes her note to Mac.

"I've found the car that killed my mother. It's an early self-driving prototype built by a company called 'WayGo.'"

She pauses. Does that sound insane? Would he chalk up her rambling to post-traumatic stress disorder? Would he think she's deranged? Or would he take her side?

She continues typing.

"I believe The Collective detected my attack and dispatched a WayGo prototype as a weapon..."

She closes her eyes.

Mac will believe me, she thinks. He'll focus the full weight and attention of the US security apparatus onto WayGo.

She sighs, dropping her hands to her lap. Once the FBI moves in, they'll find the Seymour-Zahra connection, one the NSA has long suspected but never proven until now. And once they have Seymour in their sights, they'll dig up all his other activities, his unsavory leftist friends, his crimes of conscience. They'll gather the levers required to compel his cooperation, even if he has nothing to offer. And he'll know who did this to him, who brought so much sorrow to his life.

Tears roll down her face. She continues typing.

"If our analysts help the FBI to perform a deep and exhaustive investigation of the WayGo systems and records," she types, "I am certain they'll find artifacts and inconsistencies that explain how a WayGo car was controlled by my old comrades in The Collective."

She looks up from her screen to see a mother pushing a stroller and a young couple holding hands as they walk along the waterfront. How far will she go to get her life back? Will she betray Seymour, the quirky, infuriating man she used to love? Will she destroy his life to secure her own freedom?

A chirp from her laptop interrupts her thoughts. It's an incoming message...

```
From: alasbarricadas420
To: fuzzylogic666
Subject: That thing you asked me
about
Come back to my place tonight.
It will be worth your while.
```

She reads the note twice, her heart racing. Is Seymour

ready to talk? About what? Should she hold off on sending this note to Mac? Or is time too precious, the stakes too high? She stares at Seymour's note for several seconds, then, with a sigh, slowly closes her laptop. The NSA can wait one more day.

.

# HARD CONVERSATION

SEYMOUR OPENS THE DOOR, glancing around before meeting her gaze.

"Did you bring your pig friends?"

She shakes her head emphatically.

He motions her inside and leads her to the kitchen. Like the rest of his house, it's devoid of decorations or even appliances. Instead, a computer and oversized monitor rest on an otherwise empty kitchen table.

"Up all night?" she asks.

"You gotta see this," he says, pointing to a page on his screen titled "Status Report." It includes an image of a silver, egg-shaped car with windows the color of smoke. A chill runs down her back.

"That's prototype M64B build number 4," he says. "Soon to be retired, now that the D and X models are in pre-production."

"That's the car," she says softly.

He nods and points to another window on his screen. It contains a list of dates and events with descriptions like "Powered up" and "Moved to Garage 8". He points to the last event, dated February 17. The caption reads: "Fault: Communication Lost."

"The day mom died," she whispers.

"The car went offline," he says, "but nobody cared because it was scheduled to be demolished, and they figured fixing a junker was a waste of time. But I can't actually find the original demolition request. Nobody knows who wanted the car to be retired."

"Did somebody hack the request?"

"I wasn't ready to believe your crazy story based on that glitch alone," he says. "There was still the little question of how a prototype could have made the 40-mile trip from Mountain View to San Francisco without being spotted. But it was enough to spur me to keep digging. Then I found this error log."

He opens another document.

"It's the log from one of our car carriers, the big robot trucks we use to move our vehicles between sites. They're completely autonomous and licensed to operate along state-approved routes."

He summons another document titled "retrieval request" and highlights the dates and times at the bottom.

"The truck picked up prototype M64B-4 on February 17th at 4:30 PM, then carried it to our South San Francisco paint shop."

"South San Francisco is close to Mom's house."

He nods.

"The shop noticed the car was scheduled to be demolished the next day and figured the whole request was a mistake. They sent it away, and five minutes later, both the truck and car went offline."

"My God," she whispers.

"Dispatch sent a team to find the missing truck, but both vehicles came online on their own, and the search was canceled. The truck delivered M64B-4 to our Oakland demolition center just after 8 PM, and the team destroyed the car the next morning.

"So at six o'clock on Tuesday, February 17th," she says, her face growing hot, "a WayGo robot truck carried your prototype to within a few miles of mom's house?"

"Look at these notes," he says, pointing to another document.

She places a trembling hand on his shoulder and forces her wavering eyes to focus on the screen. The computer displays an interoffice memo:

```
From: WayGo Demolition Team,
Oakland Yard
To: Dispatcher
Subject: What a mess!
M64B-4 was already trashed when
it got here. What did you guys
do to it? Anyway, we demolished
what was left, as requested.
```

"The car smashed into Mom's house twice," she says softly. "It was crumpled and bashed when it finally left."

He shrugs.

"We built the M64 prototypes with extra heavy bodies to withstand our rigorous test schedule. But even so, I'm amazed it was still operating by the end."

"Is there anything left of it?"

"A block of compressed steel on a slow boat to China."

"But you believe me, right? The coincidence is too big to ignore!"

He says nothing and continues to stare at his screen.

She pulls out her own laptop and shows him her day's work: the email and other data she stole from WayGo.

"Does this stuff look familiar?" she says.

"What the hell?"

"Your servers are totally compromised, Seymour. Apache, Outlook, and a dozen other systems are owned by The Collective. WayGo is Zahra's bitch."

He folds his arms and sets his jaw like a pouting child. And suddenly, she sees it: something that should have been obvious from the start.

"You already knew The Collective owns WayGo," she says quietly. "You probably helped them."

There's no other reason the company could be so completely ransacked; no other way Seymour would have missed all the signs.

"You left us," he says after a pause. "You left *me*."

"And Zahra filled the gap?"

"It wasn't like that," he says, staring at the floor.

"She promised you a new adventure, right? You could be a tech bro and a radical revolutionary at the same time. Was that the deal?"

"That's always the deal!" he says defensively. "The same one you signed up for. Do good for The Collective, and make money for yourself!"

"I'm not judging," she says, "But what could Zahra give you that you didn't already have? Money? Freedom? Tech?"

"After I worked at WayGo for a while, I found the whole corporate tech scene too soul-crushing. So I started helping the Cyber Army in my free time."

From her work at the NSA, Emily is slightly familiar with the Cyber Army. A group of small-time anarchists that specialize in stealing money and secrets from right-leaning politicians they consider too reactionary.

"But they're total amateurs compared to The Collective," he continues. "Not one-tenth the mojo."

Unlike The Collective, the Cyber Army is not a money-making venture. Hence the group's more limited resources.

"Zahra and Kaylin approached me with an offer. I could occasionally borrow the APRIL botnet and task it with Cyber Army missions…within reason, of course. In exchange, I agreed to help them with their latest project."

"Zahra loaned you the keys to APRIL?" Emily says, awed.

The same gullible idealogue. The same Seymour she loved. The same Seymour she could never quite trust.

"What did they want in return?"

He walks to the kitchen window, hands in his pockets.

"I've already admitted too much," he says. "Enough to screw myself and all other comrades forever."

"You gave them your cars, which they used to kill my mom," she says, trembling with unexpected anger. "What else compares to that?"

He sighs, staring at the sink for several seconds before turning to face her.

"I built them a new language model," he says. "I gave APRIL the power to watch for trouble."

"To watch for… what?"

"The collective has this great little scam of stealing computers. From Lenovo alone, they take nearly one laptop in ten thousand. And they steal from plenty of others too."

She nods. She and Ben long suspected this was happening but hadn't gathered enough evidence to interest the FBI.

"The scam's simple enough," he continues. "Hack the package courier companies, reroute the occasional shipment, then flag the computer as "lost." Of course, eventually, the companies noticed the elevated levels of theft, and Lenovo built a firmware patch to make newly unboxed machines check to see if they were lost. Lost machines reported their GPS coordinates to the cops. The partners The Collective hired to retrieve the stolen merch started having people arrested. It was bad.

"An audacious scam," Emily says, not fully able to suppress her admiration.

"Rather than give up the revenue," he continues, "Zahra chose to enhance their target surveillance."

"With wiretaps?" Emily asks incredulously. "Double agents?"

"This is The Collective," he says with a smile, "which means the solution was pure geek."

"That's where you came in."

"I expanded the machine learning language models and elevated APRIL's ability to understand human correspondence."

"The botnet reads Lenovo's corporate email?"

"And text messages, and Word documents, and even phone conversations. It uses the intel to predict new anti-theft risks before they can harm Zahra's operation."

"Which makes stealing easy and convenient."

He scoffs.

"They'll keep expanding until APRIL watches everybody and steals a little of almost everything."

Which is why she fled Zahra and why Seymour should stay away. Because nothing is ever big enough or audacious enough for Zahra.

"So you're still in contact with them? You know how to reach them?"

"I won't help you trash The Collective," he says with a shake of his head.

"Because my mother's death was an acceptable murder?" she says, her anger growing. " Just the cost of doing business?"

He meets her gaze, his large eyes drooping and bloodshot. He looks as tired as she feels.

"The Collective cut me off from all secure chats, messages, and encrypted email," he says. "They just went dark."

"So you pissed them off too?"

He shrugs.

"Maybe I declined too many of their gig requests. Maybe they decided I wasn't reliable or useful enough. All I know for sure is that four months ago, they quit responding."

She slumps into a nearby chair. For just a moment, it felt like she was getting somewhere. Now it's another dead end.

"I just wish I could ask Zahra why," she says. "Why did she feel the need to kill me? How would that help her?"

He sits down beside her and heaves a sigh.

"My last gig for them was hardening APRIL's command and control. Minor stuff, really. Kaylin worked with me on it."

It's not surprising that his last gig was with Kaylin. Emily's cousin was always partial to Seymour. Not in a sexual way, Zahra fulfilled that side of Kay's life. No, her partiality to Seymour was about style—their minds just worked alike. Kay always said that Seymour made every problem seem trivial.

"So even though the others cut you off, you maintained contact with Kay?"

It hurts a little to know that Seymour still has contact with her cousin. Emily herself hasn't heard from Kaylin in years.

He shakes his head.

"She cut me off as completely as the others did. But prior to that break, I was helping her test a new onion router, something to obscure APRIL node locations. In the course of our work, I accidentally discovered Kaylin's physical address.

"Did you admit that to her?"

"I kept it to myself. You know how squirrely she can be."

"Is that why they cut off contact with you? Did they realize you had Kay's address and figured you'd gone turncoat?"

*Just like I did?* She doesn't add.

"Possible," he says with a shrug.

"But you have her address?"

"More or less."

"And you'll share it with me?"

He gives her a long look, dark eyes serious.

"The knowledge would be for you alone," he says. "You can't give it to your pig bosses."

"Is Kay still in Hong Kong?"

He nods.

Such a long trip, and Kaylin might not even reveal anything useful. She might refuse even to speak with Emily. Still, Mac did ask her to forget about her hacking skills and to use her human contacts instead. What closer contact does she have than her own cousin?

"I'll go to Hong Kong myself," she says, "and I won't tell the NSA anything."

# FLIGHT

EMILY TUGS the handbrake and switches off the ignition. Nemo gives a last gurgling shudder and grows quiet. She wipes the sweat from her burning forehead and opens the door. Throngs of day-tripping tourists amble past, laden with shopping bags and the occasional ridiculous mariachi hat. She tries to lock the door, fumbling with Seymour's key, but the ancient lock is frozen. A quick survey of the interior shows nothing but drink cups and fast food bags, so she shoulders her pack and walks off. Hopefully, Nemo will be fine here, however long the trip might be.

She follows the herd to the San Ysidro border station. The border agent barely glances at her passport and impatiently waves her past. She leaves the facility and steps into the Tijuana afternoon sun which blazes like a prairie fire. She hails a taxi and hurries to the nearest mall, where she purchases a cheap suitcase and some travel clothes. She haggles with a shopkeeper, trading dollars for pesos without involving any pesky, and potentially monitored, currency exchange. Then she catches another cab to the airport and finds the AeroMexico ticketing desk.

"Round trip to Hong Kong, please," she asks the smiling agent, "for today if you have space."

"Your return date?" he asks politely.

"Friday," she says, forcing herself to match his smile.

His thick eyebrows raise. "A short visit?"

"Business. Wish I could skip it."

He nods absently and enters her itinerary into the computer. She has no firm return date but can't admit that without arousing suspicion. She hands over the pile of pesos as payment. Using cash should avoid yet another electronic breadcrumb.

"Passport, please," the agent says. She looks sadly at his outstretched hand. If only there were a way to avoid this step, she might stay off the radar entirely.

"Madame," the agent asks again, more firmly this time, "I will require a passport to complete the sale."

"She digs through her pack and hands him the little blue book with a sigh, watching as he holds it over a scanner. She hopes to get as far ahead of her electronic trail as possible, which means minimizing the digital artifacts she creates. At least this passport scan will go into an airline database rather than a government system. And since it's a foreign airline, the data might sit for days, even weeks, before NSA signal intelligence vacuums it up. By then, her business should be complete.

Four hours later, she's sitting in an Aero Mexico cattle car, wedged between a snoring man who must weigh at least 300 pounds and a teenager whose earphones are cranked to hearing-loss level.

This will be worth it, she reminds herself, if I find Zahra.

But it all depends on how pissed the agency, and Mac, will be when they figure out what she's done. Hopefully, the trip will be short, just a few days, and she'll be back with something useful before they even know she's gone.

She adjusts the overhead air vent to slow the cold gale blowing on her head. When that's not enough, she wraps herself with the complementary tissue paper blanket, closes her eyes, and struggles to ignore the music escaping from her neighbor's ear pods.

She considers her cousin Kaylin, with her worn cardigan and glasses perennially askew, the easygoing, smiling, optimist, prone to seeing the good in others. Yet even Kay was unforgiving the last time they spoke, the day Emily admitted she was switching sides.

"After everything Zahra's done for you," Kay told her, voice shaking with anger and disappointment, "and after all the trust we've put in you?"

"Zahra was supposed to meet the Lanza family," Emily replied, surprised and hurt by Kay's ferocious response. "But at the last minute, she volunteered me to go in her place. I got to meet the mobsters who, as it turns out, were cooperating with the FBI."

"She was needed in Hong Kong," her cousin shot back, a little too emphatically.

"It was a trap, Kay, and she knew it!"

"She was heartbroken," Kaylin says with her usual fervor. "She'd *never* sacrifice you."

Kaylin trusts. Emily, not so much.

———

SHE'S jolted awake as the wheels strike the tarmac. She opens the shade, marveling at the green mountains and glittering towers of this tiny, dense metropolis, the place she called home during her high school years, the years Audrey was in prison. She can't face Hong Kong alone or find her cousin Kaylin without help—at least not without creating a trail of evidence that the NSA and Chinese can easily follow. To move quietly, she needs untraceable money, an ID, and places to hide. And she knows only one person in post-colonial Hong Kong who can give her those things.

"Frank," she murmurs aloud.

Frank Ng, Uncle Ip's younger child and, after her Uncle's death, inheritor of the vast Ng empire. Frank didn't exactly get the job through primogeniture; Kaylin could have fought for the role, despite being a gay woman. But the odds were stacked against her, and she'd already decided that The Collective was more honorable and lucrative than a big, messy franchise in Hong Kong's waning triads. So Kay became an uber-hacker, Frank became Godfather of the Ng clan, and Emily took pains not to play favorites. Hopefully, Frank remembers that.

She gets through customs, snags a taxi to the New Territories, and travels to Frank's high-rise apartment building. As she rides the elevator to the penthouse level, she conjures a memory of her younger cousin: heavy-set, wide-faced, and smiling. He strongly resembles his late father, Ip, except that Frank always seems more world-weary, more burdened by the demands of power. Will he still feel like a brother to her? Or will their divergent choices have made them grow apart?

The elevator doors slide open, and she steps into an airy foyer containing a single bronze door. She rings the bell, and it opens abruptly. Frank stands there, more rotund than she remembers, dressed in a billowy shirt and wearing a wide grin on his fleshy face.

"Emily!" he says, grabbing her in a bear hug. His cologne only partially covers the smells of sweat, fried food, and hard liquor. Was he up all night?

He steps back, holding her at arm's length, eyes sweeping over her in an appraising fashion.

"You're all grown up!"

His Queen's English is more precise than she remembers, his Cantonese accent more subtle.

"I was about to eat a little breakfast," he continues, motioning her to follow, "let's see what the cook left us."

Her stomach twists at the thought of food.

"I ate on the plane," she says politely.

"Airplane food," he agrees, "is terrible, and the portions are small!"

He disappears around the corner, chuckling at his little joke.

"I bet you're dehydrated from your flight," he calls from the other room, then reappears with two open bottles of Young Master beer. He holds one out to her, and she accepts it doubtfully, doing her best to hide her revulsion at alcohol before 9 am. He flops onto a long couch, and she takes her own seat across from him, sipping the beer tentatively. It's surprisingly pleasant against her travel-worn throat.

"Is this a business trip," he asks, "or a holiday?"

"Let's call it business."

"They promised the internet would replace travel," he says, shaking his head, "but I spend half my time wandering the planet, meeting people who think we're friends because we spoke on Zoom."

Gun runners? Drug dealers? Or did he succeed in pulling the business away from its traditional profit centers and toward something more legitimate?

"Thank you," she begins haltingly, "for seeing me on such short notice."

He shrugs. "I've got nowhere to be on a Sunday morning."

Do gangsters get Sundays off? Does crime take a holiday?

"It's just," she begins uncertainly, "that my mother died last week."

She briefly describes the events surrounding Audrey's death, sticking to the bare facts and omitting her later revelations about The Collective and the car. Frank's face grows redder with each passing detail. Finally, he erupts, pounding his fist on the coffee table.

"No Ng deserves to go out like that!" he shouts.

Emily flinches at the outburst, and he seems to notice her discomfort. His expression softens.

"I mean," he stammers, "your mom was a good person, even if she and Dad didn't get along."

"Thank you," she says softly.

It's coming back to her that mood swings are one of Frank's defining traits.

"Is that why you're here?" he continues. "Is Aunt Audrey's murder related to Hong Kong or the family somehow?"

"I was the actual target," she says softly.

His eyes narrow.

"Is this about The Collective? Is Kay mixed up in it?"

"I need to talk with her," she replies.

He looks at the floor.

"My sister and I aren't speaking. I don't know how to reach her."

Frank's succession to head of the Ng empire made things tense between him and his sister. Apparently, the situation has only worsened.

"I think I know where she lives," Emily says. "But I need some help before I visit her."

His eyebrows raise.

"Like?"

"I'm a little short on cash, and if I use the local ATMs, I'll leave a digital footprint. I was hoping you could give me a loan."

"I'll just give you the cash," he scoffs,

"And I need a valid Hong Kong ID," she adds. "So I can get a hotel and conduct business without being flagged."

This second request is a more overt reference to his unsavory connections. In the new, closely surveilled Hong Kong, only a major criminal can conjure a usable, high-quality, fake ID on short notice.

"Aren't you some kind of government agent?" he asks. "Can't your people set you up with that stuff?"

"Sneaking around Hong Kong is above my pay grade."

"Your employers don't know you're here?"

She shrugs

"You don't exactly blend in," he continues. "You're a striking woman and…" he pauses, his eyes settling on hers, "obviously not Chinese."

She averts her gaze, her face warming with self-conscious-ness. Not being one thing or another is her life's story. As a girl, she was ashamed of her hazel eyes, so spotty and discolored, and also her dark skin, both gifts from the father she never knew.

"Hong Kong is a cosmopolitan city," she retorts, "filled with all kinds of people."

"In the tourist zones," he acknowledges, "and the business districts. But if you journey deeper into the territory, you'll be a parrot among crows. And unless you've been practicing your Cantonese, people will hear your terrible accent. You *will* get noticed."

"I'll wear sunglasses," she retorts. "I'll keep my mouth shut."

"Just to talk with my stupid sister?"

Frank isn't usually this belligerent. Volatile, yes, but not argumentative. Does her plan annoy him that much? Have he and Kay become like Uncle Ip and Audrey? Has the next generation of Ng siblings grown just as belligerent as the previous one?

"I need Kaylin to help me find the truth," she retorts.

"The truth's not always liberating."

No doubt that's good advice for a gangster, but she's charting a different path from both her mother and her Hong Kong family.

She clasps her hands together and meets his eyes, revealing all her vulnerability and desperation.

"How can I convince you to help me?"

He gives a tired smile, a bit of his easy-going nature seeming to return.

"You can give Kay a message," he says. "Tell her I'm willing to square things with Zahra, but only if she meets me halfway. Will you tell her that?"

Since when does Frank's business overlap with Zahra's? And what needs to be squared?

"I'll tell her," she agrees, "and thank you."

He chuckles and downs the rest of his beer.

"Since when could I deny you anything, cousin Emily?"

# FRIENDLY VISIT

MAC EMERGES STIFFLY from the rental car, stretching his cramped legs and tossing the paper coffee cup to the curb. The overpriced coffee didn't relieve his headache or reduce the grinding fatigue leftover from that 4:00 AM flight. He glances at his wristwatch, squinting as the west coast sun glints off the dial. He tilts his wrist: it's 8 AM here in paradise. Is that too early to pay a visit to this Seymour character? Should he worry about hurting the little bastard's feelings?

He looks toward the man's precious little house. The place is Brady Bunch meets Mother Goose. Back in Maryland, a dump like that would be bulldozed and replaced with an honest home, something with a big garage and five or six bedrooms. Out here, they call these post-war starter homes "cute" and sell them to overcompensated hipsters for millions.

He tromps across the rock garden, taking no great care to avoid crushing the delicate cacti and grinding the bright green aloe under his heels. If he'd been a lesser man, he would have moved to California and joined this money-grubbing tech royalty. Marcia, his soon-to-be ex-wife, had begged him to go into the private sector. She never understood the importance of his work, never appreciated the value of service to one's country.

Emily, by contrast, fully understands the special mission of the NSA. As the daughter of leftist terrorists and the niece of a notorious Hong Kong gangster, she appreciates how dangerous the world is and how badly the country needs dedicated public servants to restore order. If he ever gets this mess straightened out, he'll fight to keep her at the agency and restore her faith in a system that, lately, has repaid her dedication with grief.

Mac strolls up to the front door and regards its gaudy coral-colored doorbell. Why did Director Chip assign him to make this visit? Mac is no field agent, he's an overweight hacker-turned-manager in a rumpled suit—a desk jockey cosplaying as Eliot Ness.

"You're perfect for the assignment," Chip had crooned, "Your unique connection to Ms. Hernandez gives you special insights into her world and, therefore, into Seymour Frey's world as well."

A cold pang of worry stabs his chest. What did Chip mean by "unique connection" to Emily? How much does the old man understand about his feelings toward her? Is he that transparent?

He jams his finger into the doorbell and listens as a chime rings from the far side. A dog barks behind the neighbor's fence. He loosens his tie.

*Maybe Frey isn't here,* he thinks. *Maybe I can go home without having to talk to him at all.*

Mac withdraws his phone and rechecks his messages. Dammit. The surveillance team just sent another photo of Seymour peering out his kitchen window like a sad puppy. This picture is only ten minutes old, which means the stupid terrorist must surely be at home. Why is the FBI keeping such a close eye on him, anyway? Are they still pissed at how easily Emily slipped their surveillance?

He pounds the door, then jams his finger into the doorbell a second time. He releases it in exasperation, steps back, and sighs. He was the wrong man to send on this goose chase. Director Chip should bring in the experts.

Mac turns and takes a single step into Seymour's rock garden when a voice calls from behind.

"May I help you?"

He whirls around. A slender black man with a mop of dark hair and wide angry eyes regards him from the doorway. Mac composes himself, affecting his best expression of sympathy and professional concern.

"Good morning," he says with all the politeness he can muster. "I was hoping I could speak with Mr. Seymour Frey."

He's talking to Frey, of course. The punk looks just like his photos.

Seymour's expression shifts slightly from pure annoyance to something more tentative.

"I'm Seymour."

Mac extends his hand.

"The name is Lawrence MacCarthy, though most people call me Mac."

Seymour's eyes widen briefly as if in recognition. Then, just as quickly, they return to a neutral expression.

"So?" he says, ignoring the outstretched hand.

Mac drops his arm.

"I'm with the National Security Agency," he says, producing his business card.

Frey takes it reluctantly as if the card was soaked in rat poison.

"I didn't know the NSA made house calls," he says. "In fact, I didn't think you could conduct any operations inside our country."

Of course, the little fucker would know that. He's a domestic terrorist who spends his free hours hacking legitimate businesses and trashing the country in the name of his pinko creed. He has to understand the law in order to flout it.

"I'm not here," Mac replies, struggling to retain his businesslike demeanor, "in relation to any case my agency might be pursuing. I'm here to address a human resource issue."

Seymour's frown deepens.

"What does that even mean?"

"We have an employee, Ms. Emily Hernandez. Do you know her?"

"We're acquainted."

"I was hoping," he continues, "that you might have a minute to chat about her situation. May I come inside?"

Seymour's fingers tighten around the edge of the door, and his knuckles whiten. He looks ready to slam it and run away.

Go ahead, little boy, Mac thinks. Run so I can turn you over to those FBI dogs. You'll enjoy their company much more than mine.

"Why not?" Seymour says abruptly and steps back, revealing a spotless white hallway.

Mac follows Seymour into a spacious living area which, bizarrely, is mostly devoid of furniture. There is, however, one prominent decoration: A set of twin flags plastered to the far wall, one black, the other red, the symbol of Antifa-affiliated terrorist groups, the sort of organizations Mac loves smashing to bits.

Seymour follows his gaze, seems to notice his interest in the flags, and smiles. Mac faces him, squaring his shoulders.

"Have you seen or spoken to Ms. Hernandez lately, Mr Frey?"

"We've already established that you have no jurisdiction within the borders of the United States," Seymour says. "Which makes me wonder why you think you can ask these questions at all?"

Mac forces a sad smile.

"I have no particular authority, Mr. Frey. And no right beyond a genuine concern for Emily's well-being. Have you heard about her mother?"

"I suppose you'll tell me?"

"The poor woman died in a bizarre accident. The shock was, well, more than Emily could absorb. It took a toll on her state of mind, and I made her promise that she'd stay in touch during her period of mourning. A few days ago, she went radio silent."

"Maybe she didn't want to share her grief with a bureaucrat middle manager."

"I grew so worried," Mac continues, ignoring the jab, "that I asked a family friend to stop by her home."

That "family friend" was actually an FBI agent. And the 'worry' he felt could more correctly be described as escalating panic.

"Isn't the NSA based in Forte Meade, Maryland?"

"That's right."

"So, you traveled all the way from the east coast just to tell me this story?"

"Emily and I have become… close, I suppose you could say. It's the product of all those long hours of working together."

Should he be admitting that? Has he said too much?

Seymour's nose crinkles like he smells dogshit.

"How nice for you."

Now for the job that Director Chip actually sent him here to perform.

"I know she harbors a lot of shame regarding her time in The Collective."

"The… what?" Seymour says smoothly as if he's never heard that name before.

Mac gives a theatrical sigh.

"It's a cyberterrorist network led by a dangerous outlaw named Zahra Kartal. Perhaps you've heard of her?"

Seymour stares, stone-faced, saying nothing.

"Zahra's group claims to be a band of cyber Robin Hoods, but they keep most of what they steal."

"Sort of like the federal government."

"During her time in The Collective," he says, again ignoring the snark, "the other members abused her psychologically, threatened her, and subjected her to destructive, co-dependent –"

"Is there some reason," Seymour interrupts, dark eyes sparkling, "that you're telling me this rather long story?"

Mac suppresses a smile. He's getting to the kid.

"Emily believed that her mother's murder was connected with this so-called collective," Mac continues with all the earnestness he can muster. "We believe she's re-establishing contact with them in a misguided attempt to gather intelligence. We have to find her before she gets hurt."

Seymour's face is a barely disguised scowl. His distaste is palpable.

"The criminals are the people working in the NSA, Mr. MacCarthy. Which is why Emily and I haven't spoken for years."

Mac's sour stomach aches. The flight, the coffee, and his need to play this part have taxed him to the limits of his fairly modest abilities. He'd love to pull one of those communist flags off the wall and wrap it around Seymour's pencil neck.

He shakes his head, collecting himself. A living and over-confident Seymour is the only ace he's holding right now.

"Our culture of secrecy is sometimes a curse," he says, doing his best to hold onto the stoic professional act. "We've kept too much from Emily, told ourselves it was for her own good. Now I fear she doesn't understand the risks she's taking or see how much her actions could harm both herself and the NSA."

The blazing sun falls in through the floor-to-ceiling

windows, hurting his eyes. His pulse beats in his temple, each heartbeat like a chisel to his skull.

Seymour walks to the door and pulls it open.

"It's been an interesting visit, Mr. MacCarthy."

Mac nods and trudges into the brilliant morning, pausing just beyond the threshold.

"Perhaps you can tell Emily something if you see her again."

"Won't happen."

"Tell her," Mac continues, "that she's becoming part of these events rather than just a victim of them. If she continues down this path, she'll be worse off than when she worked for Zahra. Will you tell her that?"

Seymour glances at him once more, his dark eyes burning, then slams the door.

Mac shoves his hands into his pockets, his body suddenly lighter, his headache a little less brutal. He strides across Seymour's rock garden, taking care to crush a fresh sage plant that he missed on the way in. He whistles a little song as he strolls past the white van that is obviously FBI. The G-men will have to up their game if they want to seize the opportunity he saw here today.

He fumbles with his keys, unlocks the door, and drops into the car seat. When he gives his report to Director Chip, the old man will claim that Mac revealed too much and got too little in return. Chip will demand that they mobilize the FBI and that Seymour be interrogated. Mac will counsel patience.

He closes his eyes and grips the steering wheel in concentration. Seeing Seymour's reactions today, the punk's doe-eyed devotion to Emily, was a punch in the face. But part of him relishes these feelings of jealousy. They feed his anger and focus his mind. He recalls that rainy evening in Annapolis, Emily shivering underneath the sheets, pressing her naked body close to his, squeezing away his guilt and self-loathing.

He glimpses his bloated, grizzled face in the rearview mirror—a hideous old face, especially when compared with Seymour's.

*So why does she love me?* he thinks. *Am I the father she never knew?*

The idea disgusts him. But he'll play any role if it brings her closer to him. Without Emily, he's drowning, lost in this sick and twisted world. She's the only good thing, the only true light that guides him through the shadows.

His mind returns to Seymour, arrogant and ignorant, unaware of his own vulnerability. It should take only a few more taxpayer dollars and a slightly subtler level of surveillance to trick the kid into thinking he's unwatched. That's when Seymour, in his earnestness and naivete, will cast caution to the wind and lead him to Emily. Then Mac can dispose of this stupid Antifa terrorist, extricate Emily from her nightmare, and run off into the sunset. Once he has Emily, once Seymour is gone, he can become the hero that she's always wanted him to be.

# CHOI HUNG ESTATE

EMILY CLIMBS from the subway and glances around. Half a dozen residential towers loom ahead, their walls painted orange and yellow on the lower levels, turquoise and blue through the middle, and deep purple along the top. They look like a cluster of massive, flattened rainbows, which is by design since this is the Choi Hung Estate, literally the Rainbow Public Housing project. Her cousin Kaylin lives in this sprawling miniature city; she just has to find her.

Emily follows the afternoon crowd, moving with the mass of humanity that flows from the subway to the plaza at the center of the complex. As she draws near, the rainbow illusion fades, challenged by the reality of peeling paint and lengths of hanging laundry.

"I can't isolate Kaylin to a specific building," Seymour told her, "so look for the hottest hotspot among the local networks. That will be her."

This means connecting to a wifi that's tied into the building's fiber optic backbone. But whose wifi? She slows her pace as streams of residents flow past and break into smaller clumps, each vectoring toward a different tower. The closest estate has a row of shabby businesses along its base, including a nail salon, fruit stand, and a boba shop. She makes her way past milling teenagers toward the boba shop whose name, "The Land of Oz," is written in emerald letters above the front door.

"Small tea, please," she tells the bored-looking clerk in what she hopes is passable Cantonese. The girl's eyes widen, perhaps confused by her horrible pronunciation. But as Emily lays the money on the counter, the clerk appears to understand and fills a plastic cup. Emily grabs a table, connects to the store's wifi, and sips her sugary drink. The network uses woefully out-of-date software, which is good because older routers were long ago hacked by APRIL, the Collective's botnet. Emily uses her knowledge of APRIL to locate a back door and, within minutes, has access to the router's internal controls.

"Thank you, Zahra," she mutters as she reviews the statistics, looking for clues about Kaylin's presence. An hour and two bobas later, she sees it: A network segment, three hops from her own, a data bonfire among an otherwise dark field of fiber optic cable. That segment, labeled "丹鳳樓 – 18", must be Kaylin's.

She translates the Chinese and learns that it's a building called "Tan Fun House." She approaches the shop girl who is staring at her phone.

"*Excuse me*," Emily stammers in her broken Cantonese, "*I want find Tan Fung House? Where is?*"

The girl gives her a withering look, then points out the window.

"Across the plaza," she says in perfect English.

Emily packs her things and joins the throng of school children and returning workers filling the sidewalks. Propelled by this river of humanity, she slips through the front doors of Tan Fung House and into the nearest elevator, managing to hit the "18" button before being shoved to the back by a press of sweaty bodies. The car stops on every floor and is mercifully empty by the time she reaches level 18. She steps off to find a battleship gray hallway arrayed with dozens of separate doors, each covered by a metal gate. Security gates are a common feature of older Hong Kong apartment doorways, but they make the floor feel like a cell block.

She tiptoes down the hallway, hoping to avoid notice. She doesn't know which door to approach or how to proceed, so she passes gate after gate, head cocked, hoping to catch a snatch of Kaylin's reedy voice. Behind the first, a man and woman shout at each other in an apparent domestic spat; behind the next, K-pop blares, rattling the hinges. The hallway is alive with sounds: barking dogs, squealing children, and beeping microwaves. Yet within this cacophony, she detects no hint of her cousin.

*Should I knock on a door?* she thinks. *Should I ask if anybody's seen the little woman with the thick glasses?*

She approaches the grimy window at the far end of the hall and looks down. Children play basketball in the courtyard, their happy voices still audible 18 floors below. She sighs. There's nothing to be gained by lurking here in the hallway; either she knocks on some doors, or she just goes home.

She approaches the nearest doorway and raises her knuckles, ready to pound the metal bars that cover it. But a glint in the corner of her eye gives her pause. Two doors down is a different sort of gate, one she didn't notice on her first pass. It's thicker than its neighbors, a chromium bulwark anchored with dozens of sturdy bolts. A mound of letters rests at its base as if the occupant hasn't checked them in months.

She steps toward the gleaming metal, certainty rising in her chest. If Kaylin Ng lived in Choi Hung Estate, she'd find a way to install the most impenetrable gate. And if she felt threatened, she would likely stay inside that gate for weeks, even months.

Emily pounds the bars for thirty seconds…until her knuckles ache, and the gate rings like a bell. Then she leans in, pressing her face against the cool metal.

"Kaylin!" she calls. "Kaylin Ng!"

Nobody answers.

"It's cousin Emily," she continues. "Are you there?"

A loud click from the opposite side of the hallway makes her whirl around. A middle-aged woman with salt and pepper hair stands in her own doorway, staring through her security gate, mouth twisted in a scowl.

"Visiting friend," Emily says in her toddler Cantonese.

The woman shakes her head and slams her door, hopefully mollified. Or maybe she's calling the cops?

Emily turns back toward the chrome gate with renewed fervor.

"I know you're there," she shouts. "This apartment generates more data than Netflix!"

The faintest creak emanates from the far side of the door, as if someone took a step.

"My mom died," she continues, "crushed by a car that landed right in her bedroom, if you can believe that."

There's a thud from behind the bars. The door shudders.

"I described the car to the cops," Emily says. "They said it was a Volkswagen, but I knew that was wrong, so I searched myself. Guess what I found?"

The door doesn't answer.

"It was a WayGo. Ever heard of that company?"

"Go away," a thin voice squeaks.

Emily's heart leaps with vindication. She knows that squeak.

"Here's the crazy part, Kay; guess whose bots took over that WayGo car?"

"Are you arresting me?"

Emily grabs an armful of letters from the floor and holds them up to the peephole.

"You've got mail!" she says.

"Burn it."

"Give me ten minutes, Kay."

"Does Frank know I'm here?"

Emily presses her face even harder against the bars.

"I have no idea. *Please*, let me in."

There's a shuffle, then a thud, then two loud clacks. The door swings back, releasing a stinking cloud of rotting food and unwashed socks. Kaylin Ng stands at the threshold, her face still childlike, even though she's nearly Emily's age. Her tousled hair and crooked glasses are more disheveled than Emily remembers, and her familiar navy cardigan is definitely the worse for wear. Her dark eyes peer owlishly through the round lenses, blinking as if the hallway light is far too intense. After a moment's pause, she opens the gate and motions for Emily to follow.

As Emily steps into Kaylin's cave, the odor, which was already overpowering, moves into eye-watering territory. Her gut threatens to mutiny, and she slows her breathing, attempting to contain her bubbling nausea. Kaylin closes the door and walks ahead of her into the gloom. Emily attempts to follow but trips and drops to her knees.

"Watch the books," Kaylin mutters.

Emily feels her way to the couch, then shoves aside a stack of magazines, taking a seat.

Kaylin motions toward the kitchen, barely visible in the feeble light.

"Do you want some tea?"

As if in response, a cockroach sprints across a pile of filthy dishes and then dives into the sink with an audible smack.

"I'm good," Emily says.

Kaylin's deep eyes settle on her.

"Does Frank know where I live? Is that how you found me?"

Emily swallows, holding the stench of decay and body odor at bay.

"No, but he'd love to talk with you. And with Zahra too."

"Can't help him there."

Emily sighs. This is going to be a rough visit.

"For what it's worth," Emily continues, "Seymour helped me find you."

"Fucking turncoat," Kaylin mutters.

As Emily's eyes adjust, more of the room becomes visible. The floor is littered with stacks of books, disassembled computer gear, and piles of canned food. A mattress, half buried under rumpled clothing, serves as Kaylin's bed, and the apartment's only window is apparently covered with aluminum foil. A rickety card table holds stacks of computers that expel torrents of hot air and ozone. Their flickering green LEDs illuminate her cousin's elfin features, giving her a sickly pallor. Emily restrains the urge to hug and comfort her cousin. Kaylin may not welcome the gesture. Instead, she points to the enormous stack of humming computers.

"That setup would cost me three months' salary."

"Why are you here?" Kaylin asks in a flat voice.

"I told you, a WayGo vehicle killed my mother. It was hacked by APRIL."

"I'm out of The Collective. I can't say what APRIL is or isn't doing."

"When did you quit?"

A single tear rolls down her cousin's narrow face.

"I told Zahra we couldn't survive so much exposure," Kay says, "but you know how she is."

Is this another version of Seymour's story? Have Zahra's ambitions created risks that even the dedicated comrades can't stomach? Did the danger overcome even Kay's love and devotion?

"What about Nishant?" Emily asks. "Or Horst? Did they share your concerns?"

"They got greedy," she says bitterly. "They forgot the mission."

Ah yes, The Collective's self-serving altruism, a fusion of

Zahra's opportunism and Kaylin's generosity. It was never a coherent ideology, even in the best of times.

The flicker of computer lights catches her eye. What are these machines doing anyway? And why sequester them in this disgusting bunker? Realization dawns.

"You aren't safe either," Emily says softly.

Kayin looks at the floor but says nothing.

"You're building a counterattack."

The little woman meets her gaze, eyes unblinking.

"I won't harm Zahra."

"Then you're watching her, learning who her new friends are."

Kaylin's eyes are wide and dark, her mouth a tight line.

"And you know what she's doing," Emily continues, "maybe even where she lives."

"I won't let you hurt her," Kaylin says quietly.

Emily has experience with zealots. Her mother was a tragic example.

"Are you protecting her with this?" Emily says, motioning toward the computers. "Are you helping her from afar?"

"When I can."

"Did you know somebody used APRIL to weaponize that self-driving car?" Emily asks, her voice now trembling with frustration.

"I've noticed… changes," Kay says, her mousy voice barely louder than the computer fans. "New botnet messages I can't decode and neural network updates that I can't reverse engineer. It's Zahra's new partners, I suppose."

"Who are they?"

"The Chinese," Kaylin says with a shrug. "Or maybe the Russians."

"Help me find Zahra."

"She thinks you're the devil."

Emily breathes a long sigh. Kaylin's devotion to Zahra

feels so familiar and also so perverse. It's the same devotion Emily's mother held for Emily's father.

She works her way to the far end of the room, navigating the piles of books and garbage, then pauses by the window.

"My father, Sebastian, was a revolutionary," she says. "He believed that armed struggle molds humans into better creatures, that strife makes the rich generous and the hateful loving. He thought humanity just needed tempering, a brief period of conflict, and our eyes would be opened! I never knew my father, but I sometimes talk with him in my dreams. I always tell him about my life, about how badly things worked out for Mom and me."

Up close, Kaylin's window covering looks like a second grader's art project: sheets of aluminum foil secured by strips of masking tape. Emily picks at the tape with her fingernail.

"Leave that alone!" Kaylin cries, struggling to her feet and knocking over a pile of books.

"Zahra is like my dad," Emily continues. "She has a big vision."

Emily rips away a sheet of foil, exposing a dazzling band of sunlight. Kaylin, long used to darkness, clamps her hands over her eyes.

"Stop!" she says.

"She claims that we're building a better world," Emily continues, then rips away a center strip of foil. Choi Hung Estate's rainbow towers glimmer outside, framed by the evening sun. Kaylin falls to her knees, overwhelmed by the brilliance.

"She says we're ushering in a new golden age where minds and bodies are freed from repetitive tasks. Humans can concentrate on pure creativity while machines do the grunt work and even the grunt thinking. The Collective is the vanguard of Zahra's project, using stolen money to make her vision a reality."

"It's a good vision," Kaylin says weakly.

Emily tears away the last strip, exposing the entire window in its dingy brilliance. She balls up the foil and throws it to the floor.

"My dad's vision and Zahra's vision are both bullshit," Emily says, struggling not to raise her voice. "Do you know why?"

"I don't control her," Kaylin says.

"My dad's vision screwed up people's lives," Emily says, answering her own question. "Mom went to prison because of it, and I became an orphan. But Zahra's vision is even worse; it involves straight-up killing people."

"She didn't kill anybody," Kaylin says, red eyes staring directly into the light.

"Let her tell me that herself, Kay. Let her explain how my mother died."

For the first time today, Kaylin meets Emily's eyes, a tear trickling down her bony cheek.

"If she agrees to meet you, if she proves that she's innocent, then will you leave her alone?"

Zahra obviously sent that car. Who else possesses both the will and the means? And Emily has come too far to let Zahra off the hook; her very survival depends on capturing her old boss.

"I just want to talk with Zahra," Emily says with all the earnestness she can muster. "I want to hear her side of the story."

Once the NSA and CIA take out Zahra, The Collective's grand vision will dissolve, and the group will disperse. It'll be hard for Kay at first, watching her friend and lover go down in flames. But in time, she'll see that the world could never be sane with Zahra on the loose.

"Alright," Kaylin says. "I'll tell you how to find her."

# HEADQUARTERS

EMILY ELBOWS through the crush of humanity, making her way along Pedder Street toward Queen's Road Central, an urban canyon formed by rows of steel skyscrapers. The buildings block all but a small patch of sky, leaving the streets in nearly perpetual shadow. A red river of taxis crawl through this canyon, honking and swerving as they navigate the gridlock. She approaches the Cheung Kong Center, a modern tower clad in blue-gray windows that disgorges a stream of workers from its revolving doors. She pushes past the mass of humanity and into the lobby. Behind the desk, a man in a crisp blazer looks up.

"May I help you?" he says in officious Cantonese."

"I'm here to visit Thoughtful Industries," she responds in English.

According to Kaylin, Thoughtful Industries is Zahra's latest shell company and the place she's agreed to meet Emily.

The guard folds his hands, unsmiling.

"You have an appointment?"

"I'm Kaylin Ng," she says, holding out a business card she printed ten minutes ago.

"Who are you here to see, Ms. Ng?"

"Elif Osman. That's O-S-M-A-N."

Zahra's latest alias.

The guard dials a number on his phone.

"This is lobby security," he says, "are you expecting a Ms. Kaylin Ng?"

He pauses, then nods.

"Very good. Thank you."

He motions toward the bank of elevators.

"Floor forty-six, suite eleven, which will be on your left."

She boards the gleaming elevator, which, unlike the lift at Choi Hung Estate, contains no sweaty riders or flickering lights. It deposits her in a marble hallway where she quickly finds a set of black double doors etched with the moniker "Thoughtful Industries." She presses the doorbell button, and after a brief pause, a narrow-shouldered white man in a brown suit appears.

"You're not Kaylin," he says brightly.

"I can explain," she begins, "you see, Kaylin couldn't –"

The man grabs her hand.

"Emily Hernandez," he says, "it's so good to meet you finally!"

She stands, confused, as he pumps her hand up and down. Does she know this man?

"You're one of Zahra's old business partners," he says as if hearing her thoughts. "From her time at Automated Intelligence, I believe?"

Another of Zahra's shell companies, dating back to Emily's own days in The Collective.

"That's right," she says weakly.

"Jeremy Greaves," he says, smiling widely. "I'm the office manager for Thoughtful Industries and know everything about everyone!"

They pass through a wide waiting room with elegant chairs and a modern glass desk.

"The boss said you're the brightest person she ever

worked with," he continues. "A genius at all that computer stuff that makes her so rich!"

Perhaps Zahra called Emily a genius once or twice. But she had some other names for her as well: back-stabber and stool pigeon, among them.

"Zahra's here then?" she asks nervously.

"You already know the answer to that," Greaves says with a sly smile.

He opens a second black door and leads her past rows of empty glass conference rooms and then past an expansive open office filled with low desks, each equipped with a high-end workstation and a sleek chair. The place is prepared for a software army, but the troops haven't shown up.

"In a month or two," he says over his shoulder, "this facility will feel very different. Very different indeed."

She nods, her mind whirling with confusion. What does Greaves think she's doing here? And why does he expect *her* to know Zahra's whereabouts?

They approach another door with the title "Zahra Kartal, CEO" etched in gold letters. Apparently, an alias is unnecessary for those who get this deep into her realm. As they pass through the door, Emily is unable to stifle a small gasp. Zahra's office is beyond sumptuous, with soaring ceilings and a wall made entirely of floor-to-ceiling glass. And beyond the glass, the spires of Hong Kong are framed by the glittering waters of Victoria Harbor. There's also a massive desk along the far wall, more throne than a workspace.

"You like that monstrosity?" Jeremy asks skeptically, noticing her interest in the desk.

"It's, uh, very imposing."

"It's horrid and tacky. When they brought it this morning, I told them just to return it. But Zarha already paid in full, the silly girl. When she gets back, we'll have words about this appalling lapse in taste."

He strolls to the side of the office, where he flops down on a leather couch.

"In the meantime," he says, patting the cushion next to him and smiling widely, "I was hoping we could chat."

Her arms prickle. Who is this man?

"When's Zahra coming?" she asks timidly.

"Oh, we'll see her today, as I think you know, but not for a few minutes yet."

The man's obtuse assertiveness is disconcerting. He's like a younger and gayer Mac. She reluctantly perches next to him, just beyond easy reach. He slides closer.

"Did you already know Zahra was back in town?" he asks confidentially.

"Back?" she says, confused.

"Because Kaylin called me to ask about a meeting," he continues, "and then, not twenty minutes later, Zahra texts to say she's come home! That, at long last, her journey is over."

He leans close, his shoulder lightly touching hers. His cologne is distinct and multifaceted, with notes of citrus, magnolia, and something else... maybe freshly cleaned linen? He folds his smooth, manicured hands.

"You had *no* idea that Zahra would return today?" he asks slyly.

Waves of cold unease rise through her gut. It's as if she's being written into somebody else's story...like her actions are being choreographed without her permission.

"I didn't know she was gone."

"What, if I may ask, is the nature of your visit? How should I tell her to prepare for her discussion with you?"

His smile is warm, but his eyes are intense.

"How... long has she been gone, Mr. Greaves?"

He blinks, and, for a moment, his smile falters.

"A considerable time, I'm afraid. It's been a solitary existence here at headquarters."

"Months?" she asks, struggling to sound casual. "More than a year?"

His muscles tense under the smooth fabric of his silken shirt. There's not a gram of fat on the man's small frame. He could easily overpower her.

An air conditioner kicks on somewhere, its soft thrum surprisingly loud against the deathly silence of Zahra's office. If she screamed, would anyone hear?

"Let's take turns," he says suddenly. "I'll answer one of your questions, you answer one of mine."

She eyes the open door. She could make a break for it, just dash away. But that's insane, isn't it? She's here to talk with Zahra, right?

She meets Jeremy's unflinching gaze.

"That sounds fair," she says.

"In answer to your first question," he says, "I haven't seen Zahra for nearly fifteen months."

She struggles to keep her face neutral, to hide her growing panic.

"What's she been doing?"

Jeremy waggles his finger.

"My turn for a question, Ms. Hernandez. Why did *you* come here today?"

"I doubted Zahra would talk to me through email," she says truthfully.

"An evasive answer," he says with a frown. "And after I gave you such good and specific information."

Emily sighs. She's not holding many cards, but maybe she can give just a little more.

"I'm hoping Zahra will demystify some strange events that have occurred in my life."

Though hardly more informative than the previous response, it seems to satisfy him. His face brightens, and he nods.

"Your turn then," he says.

"Where has Zahra been during this absence?" she asks. "What cities or countries?"

"I heard she went to Istanbul for a few weeks," he says with a sigh, "probably to visit family. Then on to Stockholm, Silicon Valley, Bangalore..." he looks thoughtful, running through an inventory in his mind. Finally, he nods. "I think that's it. Does that help somehow?"

More than a year of continuous travel! Since when does Zahra conduct so much of her business in person?

"My turn again," he says. "These strange events you mentioned. Did you cause them? Or did Zahra?"

An interesting question.

"A little of both, but I believe it was mostly Zahra."

Jeremy shakes his head.

"I'm being so open with you," he says in a vexed tone. "And you repay me with riddles."

"That's all I can say on that topic. But you can ask me another question."

"Hmmm," he says, still looking irritated. Then his expression brightens.

"I know you work for the NSA. So is this an official visit? Is she in trouble with the feds?"

She tries to hide her surprise, but her poker face has always been terrible.

"This is a personal visit," she says, "not official at all."

Jeremy's eyebrows raise, and his smile returns.

"I believe you," he says. "You don't act like you have the full faith and support of the US government behind you."

Is she that transparent? Is her desperation that obvious?

"My turn," she says. "Why did Zahra visit so many places? What is the purpose of her travels?"

Jeremy shrugs.

"Recruiting new engineers, meeting the worldwide development team, talking to investors... all that businessy stuff."

Is Thoughtful Industries more than just a front? Is Zahra creating a legal business this time?

"Recruiting and fundraising required more than a year on

the road?"

His light skin reddens slightly.

"I only know what I'm told," he says defensively.

"My turn again," he adds. "Do you believe this is a real business?"

Maybe Jeremy isn't as gullible as he looks.

"I have no idea."

"You're a government spook, for God's sake," he says with exasperation, "you have an opinion!"

She draws a long breath, calming the tremors in her arms and chest. This little man is the latest of Zahra's endless string of victims. She's spun him a vision of being on the ground floor of a huge opportunity, of being her right-hand man, her consigliere. If Zahra has a superpower, it's her ability to appeal to a person's greed and hunger for importance.

"Her projects always exist in the shadowy realm between legitimate and criminal," Emily admits.

He crumples slightly, shoulders sagging as if gravity just doubled.

"I have stock options," he murmurs, "equity."

"My advice, Jeremy –" she begins, but a buzzing interrupts her.

His head snaps toward the sound, and he jumps from the couch like a dog running to his master. A moment later, he's talking, his voice high and shrill, answering another voice that is deeper and angrier. Then he's back, his face flushed.

"Would you mind," he says, voice cracking, "waiting in one of our conference rooms?"

"Mr. Greaves?" says a gravelly voice with a thick Chinese accent.

Jeremy's eyes widen. He glances down the hallway, then back to her.

"Please, Ms. Hernandez," he says, "this way."

He leads her to a glass conference room and then steps quickly away, pulling the door shut behind him. She stares through the glass, watching as he skips out of sight. Moments later, muffled voices echo up the hallway amid his protestations.

"I suppose you could wait in Zahra's office," he's telling his new guests, "if that would be more comfortable."

"That will be acceptable," says a smooth deep voice in crisp Queen's English.

Jeremy appears, leading a group of Asian men dressed in slacks and Hawaiian shirts. At the center is her cousin, Frank Ng, jaw set like he's grinding bullets between his teeth. She jumps up in surprise, ready to ask what he's doing here. But he's past and out of sight before she reaches the door. She returns to the conference table and racks her brain. Since when does Frank have contact with Zahra? Did Kaylin introduce them? What sort of business might Frank's criminal operation conduct with The Collective?

She returns to the door, opens it quietly, and sticks her head into the hallway. Muffled voices shout from behind Zahra's closed door. She steps into the hallway, still uncertain. Frank's voice rings out.

"If you think I'm angry," he's saying, "wait till you hear from the Wangs. Or the Fungs!"

"Zahra has already assured –" Jeremy begins in a pleading tone.

Frank cuts him off.

"We're done with assurances, Jeremy."

She steps back into the conference room and shuts the door with trembling hands. What could Zahra have promised Frank? Is it related to her mother? Could he have known about her mother's death before she even arrived in Hong Kong?

Footsteps in the hallway interrupt her thoughts. Jeremy steps into the room.

"I need to ask..." he says, voice trembling, "whether you've spoken with Zahra recently?"

Does this count as one of Jeremy's questions? Is it his turn to ask? His wide eyes and flushed cheeks suggest that perhaps she shouldn't push the point.

"Not in years."

"Because," he continues as if she hadn't spoken, "she should have been here hours ago."

*Hours ago?* Is that why Jeremy was so talkative? Was he stalling? Hoping Zahra would make one of her signature late entrances? Or did he suspect, even fear, that she wasn't coming at all?

Jeremey is already heading down the hallway toward where Frank awaits.

A shiver rushes up her arm. Does her cousin understand that Jeremy is an innocent bystander in Zahra's game?

There are sounds of a scuffle. Jeremey's voice rings out.

"Please, Mr. Ng," he's saying, "I really don't –"

Emily leaves the conference room and strides down the hallway. She stops at the entrance to Zahra's office and listens at the door.

"Try harder," Frank is saying. "You last saw Zahra when?"

"I – I already told –"

This has to stop. Frank's got to be told that Jeremy is a victim, just like the rest of them.

She pushes the door open.

Jeremy is on the floor, face pressed to the carpet, eyes squeezed shut in pain. One of the bigger Hawaiian-shirted men kneels atop him, holding a knife against his upturned cheek. A long red line of blood oozes at the knife's edge. Jeremey's eyes meet hers.

"Help me," he squeaks.

Emily's legs are frozen, pinned by fear and indecision. Frank is her cousin, almost her brother. He got her a place to stay in Hong Kong, helped her with money, and obtained a fake ID. But what is he doing to this poor man? Why is he here at all? Did he follow her?

Frank rises from the couch, eyes wide.

"Emily," he says, "I didn't want you to –"

Emotions spring from her chest like bees from a hive: rage and indignation at Frank's intrusion, pity for poor clueless Jeremy.

"What are you doing to him?" she shouts.

Frank's eyes narrow, darting briefly from Jeremy to her.

"This isn't what it looks like," he says, taking a faltering step. "I needed him to tell me…" his voice trails off.

But this is exactly what it looks like. This is the Ng family that her mother warned her about, the side of the family that Uncle Ip took great pains to hide. But she's an adult now, and there can be no more hiding.

"Are you going to kill this poor man?" she says, her anger rising.

She doesn't wait for an answer but turns on her heel and dashes from the room.

"Wait!" Frank shouts.

But she won't wait, won't be a party to torture, won't stand by while they carve Jeremy up. She isn't big enough to grab the knife from those men, but she saw a phone in the conference room. She'll call the cops.

She locates the phone atop the conference table and picks up the receiver, her finger poised over the operator button.

Frank appears at the entrance.

"Wait," he says again, his forehead furling with obvious concern. "Please, Emily. Give me a chance to explain. I wasn't going to –"

But his sentence is interrupted by a thunderclap that sweeps him aside like a sheaf of paper in a hurricane. Fire rolls down the hallway, and superheated air rushes through the door, flipping the table over and throwing her down. Her head slams the carpet with a brain-scrambling 'crack.' She's insensible.

# SUDDEN DEPARTURE

EMILY OPENS HER EYES. On the ceiling above, flower-shaped nozzles spray water through swirling clouds of smoke. The distant "honk, honk" of a siren rises above the ringing in her ears. A woman speaks in a computerized voice.

"There is a fire in the building," the voice is saying, "Please seek immediate egress. This is not a drill."

It repeats the message in Cantonese as the air grows opaque. The room stinks of burning plastic and overdone meat. She scrambles to her feet and gags as the smoke suffocates her. A memory returns, a fireman visiting her elementary school, instructing the children to stop, drop, and roll.

"Crawl like a dog," he told the children, "stay under the bad air."

She falls to her stomach, pressing her face into the water-drenched carpet. At floor level, the air is still acrid, but her head clears a little. She perceives the rectangular outline of the doorway, intermittently visible through the billowing smoke. She pulls herself forward, hand over hand, then shudders as pain stabs her skin. A shard of bloody glass protrudes from her palm. She plucks it out and continues more carefully, watching for dangerous debris. She clambers around the overturned table, and the doorway reappears, backlit by a wavering orange light. The door itself is torn from its hinges and lays askew in the hallway.

*Where are the others? Are they hurt?*

"Frank?" she calls. "Jeremey?"

The only answer is a growing rumble, the fire, now disturbingly close. She peers around the doorway, and the heat of a dozen campfires burns her face, making her shriek in pain as she withdraws. Zahra's office is completely aflame. Is Jeremy still in there? What about her cousin?

"Frank!" she calls again, her voice cracking from fear and lack of oxygen.

The air thickens. There's little time left.

She rests for a moment, letting the sprinklers pour cool water on her neck, then breathes deeply, gathering as much usable air as she can hold. Once she's in the hallway and fully exposed to the heat from Zahra's office, she'll have just seconds before she succumbs. She draws a final scrap of air and then lurches through the door. The heat stings like a swarm of bees, and the stench of burning hair, her own hair, fills her nostrils. Then she's at the lobby door and dashing through. Her foot strikes something soft, and she tumbles to the floor, finding herself staring into Frank's blackened face. The blast must have thrown him here. His eyes are closed, and his cheeks are blood-spattered.

"Frank!" she shouts.

He remains motionless.

She staggers to her feet and squints at the approaching fire. In a minute, they'll both be engulfed. They have to move.

She opens the lobby door, and blessed cool air pours in, a balm to her burning skin. But the fire, fed by fresh oxygen, lurches toward them. She props the door open with a chair and tugs on Frank's arms with what's left of her waning strength. He's easily two hundred fifty pounds and as immobile as a dead bear. She wraps her arms around his shoulders and pulls with all her might. He moves...but not far, just a few inches. She tries again, choking as the lobby fills with smoke. Inch by agonizing inch, she moves him through the doorway. When his feet finally clear the threshold, she slams the door and seals off the raging fire. Then she falls to her knees, weeping from pain and exhaustion.

Yet there's no time for recovery. Frank is in trouble, maybe even dying.

She reaches for her phone but finds it missing. She puts her head on his chest and listens for a heartbeat. She's no doctor, and his chest is thick, but it seems too quiet. She puts her ear to his mouth. There's no breath.

"Not you too, Frank!" she says. She recalls a long-ago CPR course that Uncle Ip made her take, then pinches Frank's nose, covers his mouth with hers, and breathes out with all her might. She listens again. Is he breathing or just exhaling the air she gave him?

"Goddammit, Frank," she says through her tears, "why were you even here?"

She continues the amateur mouth-to-mouth, unsure whether she's helping or killing him. A loud bang draws her up short. A giant man, well over six feet tall and dressed in a flowing Hawaiian shirt, steps through the front door. His wide shoulders fill the entire entrance.

"I'll take Mr. Frank," he says. His voice rumbles like a bass violin.

The giant effortlessly lifts her cousin, then turns toward the exit. A gray-haired man also dressed in a Hawaiian shirt, steps up from behind.

"Ms. Emily," he says, "we must leave immediately."

"The others!" she shouts, gesturing toward the office entrance.

The gray-haired man places his palm against the door, then flinches.

"Too hot," he says. "Can you walk?"

"Yes, but –"

He takes her arm.

"Please follow," he says, pulling at her.

"The people!" she shouts, resisting his steel grip. But her depleted strength is no match, and, in a moment, they're at the end of the hallway.

The giant flings open a metal door, and they step into a stairwell filled with workers in office attire. Everyone is marching downward, making their way to safety.

The gray-haired man pushes her into the throng. She collides with a harried-looking gentleman in a pin-striped suit. The man turns toward her, his expression shifting from irritation to surprise and then to horror. Instinctively, she follows his gaze, looking at her own blouse and skirt, then gasps. Blood and water cover her arms, her silk blouse is torn in several places, revealing her bra, and her gray skirt is nearly black with soot.

"Are you injured?" the man asks in Cantonese.

"I'm fine," she says in trembling English, "but others are still trapped!"

"This woman is indeed badly injured," the big man announces, "and also confused. We're taking her to the authorities!"

The man in the pinstripe suit nods. Clearly, this disheveled foreigner is out of her head.

But she isn't. Jeremy Greaves is trapped up there, along with at least six of Frank's men. And nobody cares!

She rounds on the giant, who still cradles Frank in his thick arms.

"They're your co-workers!" she shouts. "You should save them!"

His face reddens.

"They can't be helped."

The gray-haired man withdraws a walkie-talkie from his jacket, mutters a few phrases in Cantonese, then holds the device to his ear.

"Firemen coming up stairs," he says.

Moments later, a line of first responders appears, outfitted in raincoats, yellow helmets, and oxygen tanks. They push their way through the crowd, their faces stern.

"People are trapped on the forty-sixth floor!" Emily shouts to the nearest one.

His eyes sweep over her tattered clothing and bloody skin. "Do you need medical attention?" he says in English.

"We take her to authorities," the gray-haired man replies, then repeats his intention in Cantonese.

The fireman nods and continues his ascent.

They march downward, passing landing after landing, flowing with the stream of evacuees. And all the while, the gray-haired man keeps his hand firmly clamped to her arm.

*I'll get rid of you when we reach ground level*, she thinks. *I'll scream to the cops.*

His radio crackles, and he mutters into it. She makes out the word "neoihai," or girl. Is she that girl? What are they planning?

As they reach the eleventh floor, a frazzled office worker emerges from a door and joins the crowd, apparently late to realize that this is no mere drill. Emily wrenches her arm free and bolts for the closing door. But powerful fingers grab her and yank her back.

"We not at ground level, miss," the gray-haired man says, his teeth bared and his eyes bulging. "Ten more floors!"

A woman jostles the man in front of her. The man jumps the railing and drops into the crowd below amid shrieks of outrage and pain. These people are already panicked. If she keeps acting out, she might cause a stampede.

When they reach the third floor, a door abruptly swings open and gloved hands pull her through. In less than a second, she's surrounded by a group of Hawaiian-shirted men who are hustling her down a quiet corridor. She shouts, but there is nobody to hear.

"We're almost there," the gray-haired man calls from the back of the scrum, "just a few minutes now, Ms. Emily."

They descend a long flight of stairs and arrive at a loading dock. Two vans sit with their side doors open and flashers blinking. A woman across the street glances in her direction. Emily catches her eye.

"Help!" Emily shouts, "These guys are kidnapping me!"

Before the woman can respond, her captors shove her into the van and slam the door. The driver guns the engine. The van lurches from the curb.

"All will be well, Ms. Emily," the gray-haired man says. "We safe now."

# WHAT TO DO?

"SIGNAL INTELLIGENCE FLAGGED this news report at about 4 am today," Mac says, pressing a button on the remote.

An image appears on Director Chip's wall screen displaying a female TV announcer speaking Chinese. An inset behind her shows Emily, filthy and bloody, dragging a corpulent man through a sea of flame.

"What am I looking at here," Chip mutters, "and why is our junior analyst in that hellscape?"

Mac freezes the image. Emily's face is contorted with fear, and her clothing appears burned.

"A sizable explosive detonated in a Hong Kong high rise just after 2 pm yesterday. Emily was there."

"Is she in custody?"

"Missing. And she's got the whole Hong Kong police force looking for her."

"Who's the fat guy?"

The director has been known to occasionally shoot the messenger if the news is bad enough. This news is terrible.

"Frank Ng," he says softly, "scion of the Ng crime family and mid-level operator in the 14K triad."

"So she's *actually* working with her mother's family? That isn't just a story?"

"It gets stranger," Mac continues. "The office where this footage was captured is leased by a boutique consultancy out of Barbados named Thoughtful, Inc."

Thinking Machines, Mindful Systems, and Mind Games are all Barbados-based shell companies The Collective has used to blend legal and illegal activities. Thoughtful, Inc. would seem to fit the pattern.

"Zahra," Chip whispers.

"Cops found the remains of seven bodies. They've identified six as being part of Frank's crew. Only a few fragments of the seventh remain, but DNA indicates the victim is male."

"Any clues about the bomb?"

Our contacts within the Hong Kong police say it was ammonium nitrate and fuel oil. An ANFO mixture, the type used by mining companies."

"An unusually bulky choice," the director observes.

"A large metal desk got delivered the previous day. Fragments suggest the ANFO was encased within it. Nobody's figured out who shipped it there."

Chip's bloodshot eyes meet his.

"How the hell did Emily slip so far away from us and so deeply into," he motions toward the screen, "whatever *that* is."

"She knew the NSA airline sweeps would lag on flights originating outside the US. She crossed into Tijuana and bought plane tickets with cash. That got her several days ahead of our radar."

"Clever," the old man says sourly.

And desperate. But they had wanted Emily to become desperate, hadn't they? They'd wanted her to find Zahra for them.

"It's starting to look," Mac says, heart sinking at the betrayal he's about to utter, "like she *is* a player after all."

"Sometimes life imitates art," Chip says, the hint of a smile curling the corner of his mouth, "which makes her a dangerous pawn."

Mac glances again at the frozen image on the screen. Emily seems haunted, her skin drawn tightly over delicate cheekbones, dark rings encircling wide eyes. Caring for her difficult mother, being told she might be fired, watching her mother die, and then being pushed by that FBI bastard... she's had to endure more than any person should. Director Chip will sacrifice anything to bring Zahra under his control.

"It may be time," Chip continues, eyeing him carefully, "to bring more resources to bear."

"No," he blurts before he can stop himself. "Our plan can still work. We should just utilize the assets already in play."

"Such as?"

"Seymour Frey, for one."

Chip scoffs. "The anarchist hacker boy? Ms. Hernandez's love interest?"

The taunt irritates him more than it should.

"Two hours ago," Mac says, struggling to maintain his disinterested tone, "Seymour boarded a plane for Hong Kong."

The director's eyes widen momentarily, then his shoulders relax, and his crooked smile broadens, revealing a row of yellowing teeth.

"Little Seymour's invited to the party too? Have you informed the Hong Kong Chief of Station?"

"Fong will be on him the moment Frey sets foot in the territory."

The director steeples his fingers and leans back in his chair.

"Do we know whether Emily summoned little Seymour? Or is Zahra pulling the strings?"

Mac shrugs.

"The FBI didn't have a warrant to bug Seymour's home,

and his use of high complexity lattice multivariate encryption means we can't decode his messages."

"Run it through quantum computing."

"It'll still take weeks."

"Add more resources."

"We'll need signoff from the cryptography directorate, and they'll want to know why this is a priority."

Chip grips the arms of his chair.

"We've got one of our own analysts running loose in Hong Kong and appearing on the evening news. Do you think there's any chance I can keep this from senior management?"

Mac resists the urge to step back. This situation is panicking the old guy more than he realized.

"Well, no, I don't suppose –"

"I'll have to invent a story," Chip says, his thin voice growing shrill, "imply the girl still works for Zahra while also explaining how such an oversight was possible in a well-run department like mine."

*Ah, Emily, how will I get you back now? What the hell are you even doing over there?*

"Who else is coming to this Hong Kong party?" Chip continues, rising and strolling to the window. "What about Ms. Hernandez's other cousin... what's the woman's name?"

"Kaylin Ng. We haven't found her, but we don't think the Chinese have either."

Chip's face reddens.

"And that old hippie? Can we expect him to show up as well?"

Mac releases a slow breath. The director's fixation on Ben Katz is... interesting. Prior to recent events, he never mentioned Ben's name nor showed the slightest interest in the man's often groundbreaking work. Is this new focus merely due to Ben's strangely timed disappearance? Or does Chip know something more?

"He's fallen off the map," Mac says.

The director slaps his hand on the desk.

"Our enemies are threatening us, and if this goes side-ways…" his voice trails off, the threat hanging, unspoken.

A year ago, even six months ago, Chip's threats might have held some potency. Now they feel tedious. Still, the old man's obvious panic represents an opening of sorts.

"There's no evidence connecting Ben with Zahra. For all we know, he's off in Dharamshala howling at the moon. On the other hand, we have a good shot at finding two, and maybe as many as four past or present members of The Collective."

"Finding them's not enough," Chip says, his voice quivering with anger, "we need to bring them under our control and engage them in our search. Otherwise, we'll be forced to activate Pryce."

A cold spike of fear spreads up Mac's spine, damping what had been rising spirits. Pryce is the nuclear option. If Chip is willing to deploy his cat's paw, then this is a scorched-earth operation.

"The situation is not beyond salvaging," Mac says soothingly. "I can still turn Emily. I just need to go in myself."

The director raises a scraggly eyebrow.

"Just yesterday, you told me you weren't cut out for field work."

His pulse accelerates. He has to make this sound like he means it.

"This time, I have to be the one to go. There's no other choice."

"And why's that?" Chip asks, his watery eyes narrowing.

He's gone too far, he's triggered the old man's suspicions. But there's no going back.

"I'm her boss Leonard, and her mentor. If I go out there in person, it'll be a sign of goodwill, proof that we still care about her, that we haven't written her off, despite this latest fuck-up."

The director's eyes seem thoughtful. After a moment, he nods, and the crooked smile returns.

"She might be desperate enough to buy that."

"And once we've gotten her side of the story," Mac continues, growing bolder, "we may realize that her reasons were good ones. Who knows? Maybe we really will bring her back in from the cold."

Chip bursts out laughing, a hiccuping, cackling sort of laugh.

"Not a snowball's chance in a nuclear holocaust," he says between gasps.

The old man recovers himself, and his smile fades.

"But I see your point. A target is easier to acquire when it's not fighting us."

Mac nods, doing his best to keep his expression neutral. If he wants Emily safe and whole, then he needs to keep Chip from sending Pryce, even if that means playing the director's wicked game a little longer.

"On the other hand," Chip continues, "your presence could generate unwanted interest from our leadership. I'll need to give them a logical-sounding justification."

"Tell them that I'll be providing on-the-ground guidance to the local CIA station," Mac says, wiping the sweat from his forehead.

"Do you really intend to provide intel to the local CIA station? Why take that risk?"

Mac smiles inwardly. For once, the old man isn't seeing all the angles.

"They're already deeply involved, which means somebody needs to guide their understanding and lead them toward the right conclusions."

Chip nods, and the deep furls on his forehead seem to smooth out a little.

"This is why I took you into my confidence, Mac. You think like me."

"Thank you, Leonard," he says between gritted teeth.

Being taken into the director's hall of mirrors was the greatest mistake of his life, which makes saving Emily from Director Chip all the more urgent.

# THE PRISONER

EMILY OPENS HER EYES. Dazzling brightness blinds her, and she squeezes them shut again. She slowly opens just her left eye, then her right. Tall windows wash the space around her with sunlight. She's in some sort of bedroom, lying in a massive bed, buried up to her neck in heavy, smothering blankets. She's roasting, and her body is damp with sweat.

*Where is this place?*

She sits up, and the room immediately spins. A cauldron of bile bubbles deep within her gut. She rolls from the bed and hits the floor just as hot liquid burns her esophagus. She locates a garbage pail and brings it to her face. Her stomach expels everything she's ever eaten, heaving and retching until she's shivering with pain, and there's nothing left to purge. She grips the pail, panting, as fresh images flash through her mind: Zahra's office, fire and searing heat, Frank's unconscious body, and a van full of thugs. She's been kidnapped. This is a prison. But whose?

A gentle knocking from the ornate cream-colored door interrupts her thoughts—a gray-haired man in a dark suit steps into the room.

"Do you need assistance?" he asks.

She's seen him before, only he was wearing different clothes. He was the man in the Hawaiian shirt, the one who held her arm and forced her into the van.

She struggles to her feet, swaying drunkenly.

"Stay away," she slurs and takes an unsteady step.

He holds up his hands placatingly.

"I am only here to attend to you."

She focuses her wobbling eyes, forcing them to give her a clearer sense of this man. His expression is grave more than hostile, and his flat mouth is stern more than angry.

"I get help," he says and retreats through the door.

She drops to the floor, too dizzy to stand another second, then surveys her surroundings. The space is excessively decorated, with ornate woodwork, elegant armchairs, and floral patterned draperies. She stumbles to a window and throws back the curtain, revealing lush hedges and verdant gardens beyond. This is, without a doubt, the most opulent prison she's ever seen. She pushes on the sash, hoping to open the window and make her escape. But the frame is immovable, and her exertion reactivates her stomach's contortions. She gets back to the garbage pail just as the heaving starts again.

"May I help?" a gentle voice asks.

A trim, smiling woman in a white nurse's uniform stands over her. The woman's lips are bright red, and her smooth black hair is mostly covered with an elegant silk hijab.

"I'm really nauseous," Emily admits, "I get that way sometimes."

"Those men," the nurse gestures toward the door with evident disdain, "attempted to sedate you. They certainly aren't doctors."

She dimly recalls receiving a glass of water in the van. That's when the world went fuzzy.

"Perhaps you should return to your bed," the woman suggests.

"Who are you?"

"Nurse Farah, the person charged with helping you regain your health and strength."

"Is this a hospital?"

"This is Mr. Ng's country estate."

Mr. Ng? *Frank* Ng?

"May I see him?"

The nurse shakes her head, then opens a door on the far side of the room, revealing a white-tiled bathroom.

"The lavatory is there," she says, "along with fresh clothing. Once you are fully yourself, we can consider next steps."

Her accent is unfamiliar. Malaysian perhaps? But she's friendly enough, and her eyes convey more pity than malice. Still, she's an accomplice in Frank's conspiracy, whatever that is, and can't be trusted. Emily stumbles toward the opposite door, the one the gray-haired man used, and tries unsuccessfully to twist the knob, an effort that activates a fresh wave of dizziness. She topples to the floor.

The nurse comes to her side, cradling her shoulders and placing a cool palm on her overheated forehead.

"You can shower," the woman says, "and Mr. So will bring you a light breakfast. Then we can see if an audience with Mr. Ng will be possible."

The nurse helps Emily to the bed and then walks briskly to the door, uttering a few words in Cantonese. The gray-haired Mr. So opens it, allows the nurse through, then pulls the door firmly shut. There will be no escape by that route.

Emily accepts Nurse Farah's advice and takes the prescribed shower, letting the water wash away blood, sweat, and soot. She dresses in the comfortable and perfectly fitting clothing that her hosts have provided, then explores the room with clearer eyes. While she was showering, somebody removed the vomit-filled can and left her cleaned backpack, which, surprisingly, still contains her laptop. There's also a bowl of chicken broth, warm and steaming. Hunger forces her to sample the food, despite the potential risk of being sedated a second time. With her belly becalmed, she curls up in one of the window boxes and finishes the broth while gazing across the lush English gardens. Is this still Hong Kong? Is this one of the many Ng estates she never visited as a girl? There's so much about the family empire she has never understood.

She finds a wifi password on a sticky note and checks her messages. There's one from Mac, which she ignores, and another encrypted message from Seymour. It contains just two sentences:

"On my way to HK. Here's my flight info…."

She glances at her watch. Seymour will be in Hong Kong in less than five hours. The idiot. Has he no sense of self-preservation? No fear about what he might be bumbling into?

A soft rapping interrupts her thoughts. Mr. So steps in.

"Mr. Ng would like a few minutes of your time," he says in his gravelly voice.

She eyes him, quelling a growing panic. This man's recent rough treatment of her is still a visceral memory.

"If now is not convenient," he adds, "we can choose another–"

She nods vigorously.

"Now is fine."

She follows Mr. So through several hallways, arriving at a sort of royal sleeping chamber. An immense bed squats in the center of the room with Frank sitting atop it, his head bandaged, and an IV drip taped to one arm. The other arm is also bandaged, and the surrounding skin is red and mottled.

"My unexpected savior," he says weakly.

She rushes to him, eyes welling with tears, and gently takes his unbandaged hand.

"You're safe," she says, surprised at her own intense relief.

"It's not every day I'm almost cooked alive," he agrees, "but I would have been a goner if you hadn't dragged me out of there."

"The others?" she asks, already knowing the answer.

"Six of my best men," he says quietly. "And that poor little fool Greaves."

They sit for several minutes without speaking, his hand in hers.

"Was that Zahra's latest attempt on your life?" he asks finally.

She shrugs.

"It's gotten dangerous to be me."

"I've been wanting to talk with Zahra for months," he admits, "so when I realized you might be meeting her, I had to act."

His dark eyes are sad. He seems genuinely sorry for the betrayal.

"How did you get mixed up with her?" she asks. "I thought you hated all the hacking stuff."

"Kaylin, of course," he says sourly. "She and Zahra approached me with a bunch of secrets. Game-changing intelligence for my line of work."

Drug shipments? Money laundering? Counterfeiting? The triads run on secrecy. If Zahra and Kay helped Frank breach the veil of his rival's secrets, it would have been worth a great deal indeed.

"But something went wrong?"

"Several of my partner organizations got excited about Zahra's data-gathering capabilities. They wanted her to bring them facts about the government's new anti-organized crime campaign. We gave her a huge advance, but a few weeks later, she completely disappeared. My partners were…disappointed, to put it mildly."

"Was it a confidence game? Had she played you?"

He sighs, looking weary under the pile of bandages. He's an imposing figure in his giant bed, surrounded by the wealth of his ancestors, protected by his own private army. Yet there's fear in those big dark eyes—more than she's ever seen.

"Yesterday, I would have said yes, but now I'm not so sure. I mean, who can do something like this?"

He holds up a bandaged arm.

*The same people who sent that car,* she thinks.

"And you haven't heard the worst of it," he adds, turning to Mr. So, who stands quietly in the corner.

The gray-haired man reaches into his pocket and withdraws a long black object. She flinches before realizing it's just a television remote. Frank notices her discomfort.

"Mr. So and I should both apologize," he says, "for our behavior yesterday."

"So very sorry," the old man agrees in his thickly-accented English. Yet his eyes show no remorse. He presses a button, and a nearby television set illuminates, displaying the still image of a newswoman in a dark blue blazer."

"A newscast from this morning," Frank says.

Mr. So rolls the video. Onscreen, the woman speaks in crisp Cantonese. Emily understands perhaps every third word, but the meaning becomes clear as the image shifts to an overhead view of Zahra's office, apparently taken from a security camera. The scene begins with a jumble of smoke and overturned furniture. Then a figure, Emily herself, covered in soot and blood, appears in the lower left corner. She feebly drags Frank's massive, inert body across the floor toward the door on the far side of the screen.

The newscast zooms in on Emily's face, which is pixelated but recognizable. Mr. So pauses the video.

"Have they identified me?" she asks.

"Not officially," Frank says softly, "but we can assume they know who you are."

They scanned her passport when she arrived, after all. And they have old records from when she lived here as a teenager.

"The damn security cameras are everywhere," Frank mutters.

"Did they recognize you, too?" she asks.

He snorts.

"They were calling me before we even got home."

This is what comes from her clever strategies. She sought Kaylin and Zahra as though involving them would solve anything. She fell into her old, bad ways, associating with shady characters and taking shortcuts, digging herself a deeper hole. But the right answer is always the same: follow the law.

"Don't lie for my sake," she says, unable to suppress the tremble in her voice. "I'll go quietly."

"To hell with that!" Frank says, his expression suddenly hard and defiant. "They're not laying a finger on you. Not as long as I have breath and life."

Tears of gratitude fill her eyes, despite herself. Given the Ng family's history, the cops will not view his presence on that video as a coincidence. They'll hold him for months, maybe longer, hoping to garner a confession. They might even pin the whole bombing on him, especially if they can't find a likelier suspect. He could save himself by bargaining her away, by handing over his foreign NSA cousin in exchange for leniency.

"My mother had a way of taking people down with her," Emily says firmly. "That's what I'm doing to you, Frank. You see that, don't you?"

"You saved my life," he says emphatically. "It's a debt I can never fully repay. So please…" he squeezes her hand, "let me help you."

Seymour's message jumps to mind. He's flying into the middle of this mess. If she doesn't intervene, he'll be the next casualty.

"I have a friend arriving," she says. "Both the Americans and the Chinese will be waiting for him."

"Should I grab him and hide him?"

"Don't be too rough, please."

He smiles.

"We're pussycats, aren't we, Mr. So?"

The old man stares coldly and says nothing.

"And I'd like to meet up with this friend as well," she adds, "if you can arrange it."

"Naturally."

"After that, I'll be turning myself in."

"Turning yourself… what?"

"What's my end game, Frank? I'm a fugitive. I just need to tell the cops what I know."

"That's little people thinking," he says indignantly.

"Once it's over," she continues, "whether that takes months or years, I'll put all this behind me and live a normal life. But there's no other path to freedom than following the law."

"The cops will play you off as a dangerous foreign agent," he says with a scowl. "They'll say you're undermining our law-abiding Hong Kong society. And when the mainland security services realize you're NSA, they'll put you in a dark hole somewhere west of Xinjiang. Or maybe they'll just execute you."

Her over-stressed stomach gives a lurch. She'll never find her way back to normal if she's rotting in a Chinese prison.

"I've got friends in the shipping container business," he continues. "You could be on a freighter tomorrow and standing in Long Beach in two weeks. Once home, you can find any cop you want and spill your guts to them. At least you'll be navigating the American justice system."

Perhaps, but if Frank helps her escape the country, he may be digging himself an even deeper hole.

"What if I turn myself in at the US consulate?" she counters. "They could smuggle me home instead of you doing it."

"You'd be asking them to risk an international incident. They might decide it's easier to just turn you over to the Chinese. Then it's back to Xinjiang for you."

Would her government really risk letting her fall into Chinese hands? Given everything she knows?

"Help me snatch my friend," she concedes. "Then I'll figure out my exit strategy."

Whatever happens, she must extricate Seymour from this spiraling mess. Once he's safe and on a plane home, she can figure out her best option.

# NOODLE HOUSE

MR. SO'S gloved hands grip the wheel as the car rolls past row after row of monolithic apartment towers. All around them, the northern Kowloon roadway is packed with cars and motor scooters. As they approach an aging mid-rise building, Mr. So slows the car.

"Your friend here," the old man says.

He pulls up in front of a dilapidated shop. On a sign above the door, barely legible under thick grime, are two Chinese characters that she happens to know: " 麵 館 " or "Noodle House." She smiles. At least lunch is part of the deal.

She steps to the curb and gives Mr. So a little wave. He nods, and the car leaps away in a cloud of dust.

She enters the darkened restaurant, and a tiny bell tinkles overhead. The interior is tomb-like, and the atmosphere is dominated by spice and stale grease. Late-eighties chipped Formica countertops and oxidized chrome create a half-hearted fifties motif, but faded with long neglect. A middle-aged woman scowls from behind the cash register. More of Frank's happy crew?

"*Nei hou maa?*" Emily stammers in her terrible Cantonese. "*Is a man waiting for me?*"

The woman's expression remains inscrutable, but she

points toward a booth near the back. A figure moves in the gloom. A man rises to his feet, his narrow face framed by tangled black hair.

"The rest of my party is finally here," Seymour calls out. "I can finally order!"

She breaks into a run, fighting back the tears.

"You're an idiot," she shouts, arms extended, half in exasperation, half in joy.

They embrace, and his touch, his very presence, is an island of familiarity in this sea of chaos.

"Now that you're here," he says with a smile, "I'm feeling more confident that my hosts won't shoot me."

She glances furtively toward the cashier woman, who continues to stare out the window.

"Were Frank's guys, uh, gentle with you?"

He shrugs.

"They made it abundantly clear that resistance would be inadvisable. But they passed along your message, so I came fairly quietly."

She can only imagine.

They sit, and Seymour leans in, his intense stare revealing obvious concern.

"They also told me what happened, what you went through in that office tower."

He takes her hands in his.

"I should have realized how much danger you might be in if you came back to Hong Kong."

She squeezes his hands which are smooth and cool in her grip.

"You've come all this way to apologize?"

"To help."

She shakes her head.

"I'm done pretending to be a spy. Tomorrow I'm turning myself in at the US consulate."

"What are you guilty of?" he asks, brow furrowing with frustration. "Attempted martyrdom? Serial victimhood?"

"When I was doing my job and coloring inside the lines," she says, "everything was going smoothly. It was honest work, and I was making a fair wage. Things only went to shit after I reverted to my old, bad ways. That's when people started dying."

"So you're a murderer because you aren't a good little robot?"

"I violated NSA protocol and created a private attack against The Collective. They counterattacked, and Mom is dead. But instead of taking the hint, I came here as if I could force Zahra to see the error of her ways. Now seven *more* people are dead, and Frank is badly injured."

"You didn't reprogram that self-driving car," he says forcefully, "or build an incendiary device."

She sighs. Why can't he see what's so plain to her?

"Whenever my mother faced failure or setback," she says, "she always doubled down. When she left Hong Kong and ran off to America, the Ngs threatened to disown her. So she enrolled in medical school and married a Marxist. When that Marxist got himself killed, she circled the world, looking for his murderous guerilla friends, and offered them free medical care. When child services warned that her long absences were endangering her twelve-year-old daughter, she ran off to Nepal and opened a rebel field hospital. She believed that her heart was the best guide and rules were for suckers."

"Your mother was a terrorist," he says, kneading his temples. "We've been over that once or twice. But this isn't about her, it's about how you're going to survive what's being done to *you*. If you turn yourself in, they'll arrest you for her murder and for blowing up Zahra's office as well. They'll make you out to be the mastermind because that's the easiest and quickest way to cover their asses."

Will Mac let that happen? Can he stop it from happening?

"That's the hole I've dug myself."

"They'll send you back to prison, and this time for years. No parole, no deals."

"If that's the shortest path to true freedom and genuine redemption, then so be it."

His soft eyes stare for what seems like minutes…perhaps searching for any bridge between his more radical world-view and her own bleak assessment. Then his expression hardens.

"I know where Zahra lives," he whispers.

A charge of panic, like a developing migraine, flows through her head.

"Good for you."

"She owes me answers, too," he continues.

The tears return. They won't stop today.

"She'll kill you," she says, wiping her eyes.

"I acknowledge that something really bad is going on around here," he says, "and I agree that Zahra's probably mixed up in it. But I don't believe she ever signed up to execute people. That's never been her bag."

"Is she even sane any more? How would you know?"

He looks at the table and sighs.

"She hasn't been returning my messages. Not for months."

"So why do you think you know where she is?"

"Besides the whole natural language model upgrade, I also helped her build shell companies to hide her assets. The trick was hacking corporate databases so the 'beneficial owners' would have no linkage to her."

"Sounds like a Zahra kind of project."

"After you proved that a WayGo car killed your mom, I revisited those companies and reviewed their portfolios. I figured she might be living in one of their properties."

"And you found her?"

"If I tell you, you'll just pass the information to your pig bosses. Which means the only way you're finding Zahra is to come with me."

"To visit her in person? After everything that's happened?"

"We'll get her side of the story," he says, eyes wide and earnest. "We'll hear why she's been forced into this mess. And if you hate what she says, then you're still free to bare your soul to your NSA masters. But you will have heard Zahra out first."

Emily opens her mouth, preparing to tell him she's not interested, but he holds up his hand.

"Do we agree," he says, "that after tomorrow, after you turn yourself in, you'll be fucked for the foreseeable future?"

"Zahra's whole office went up in a ball of flame," she says. "I was there. I lived it. And that's what talking to Zahra will buy you."

"We were both part of The Collective," he says earnestly. "We removed power from the powerful and smashed the tools of war."

Those old mantras don't have the same impact they once did.

"We made ourselves rich in the process," she adds.

He shrugs.

"Did Zahra ever propose any violent actions or condone bloodshed in any form?"

The Collective's ethic of nonviolence, and its success in damaging the tools of violence, had been the spoonfuls of sugar that made Zahra's criminal medicine go down so easily. Emily personally sabotaged multiple defense projects by corrupting designs, siphoning funds, and otherwise throwing sawdust into the gears of the military-industrial complex. Through it all, Zahra had been steadfast: "Our methods are peaceful, and our goal is a less violent world."

"She must have changed," Emily says. "She found her inner mafiosa."

"She's in trouble," Seymour says firmly.

It's true that none of what Emily has experienced, not the car attack, nor Kaylin's odd living arrangement, nor the office bombing, feel remotely like Zahra's style. And she has to admit that confronting Zahra with her many sins would be highly satisfying, which makes Seymour's offer tempting. But what about him? How can she keep him safe?

"If NSA or CIA operatives see us together in Hong Kong or, worse if they see us with Zahra, then they'll have the evidence they've been looking for. You'll be arrested for being one of the comrades."

"That Mac asshole was at my house a few days ago," he says, "which means they're already thinking along those lines."

She should have known. Everything she does just digs this hole deeper.

Seymour seems to read her thoughts because he smiles sadly and puts his hand on her cheek.

"I'm in it up to my neck, sunshine. Which means the least you can do is see it through with me."

She broke up with Seymour because of moments like this, because of how casually reckless he can be.

She embraces his hand. His skin is soft—a man unused to physical effort, a person whose battles are fought in the electronic realm.

"You always get me in trouble," she says.

"I can definitely say the same thing about you."

"After we see Zahra, I'm still turning myself in. And I'm sharing whatever I've learned with the NSA."

"That's no less than I would have expected," he says sadly.

# THE CONSULATE

MAC STEELS himself as the receptionist ushers him toward the conference room door. The intelligence officers that he's about to meet are among the CIA's best, so he'll have to spin a story that is both complex and plausible, one that makes Emily seem guilty but also manageable. Yet, assuming they buy this story and agree to help him, then what? Once he brings Emily back to the States, does Chip just fire her? Does the FBI arrest her for participating in a criminal conspiracy? Does she wind up back in jail? He releases a calming breath. Right now, he has to get these men to help him. What he actually does with that help is an open question.

He steps through the door, and two men rise from a long conference table. Their ties are loosened, and their faces pale. The closer of the two, a square-jawed and stocky man, extends his hand.

"Ed Fong," he says, "you must be Mac."

Nominally Fong is a member of the consulate, but in reality, he's the senior CIA officer for East Asia.

"We're frankly surprised," Fong continues, "that you're making this trip on such short notice."

Mac grips the man's thick hand.

"Until two days ago, I didn't have a valid passport," he says with a chuckle.

The other man, white-haired and frail, steps forward.

"Lucas Pon," he says amiably.

Mac gently takes the bony hand. Pon's a legend in the CIA, with more than forty years in the field and numerous successes in uncovering Chinese and North Korean covert operations. He's also the person who nearly exposed Chip's extralegal operations here in the territory. Mac will have to tread carefully around him.

"And this," Fong says, pointing toward the back of the room, "is Consul General Michael O'Sullivan."

A third man, one Mac hadn't noticed, rises from the far end of the table. He's wide and pale-skinned, with florid cheeks and a scowl like a traffic cop.

"So you're the shadow factory man?" O'Sullivan says.

Mac suppresses a laugh. The phrase "Shadow Factory" is so Tom Clancy.

"Laurence MacCarthy," he says, extending his hand, "deputy director of tailored access operations."

"Is this your first time in the field, Mr. MacCarthy?" O'Sullivan asks, gripping his hand briefly and letting it go. "First time away from your cave in Fort Meade?"

"Ours is a sequestered life," Mac agrees, with forced amiability.

"So perhaps you don't know about the little festival we have every day in our front yard?"

"I came in through the garage," Mac says uncertainly.

O'Sullivan grunts, then strides to the windows, which are covered with heavy curtains. He throws them aside, revealing a courtyard where hundreds of people stand patiently in a serpentine line that wraps around the block. They clutch folders and paperwork. A few even grip American flags. Mac has seen the reports about the throngs applying for green cards and asylum, but the anguish on their faces has a larger impact in person.

"The city is experiencing a hidden civil war," O'Sullivan says, "fought between patriots who share the mainland's vision for a greater China and a smaller number of idealists who, until a few years ago, mistakenly believed they were living in a western-style democracy."

The point of this lecture is coming into focus. The State Department is giving the NSA a dressing down.

"I certainly understand," Mac says, in his most diplomatic tone, "that tensions with China make our mission challenging, that we are obliged to be cautious."

O'Sullivan glances again at Fong.

"Will you show our guest the footage?"

Fong taps a few keys on his laptop, and a screen on the opposite wall illuminates.

"This is a building surveillance video," Fong says. "An operative managed to extract it from the police records."

The video shows a bland white hallway with a tile floor and drop ceiling. An elevator along the left wall opens, and a group of men, all wearing Hawaiian shirts, emerge and fill the space. The largest of these men carries a prone figure which, Mac realizes, is Frank Ng. As the group approaches the camera, a woman becomes visible in the center. It's Emily, bloodied and covered with soot but with a look of grim determination on her face. It's not the face of a victim but of a player. Ed freezes the video.

"This was taken in the Cheung Kong Center's loading dock just minutes after the explosion," he says. "One of several high-definition videos the Chinese have of the events."

"Which seems to suggest," O'Sullivan adds, "that Ms. Hernandez is working with the triads. So how do you think the Chinese feel about that? What do they think about an NSA employee being embedded with the local crime gangs?"

The Chinese government's role has been imponderable, a variable he's tried to compartmentalize.

"I agree it's a race," Mac replies. "We've got to find her before they do."

"And if we succeed, do you believe the angry giant will just roll over?" O'Sullivan asks, face reddening. "Do you think they'll just shrug off a bombing in their downtown office district?"

"In all likelihood," Mac begins, in his most professional tone, "the Chinese believe that–"

O'Sullivan pounds the table with his fist, silencing the room.

"They believe we're subverting one of their most important and troubled cities!" he shouts. "They believe our government launched this woman, like a guided missile, straight into the heart of a powder keg!"

The long flight, the eight cups of airline coffee, and the insanity of what he's supposed to accomplish all churn his guts and make his hands tremble. He should tell this ass-kissing, bribe-taking, mistress-keeping functionary some of the things he knows. He should talk about O'Sullivan's private and undocumented yacht, his secret holdings in a Guandong hotel project, or his close ties with the Chinese Communist Party. In short, he should help Consul General O'Sullivan to see his own vulnerabilities more clearly.

Mac blinks and collects his wits. Pissing the consul general off will waste a golden opportunity. He must remember that.

"To be very honest, sir," Mac says, mustering his most contrite and respectful tone, "I've come to explain why this happened and how we will de-escalate the situation."

"Enlighten us," the consul says imperiously, taking a seat at the head of the table.

Mac falls into his own chair, gratefully accepting the glass of water offered by Lucas Pon. He sips it, focusing his fatigued mind on Chip's narrative, organizing and arranging the thread of lies that Chip has cleverly woven among the tapestry of facts. He begins with a distracting bombshell.

"Hiring Zahra Kartal's protege," he says, "was a bet that went sideways. But we can still recover. We can get Emily Hernandez back under NSA control."

Fong gasps, and O'Sullivan raises his bushy eyebrows.

"She worked for Zahra Kartal?" Fong says. "She was part of The Collective?"

Mac nods, warming to his task.

"The Collective's damage to both US business and national security was growing every year. So when the FBI caught Ms. Hernandez as part of their identity theft operation, we viewed it as more than just an isolated win. We saw a strategic opening."

Of course, catching Emily was easy enough. Zahra told Mac exactly what crime she committed and how to find her. This was Zahra's way of firing Emily, though he never knew what had caused their falling-out. Whatever the reason, the wily woman made a huge blunder, and the NSA wound up with a valuable hacker.

"You turned her?" Pon says, his old eyes sharp.

Emily's conversion from a criminal hacker to an NSA analyst was surprisingly easy. The only tricky part had been negotiating the terms of her parole—she'd insisted on only betraying just one member of The Collective: Zahra. It was an awkward compromise and, in retrospect, unworkable.

"We hoped we had," he says, "but to mitigate the danger of incorporating a criminal into the NSA, we paired her with a trusted senior analyst who would act as mentor and minder. This minder was supposed to ensure that she worked on the right projects and remained loyal to the agency."

This greatly exaggerates Ben Katz's role. He was really just Emily's co-worker. To the extent that she had a 'minder,' it was supposed to be Mac himself. But enhancing Ben's importance in this story is Chip's way of adding more pressure to the search. The old man wants every CIA operative looking out for Katz, though why Director Chip fears that strange hippie so much remains unclear.

Lucas Pon stirs, his expression unsettled, his dark eyes thoughtful.

"A report about Ben Katz came across my desk," he says. "So he's part of this conspiracy?"

Not much gets by this old fellow.

"We believe Zahra obtained leverage on Ben, perhaps by tempting him into some sort of personal or financial impropriety."

"A honey trap?" Fong asks.

Mac nods sagely, though, in reality, they have no idea why Ben left or what he's doing out there.

"Owning Katz gave Zahra a way to turn the tables and also gave her intel on the NSA's plans to catch her."

Pon leans back in his chair and closes his eyes, a slight frown wrinkling his lined brow. Fong and O'Sullivan watch him as if he's an oracle about to spout some earth-shaking prophecy. Yet Pon doesn't seem ready to prophesize. He seems confused or perhaps just frustrated.

"Take us farther back," he mutters, eyes still closed. "How did Zahra recruit Emily?"

The stale coffee takes another dangerous lap around Mac's gut. This story is a block of Swiss cheese… full of holes. He has to be careful.

"Kaylin Ng brought her in."

"Kaylin Ng?" Pon clarifies. "Former triad boss? Sister of Frank Ng? Daughter of Ip To Ng?"

"Emily is first cousin to Kaylin and Frank," Mac says, "but actually more like their sister. She lived with the Ngs from age thirteen until she went to college."

"How did that come about?" Fong asks.

"Her mother, Audrey Ng, was a black sheep and fled the family as a teenager. She came to the States, got a medical degree, and met Sebastian Hernandez, a known domestic terrorist."

"Emily's father is a terrorist?" O'Sullivan asks.

Mac nods, humoring the obviously stupid question.

"Eventually," he continues, "Audrey herself went to prison, essentially orphaning her daughter. That's when Audrey's brother, Ip To Ng, brought Emily back to Hong Kong. She became like one of his children and was especially close to his daughter Kaylin. Later, when Emily was at Stanford, Kaylin asked her to join the venture she and Zahra were starting.

"Kaylin invited her to join The Collective?" Pon clarifies.

Mac nods.

"Emily's Stanford scholarship wasn't a fluke. She's an extremely talented computer scientist. And when she quit college and joined Kaylin, The Collective had a new star hacker. Her biggest contribution was the so-called Automatic Programming, Rule-based, Intelligent Learning system or APRIL, which was the founding technology of their new botnet."

"Botnet? Intelligent... what?" O'Sullivan asks, looking baffled.

"A botnet," Pon says calmly, "is a swarm of computer viruses that run on many different systems and coordinate via the internet. Botnets are Zahra's preferred weapon."

"The APRIL technology," Mac continues, "is how The Collective's bots camouflage and reprogram themselves in response to threats and changes in their environment. It's how they're able to burrow so deeply into impregnable systems. So, as you might imagine, our first assignment for Emily was to find ways to attack and neutralize APRIL."

This story omits the fact that Chip's black operations actually funded The Collective and that his real objective isn't to neutralize the botnet but to double-cross Zahra and steal it.

Pon closes his eyes again and leans back in his chair. His

expression is a mixture of disgust and irritation as if he's never heard anything so improbable and half-baked.

"Audrey Ng's bizarre death," he murmurs quietly, "being crushed by a car in her bedroom… Who are the suspects in that murder case? Emily? Zahra?"

A drop of sweat trickles down Mac's temple and strikes the table. Is it more upsetting to fail at selling this rubbish story or to succeed? Does he even want these people to believe Chip's story?

"Zahra clearly sent that car," Mac says. "We believe The Collective views Emily as their biggest liability. They want her eliminated."

This was the part of the story Chip feared they wouldn't buy. After all, what kind of hacker organization also performs brazen, high-profile executions? Ironically, it's the part of the story that Mac himself has come to believe might be true.

"Given all Emily did for you," Pon says, "you seem rather quick to join Zahra in throwing her under the bus."

Mac struggles to hide his surprise. Does this mean Pon believes him? Or is he just humoring him? Playing along until he trips himself up?

"We're doing everything we can to save her," he says with his best attempt at heartfelt vehemence, "but we can't ignore her recent mistakes."

Pon nods thoughtfully.

"What about the man you asked us to tail? Seymour Frey, was it?"

"Did you hear how that went down?" Fong adds.

"I heard that Seymour dry-cleaned you," Mac says. "That he shook your surveillance and vanished."

"Somebody was helping him," Fong says. "They couldn't have evaded us otherwise."

"The Collective, no doubt," Mac says.

"Then it would appear that we face yet another talented and resourceful foe," Pon observes.

"Which is why I need your help," Mac says.

"I'm not sure helping you is the best way to protect US interests.," O'Sullivan says.

Mac's anger rises, threatening to burst through this time.

"I was unaware that the state department had any say in the matter, Mr. O'Sullivan. Doesn't the CIA make its own decisions?"

Ed Fong smiles sadly.

"Due to the sensitivity of our relationship with the Chinese, the state department must sign off on any covert operation in this city."

Mac sighs. Perhaps it's better this way. If he can win over both the state department *and* the CIA, then there will be more groups to share the blame when things go south.

"I'm not asking for an extraordinary rendition," he says, "or any sort of black op at all. We believe it's now clear to Emily that her Ng family influence won't protect her. We believe she'll surrender peacefully."

"I wonder if she's as cowed as you believe," Pon muses.

"What deal will you offer her?" Fong adds.

"If she provides actionable intelligence about Zahra's whereabouts, then federal attorneys will only charge her with concealing the conspiracy rather than treating her as the mastermind of it. She'll get three years rather than twenty."

"The justice department agreed to that?" Fong asks, incredulous.

"Zahra's the real culprit. They'll trade the small fish for her."

"There is too much evidence against Zahra," Pon says abruptly.

Fong and O'Sullivan turn toward the old man, wide-eyed.

"Our agents say she's in Jakarta one day," he continues, "then Lagos the next. We intercept her texts, we find her bank accounts, and we trace her real estate transactions. In one sense, she's more active and frenetic than ever. Yet it's all contrails, never hard sightings."

"She's slippery," Fong says reasonably.

"Operatives used to see her partying with Prince Mohammed bin Salman in Riyadh one week and swimming with Jack Ma in Shanghai the next. We never get those hard sightings anymore."

The old man is right. Something changed with Zahra, and not for the better. She got more cautious, more slippery. Does she have more to lose these days?

"These are mysteries that Emily will help us untangle," Mac says, pressing his point.

"How will it go down?" Fong asks.

"I've been broadcasting encrypted messages for more than a week, which she's been ignoring. But now I'm offering a live meeting and being specific about our exfiltration plan. I'm proving to her that we're serious, that we have our own skin in the game."

"That's the best your big NSA brains came up with?" O'Sullivan says. "'Meet me for lunch, and I'll take you to Leavenworth?'"

"How can you actually get her out of the territory?" Pon asks.

"A cargo plane will carry her to the Philippines. From there, the US Air Force will take her home. But I need your help evading and avoiding Chinese security."

"You're goddamned right about that," O'Sullivan says, the purple color returning to his cheeks, "because if either the Ministry of State Security or the Hong Kong authorities realize what you're doing, you'll both wake up at the bottom of a pit in Qincheng prison."

No chance of that, Mac thinks sadly. Chip is sure to have a cleaner monitoring this operation. If the exfiltration goes sideways, then the only things the Chinese will capture are corpses.

"Such a resourceful person," Pon says, "might not accept your generous offer of prison time. She might forge her own way, maybe with Mr. Seymour Frey's help."

"She's not a terrorist like her mother," Mac says, "or a triad thug like her cousin. Her life's been spent in front of a computer. She avoids physical danger."

"And yet she remains at large," Pon counters, "even though there's a citywide manhunt for her in relation to the highrise bombing."

"The irregulars want her too," Fong adds. "Russians, Iranians, not to mention the other triads. If she's such a desk jockey, how has she evaded all these folks?"

He frankly wonders that himself. Perhaps Chip's fairy tale does hold kernels of truth. Maybe the hazel-eyed woman in the frozen video is as resourceful and dangerous as outward appearances suggest.

He shakes off the thought. He's starting to drink his own Kool-Aid. Emily only appears threatening because she's struggling for her very life and because she thinks there's some other solution than a prison stay. He's here to reconcile her with hopelessness, to disabuse her of the idea that she can win, and to break her will to fight. Only then will she understand what her real options are.

"She'll take the deal," he says softly, "and we'll get her out of here before any of them can get their hands on her. That's how we'll solve your problem and ours. Without fanfare or trouble."

# VICTORIA PEAK

THE CITY BUS is nearly empty on its last run to Victoria Peak. Little is visible beyond the darkened windows, only the occasional outline of a tropical tree as they wind their way up the mountain. The bus has surveillance cameras, so they keep their sunglasses on and their hoodies pulled tight. The long ride gives her time to think about Zahra, about meeting her after so many years. Will they lapse into their old habits? Can Emily resist making accusations? Will Zahra repeat her demands for loyalty and claim Emily stabbed her in the back?

Seymour's warm shoulder rests against her, and she longs, in spite of herself, to put her arm around him. But they've been down that road before, and the fights grow in direct proportion to the hours they spend together. Being apart is the only viable option, yet here she is, sneaking glances at him, wondering what he's thinking as he stares through the smoky glass. Could he be dreading his own reckoning with Zahra? Will he re-open all his old arguments about The Collective's mission and how it should be using its vast power? Or will he confine himself to asking her what the hell happened with his WayGo car?

He straightens abruptly and glances at his phone.

"This is it," he whispers and presses the stop-request

button. The bus rolls to a halt, and the door swings open, filling the cabin with sultry air. She follows Seymour to the pavement, then watches as the bus trundles away. With a sinking heart, she pulls her hoodie even tighter over her head.

"This incognito shtick sucks," she mutters.

"Unavoidable," he says, "in a world filled with video cameras."

They proceed up the lane, approaching a row of three-storied homes, each framed by stately palms and lush tropical gardens.

"Zahra lives in the high-rent district," he says with evident disapproval.

That's an understatement. "The Peak," as the locals call it, is the most expensive neighborhood in the most expensive city on earth. Beverly Hills is nothing but McMansions by comparison.

"Being on the lam ought to mean living crappier than this," he continues.

"Crappy was never Zahra's style," Emily says. "Kaylin, maybe, but never Zahra."

"What made those two split?"

She shrugs.

"Zahra likes risk, Kaylin, not so much. It was a circle they couldn't square."

They stroll past more mansions, down a lane shrouded by trees, and around a bend where the road skirts a sheer cliff. The Hong Kong skyline glitters in the distance, its skyscrapers rising, like metal stalagmites, above the black surface of Victoria Harbor. The town seems painted in brilliant hues of pink and yellow and bluish-white, and she pauses, awestruck at the grandeur of this jewel-like city—moisture welling at the corner of her eye.

"I shouldn't have left Hong Kong," she whispers. "It was the closest thing I had to a real home."

How would her life have turned out if she'd stayed?

Would she have finished college? Would she have still felt compelled to rescue her mother from her self-inflicted financial troubles? Would she have accepted Kaylin's invitation to join The Collective? And would she have been living at Ip's house the night he was gunned down?

"You wouldn't have met me," Seymour says softly, then tugs gently on her hand. It's not safe to linger.

They proceed along Plantation Road, ascending the peak, keeping to the shadows. At the intersection with Polluck's Path, he taps her shoulder.

"That's it," he whispers, pointing to a corroded metal door embedded in a massive stone wall. Behind the wall, the tops of scraggly pines partially obscure a meandering stucco home that is surprisingly decrepit for this exclusive neighborhood. Streaks of mold stain the walls, and cracks suggest the neglect may be more than skin deep. It looks abandoned.

"Is Zahra hurting for money?" she asks.

He points to a mass of radio dishes and electronic gear jutting above the roof.

"Six different service providers connect her to the internet with microwave and free space lasers. I found this place by triangulating from their line-of-sight transmitters."

"So she spends money on networks rather than paint?"

He shrugs. "This is just a minor hub, an infinitesimal part of the millions of computers that unwillingly host APRIL's brain. So maybe it's not an important locale for her."

He steps from the shadows and motions for her to follow.

"Let's not –" she begins, but he's already striding up to the gate and jamming his finger on the call button. A minute passes. The intercom box stays quiet. He tries a second time, then raps the gate with his knuckles. She draws up next to him.

"It's not too late to catch that last bus back down the mountain," she whispers.

He shakes his head and begins walking the perimeter of

the giant stone fence. She follows him around the corner and down the side street.

"Where are you going?" she whispers.

"To the back entrance."

He puts his hands on the rocky surface of the stone fence, perhaps feeling for purchase, then glances up and down the street before scrabbling up the side. In less than ten seconds, he's at the top.

"Your turn," he calls.

When the plan was to visit Zahra at her lavish mansion, she was nominally willing to follow. But this is a home invasion.

"I'll wait here," she replies.

"Suit yourself."

He vanishes, and moments later, there's a faint "thud" on the far side.

An engine whines in the distance, and the air fills with the glow of an approaching vehicle. She looks toward the growing light, then glances at the jagged wall. When the car arrives, she'll be standing out here, loitering next to this mansion for no good reason. Should she pretend to be taking a night walk? Should she wave as the car passes by?

"Goddammit, Seymour," she mutters and clasps the jagged rocks. The mortar is badly eroded, so it's easy to find good handholds. She reaches the top just as the car rounds the corner and washes the street with brilliant light. It clatters past, hopefully oblivious to her presence.

"Did you change your mind?" Seymour calls from somewhere below.

"Help me down," she says and swings her legs over the edge, feeling for a toehold. Her foot finds an outcropping of rock, and she puts her weight onto it. It dislodges with a faint "pop," and she's airborne, hurtling toward the unknown yard below. For a moment, she imagines Seymour ready to help her, his skinny arms extended like a figure skater poised to catch his partner. Then she lands on him, and he crumples, allowing them both to topple into a mound of prickly shrubs.

"Ow, ow, ow," he whispers, his eyes wide and his hair in tangles.

"Did I hurt you?" she asks, scrambling to her feet.

He takes inventory of his injuries, then stands next to her.

"You're heavier than you look," he says.

"And you're dumber than *you* look."

The old house looms over them, taller from this vantage point than it appeared from the street. Ninety years ago, it would have been modern and grand, with wide balconies on every level and sliding doors affording the rooms with easy access to fresh air. Now it's more like a ruin than a living space, with an overgrown yard, boarded-up windows, and metalwork rusted nearly to powder. It's a house that's been left to fend for itself against wind and weather, perhaps for decades.

"I'm feeling less confident that we'll see Zahra tonight," she whispers.

He shakes his head with a mischievous smile.

"Her shell company filed plans to demolish it," he says. "But that's obvious window-dressing. I mean, look at that brand-new hardware."

He points to the conduit running from the rooftop antenna array along the side of the house and disappearing into the wall.

"It's wired for, like, twenty terabits per second."

A shiver runs up her spine as she examines the tangle of cables. What kind of condemned house needs a data center's network capacity?

"Zahra's hiding in plain sight," Seymour whispers as if reading her mind. "Slumming in the most expensive real estate on earth."

Which sounds exactly like Zahra, now that she thinks

about it. Her eyes sweep from the network conduit upward to a video camera mounted on the wall. She points to it.

"She's already watching us."

Seymour waves at the camera.

"Hi, Zahra," he says. "We're not leaving 'till you talk with us."

Emily suppresses the urge to bolt for the fence. Her most recent audience with Zahra left seven people dead.

"She left the welcome mat for us," he says, pointing toward a second-story balcony.

Emily follows his gaze. One of the patio doors is partially open. The room beyond it is dark, like the rest of the house.

"That's more neglect than an invitation," she replies, but Seymour is already grasping the railings and pulling himself onto the balcony. He holds out his hand, and she takes it, scrambling to join him.

"I didn't know you loved parkour so much," she whispers.

"Life's boring in Mountain View."

He steps through the door but abruptly turns back, an odd look on his face. She puts her own tentative foot through and immediately understands his reaction. The interior has a distinct odor, faint but foul, subtle but pervasive.

"Somebody forgot to flush the toilet," he mutters.

"Smells like the dumpster behind Hop Woo's Barbeque," she says.

"Remind me never to eat there."

Feeble moonlight filters through the dirty windows, leaving the room in near-total darkness. He uses his mobile phone light to illuminate the space, revealing a room devoid of furnishings, covered in a thick layer of dust. He opens the door on the far side, and the Hop Woo dumpster smell strengthens. She gulps, resisting the temptation to pinch her nostrils, and follows him.

The rest of the house is much the same. Empty rooms of

filthy desolation, giving every sign of a building prepped for demolition, not the hideout of a notorious hacker genius. And as they descend to the first floor, the stink becomes nausea-inducing.

"Maybe there's a rat infestation," Seymour says, his voice a little thick.

Emily pictures Zahra as she'd last seen her. Coiffed black hair streaked with gray, a tailored suit, and her favorite white pearl necklace. Zahra's age was something of a mystery— probably closer to Audrey's than Emily's. Yet the great woman had so much more style than her practical mother.

"She'd never live in this pigsty," Emily says.

"Those network links are white-hot," Seymour says. "Somebody's shoveling all those bits."

They reach a set of double doors which he pushes open. A cloud of conditioned air confronts them like a magical wall, and the stench subsides somewhat. The space beyond, which might have been a grand dining room, is bare of furniture. Plywood covers the windows, and along every wall are racks of computer systems, with blinking LED lights illuminating the space, power cables snaking across the floor, and cooling ducts punched crudely through the walls. It's Kaylin's apartment on steroids.

"Zahra's bat cave," Seymour mutters.

She finds her voice.

"How many bots can she herd with this system?"

"These are control nodes," he says, "that communicate with mid-level nodes. They're several layers up the pyramid."

So this house is a focal point for several million bots, maybe more. And since Zahra loves scale and redundancy, this is undoubtedly just one of dozens, perhaps hundreds of such control points.

The thought creates a pulse of anger in her chest, part resentment, part disgust. Without Emily's own contributions, the AI-powered core known as APRIL would never have gotten this far. Yet it's Zahra who inherited all the wealth and power. Emily got prison.

"Do your NSA pals even begin to appreciate what they're up against?" Seymour says, voice reverent.

Ben once suggested that APRIL might reach this kind of scale. She'd laughed at him.

"Botnets always contain the seeds of their own undoing," she had scoffed. "Bredolab, Mariposa, Conficker... they create too much disruption to stay hidden."

But not APRIL. Her botnet has remained quiet and largely undiscovered despite being orders of magnitude larger than her own wildest predictions.

"Just how much money do you think APRIL brings to The Collective these days?" Seymour says quietly. "

The frigid air pricks her skin. She shivers.

"Zahra's not here," she replies. "We've come for nothing."

He frowns, puzzlement evident on his thin face.

"I was so sure," he says. "All the signs pointed to it."

He strides out of the dining room and into the darkness, his phone flashlight lighting a path ahead of him.

"The owners won't let us trespass forever," she calls after him.

"There's a light on over here," he replies, "some kind of stairway."

His footsteps fade. She follows, fumbling with her own phone's light. And with every step, the Hop Woo dumpster smell intensifies. Then Seymour is calling to her, his voice filled with panic.

"Emily!" he's saying, "Oh, Jesus God!"

She stumbles, dashing toward his voice. The putrescence becomes so vile that she can barely breathe. Her throat closes, and her eyes water. Yet she presses ahead, reaching a darkened stairwell. A bluish light glows at the bottom.

"Seymour?" she calls.

She descends to the first step, but before she can take the

second, Seymour is bursting onto the landing below, shivering and eyes wide. Without warning, he doubles over and vomits against the wall, his body shaking like he's being electrocuted.

The sight of him retching, combined with the nearly intolerable stench, puts her into fight or flight mode.

*Should I run? Should I never look back?*

Yet a greater force pushes her forward, a growing certainty she cannot escape. Seymour's heaving stops, but he continues to face the wall, wheezing quietly. She steps past him, crossing the threshold into the dimly lit room.

Beyond is a concrete bunker with institutional gray walls illuminated by a bluish LED light mounted into the ceiling. The basics for survival are here: a tiny kitchenette, a petite couch, and a modest television. But the space is disheveled; chairs are overturned, and dishes are broken. And at the center is a sight too horrible and too familiar to look away from…the remains of a woman, attired in a well-tailored suit, one arm hacked away, and a good bit of the lower body missing. The corpse lies in the center of an oval stain, bodily fluids long dried in the warm air. A skeleton's head sits at the top of the business suit wrapped in leathery skin, a rictus smile revealing gaping teeth. The skeleton's head rests amid a nest of gray and black hair. A fly crawls leisurely out of an eye socket.

"Oh, Zahra," she says quietly. "Jesus, Zahra."

All their efforts, all their plans to confront her, were always destined to fail. And Kaylin had known this, or at least strongly suspected. She'd sent Emily to that office as an act of desperation, a longshot attempt to prove that her sometime friend and lover was not, as she no doubt feared, already dead. But there is no happy ending to this story. No way to wrap up the loose ends. Emily, Kay, Frank, Seymour, Ben, and Mac have been chasing a phantom. Now they must start from zero.

The foul air spins her head and darkens her vision. She grows faint, and her legs turn to jelly. She's far down a dead-end road, the same kind of misguided path her mother always followed. And like Audrey, she keeps assuming there are shortcuts, easier routes to freedom. Yet, once again, life proves that there is only one way to achieve peace and happiness. There is only one true path, the one she keeps avoiding.

She stumbles from the room, past Seymour, and up the stairway, groping toward the open door and the fresher air above. She's leaving this house, this town, this country. She has to get home and start anew. There's nothing of her existing life to salvage. She's done trying to cheat reality.

# SIDE CHANNEL HACK

SHE REACHES the top of the stairs, struggling for the filtered, conditioned air of the makeshift server room. When she reaches it, she crumples to the floor, her forehead moist, sweat dripping down her neck and back. Seymour collapses on the floor beside her.

"I've never smelled anything like that," he gasps.

The stench won't leave her nostrils. It's spoiled meat, dead possum, dog shit, all mixed together and left in the sun.

"How long has she been down there?" she asks.

"A month," he says with a cough. "Maybe two."

He's stone-faced. A few globs of vomit cling to his chin. He wipes it away with the back of his hand.

"Did you see..." he says, voice thick, "how mangled the body was?"

She conjures the image of that grimacing corpse, then shivers.

"Her arm was blown off," he continues. "Her midsection, her lower body. It was all..." he struggles for the words, "...shredded," he says finally.

"A bomb?"

He nods.

"Wouldn't the neighbors have heard or smelled something?"

"It's a big house, a big yard, and a high fence. She's got that bunker thing going on down there."

He sighs.

"I guess she really was isolated at the end."

Emily considers the beguiling, smiling woman who seduced all of them into building a hacking empire. Had that charming, maddening person finished her days like a rat in a hole?

Seymour's breathing is slowing. His eyes seem to brighten a little.

"I saw something down there," he says, "and I have to get it."

He rises to his feet and then walks unsteadily toward the basement.

What could be worth going back into that place? With that ghoul lying on the floor?

"It's a crime scene!" she shouts.

But his footsteps are at the stairs, then fading as he makes his way toward the basement. She scrambles to her own feet and dashes after him. But the cloud of putrefaction burns her eyes and twists her stomach. She clamps her hand over her mouth and steps back. She can't go down there again.

A thud rises from the basement, then a crash, then Seymour is shooting up the stairs, mouth clamped shut, eyes bulging. In his hands is an open, glowing laptop. He elbows past her, dashing toward the bright lights and relatively uncorrupted air of the makeshift server room. Once inside, he collapses to his knees and lays the prize on the floor in front of him.

"What have you done?" she says, kneeling beside him.

He points to the laptop, cheeks bulging as if fresh vomit might spurt from his mouth.

"Is it hers?"

He swallows, then nods.

"Sleep... mode... disabled," he manages to say.

Comprehension dawns. Zahra had her laptop open when whatever happened to her happened. And it remained that way, open and powered on, from then until now. In the world of hackers, this sort of find is nearly unheard of.

"It's a crime scene," she says again, face warming. "That laptop is evidence."

"A laptop in the hand is worth two on the internet," he says, regaining his composure. "And we shouldn't let it fall into the hands of the Chinese," he continues. "Wouldn't your NSA masters agree?"

Her face burns at the taunt.

"Why do you care?"

"It almost certainly contains compromising information. Stuff that would ruin lives. Kaylin's, for one."

She hadn't considered that. But this is *Zahra's* laptop, after all.

"It may also contain clues about what happened to our friend down there," he says, motioning toward the darkened stairwell.

The laptop does present a precious, perhaps irreplaceable, opportunity. It almost certainly has its secure decryption key still in volatile memory. A person with the right skills and tools could potentially decrypt the entire solid-state drive, unlocking terabytes of irreplaceable knowledge.

"We'll never get it to the right people before the battery dies," she says firmly.

He gives a small smile and then digs into his pack, withdrawing several objects, including cables, tools, and an aerosol can.

"I am the right people," he says and removes the screws from the back of the laptop.

"Are you trying a side-channel hack?"

"Sort of."

He points the nozzle of the aerosol can toward the motherboard and begins spraying.

"This stuff hurts like a bitch if you get it on your skin," he mutters.

He continues spraying until several components turn frosty white.

"A cold boot attack, then?"

He selects a matchbook-sized rectangular box from his collection of tools. It has spidery clips dangling from the bottom and a long cable protruding from the top.

"Sort of."

He withdraws his own laptop from the pack and attaches it to the cable, then presses the black matchbox onto the largest frost-covered microchip in Zahra's exposed motherboard until the array of metal clips latch onto the frozen circuitry. He returns to his laptop and types a command.

"Steve Jobs once wrote," he says, fingers still clattering on keys, "that there is no theory of protecting data that doesn't involve keeping secrets."

He lifts the battery from Zahra's computer and gives it a jerk. The power cable snaps free, and the device emits a chirp as its screen goes dark. He tosses the battery aside, then returns to his laptop, tapping a few more commands. A wide grin spreads across his face.

"And I'm pretty sure I just got Zahra's most important secret."

An ache blossoms in her chest. If his little spidery gadget really caught the laptop's encryption key, then they may possess many useful secrets, including who Zahra's new partners were and why that relationship went so badly wrong. It might prove Emily's innocence and restore her to her old job. But obtaining that knowledge is another doubling down, another step into the void.

"This is reckless," she says.

"We're seeking the truth," he replies, eyes locked onto his own computer screen.

"I was trying to have it both ways," she continues, "so, in violation of agency policy, I hacked APRIL with my own equipment from my mother's internet connection."

"You built the heart of that botnet," he says. "It's yours, and if anybody has a right to hack it, that would be you."

She can't avoid smiling at his vote of confidence, displaced though it is.

"Later," she continues, "when I feared the FBI was on the wrong track, I chose to find that murderous car myself. I thought I could do the agent's job for them."

"You realized they're idiots."

"I told myself I wasn't really bending the rules, that I had every right to make my own inquiries."

"And you succeeded where they failed," he says. "As always."

"But it wasn't enough," she continues. "Because once you told me how to find Kaylin, the easy and reckless choice was to confront her myself. Another doubling down. Another cowgirl move."

"Giddyap cowgirl!" he says, still typing on his keyboard. "Anyway, your other choice was to hand all the facts to the assholes and screw over your friends. You did the honorable thing."

She shakes her head.

"When my dad's radicalism got him killed, my mom's grief coalesced into a single-minded determination: She would carry on his fight. She would double down in the face of every new calamity and every new arrest. It was her go-to move."

He taps a final key with gusto, then looks up triumphantly.

"Got it!" he says.

"Keep it."

He detaches the laptop from his own computer and holds it out to her.

"This is your quest. See it through."

"So Mac," she says, affecting a mock professional tone and backing away from the proffered device, "I blew up Zahra's office and broke into her haunted mansion, then I pried this laptop from her cold dead hands. Oh, and my friend Seymour, the one you can't prove is a domestic terrorist? He hacked the laptop's encryption for us. So here it is, I'm sure you can trust everything you find on it. And by the way, can I have my old job back?"

Seymour's shoulders droop and his face deflates. He looks as if he hasn't slept in days, which he probably hasn't.

"I didn't come here to help you get your stupid job back."

"I'm turning myself in tomorrow," she says softly, "and you should get clear of the blast radius."

# DELIVERY DRONES

SEYMOUR WINCES AS IF SLAPPED.

"When you came to my house last week," he says, dark eyes wide with anger, "I thought you'd rediscovered some attachment to your life and future. I thought you'd remembered how to be an independent person, not some automaton cop or whatever it is you've become."

Emily opens her mouth to object but closes it again. She doesn't want to fight him or hurt him. It's been a huge relief to share this burden with somebody and to have his support when times got tough. But gratitude clouded her judgment. It tempted her back into her old habits.

He's looking at her, his sad eyes patient as ever. She resists the urge to embrace his narrow shoulders and press her face against his stubbly cheeks, to lose herself in his warm embrace. That wouldn't be fair. Not to either of them.

"It's not that I remembered, Seymour," she says, struggling to keep her voice from cracking, "it's that I forgot. I forgot my suffering as the child of domestic terrorists. I forgot what it's like to look over my shoulder all the time. And most of all, I forgot the promise I made to myself the day I quit Zahra."

His expression softens, shifting to something more like understanding or, perhaps, resignation.

"Let's at least not climb over that stupid stone fence a second time," he says quietly. "Let's walk right out the front door."

She glances around the server room.

"Should we wipe our fingerprints first?" she asks. "Yours, at least?"

Removing her own fingerprints probably doesn't matter— her face is all over the Hong Kong news, and it's hard to be more screwed than that.

"I modified the relevant law enforcement databases," he says. "My prints won't match anything."

"If they arrest you and take new prints, they'll still match this crime scene. No database required."

"I'm not getting arrested," he says with a shrug.

She takes a last look around the room, at the millions of dollars of equipment guiding the most powerful distributed computing system of all time: the APRIL botnet, a giant sponge soaking spare cycles from millions, perhaps billions, of computers worldwide. Yet even if she burned Zahra's house to the ground, the destruction of this equipment would be chump change compared to the real game being played by somebody... somewhere.

They navigate through the foyer and arrive at a broad wooden door covered with deadbolts and chains. Seymour manages to unfasten them all, then tugs on the door, which creaks loudly as it swings inward. Beyond is what might have once been a charming courtyard with a fountain, concrete benches, and a flagstone path. But the fountain is dry, the benches are cracked, and the path is choked with weeds.

"Zahra really knew how to keep up the place," she says, following him through the tangle.

"Dead people don't usually..." he begins, but his voice trails off. He cocks his head, and his body goes rigid.

"Do you hear that?" he whispers, glancing first left, then right, and finally toward the sky.

She follows his gaze but sees only stars. Yet there is a sound out there, a distant buzzing, like a swarm of mechanical mosquitoes.

Seymour's eyes grow wide. "Run!" he shouts, then dashes toward her, leaping over brambles and weeds, arms flailing pell-mell. Then he's grabbing her, shoving her earthward while, behind him, something strikes the ground with a deafening crunch.

"What –" she begins, mind swimming with pain and confusion. But Seymour is on his feet, tugging and herding her back toward the entrance. Something whirs behind him, then clips his arm before striking the ground and smashing itself to bits.

They cross the threshold, and Seymour throws the door into the path of a grayish blur that's hurtling in their direction. The object strikes the far side with a crash as if somebody just hurled a toaster at them. Seymour secures the latches and then leans against the door, panting.

"Drones," he whispers.

Her heart accelerates with realization…if you can hijack an entire WayGo prototype, then weaponizing somebody's drones would be child's play. While they've been dallying here, their enemies have marshaled a drone army to take them out.

"How many?" she asks in a quavering voice.

He puts his ear to the wood, brow furled in concentration.

"Maybe five. But more may be nearby, just in case the first wave fails.

The concept "fail" needs no explanation. The drones are here to do the job that the self-driving car and office bomb couldn't finish.

The buzzing changes and moves, and suddenly it's alongside the house, outside the boarded windows.

"Are they carrying explosives?" she asks.

"We'd already be dead," he says, examining his injured arm. His shirt sleeve is torn, and the skin underneath is gashed and bleeding.

"I think they're carrying tools, maybe knives or shears. Whatever the controllers could find on short notice."

Her heart pounds against her lungs. She struggles for breath.

"We can't stay here," she says, as much to herself as Seymour.

"If we had a way to fend them off," he says thoughtfully, then seems to remember something and dashes back down the hallway. She catches up to him just as he's entering the server room. The blinking computer towers no longer seem so benign or idle. They're sentinels, guarding this facility against invaders like them.

Seymour grabs a card table that was folded against one wall.

"This might help," he says. "We can hold it over our heads and –"

He stops, eyes wide.

"Do you hear that?" he says, his voice trembling.

At the edge of her perception, above the soft rush of computer fans, a buzzing, like tiny circular saws, grows in the hallway.

"Shit," he whispers. "They got in the same way we did."

The drones have come through the open patio door on the second floor and are moving in their direction. He squeezes himself between two server racks and motions her to follow. She presses herself in front of him, afraid even to breathe.

The whirring grows louder, now echoing down the hall-way. Her arms go numb. He grasps her trembling hand.

"Stay still," he whispers.

The buzzing intensifies, the drone is in the room, briefly visible through gaps in the server racks. It's some kind of delivery drone with the name "Tigris.com" stenciled on its plastic body. And as it drifts closer, a pair of garden shears swings into view, held in place by a metal manipulator claw. It's an improvised attack dog…obtained on short notice to neutralize the invaders.

It floats her direction, rotating slowly, perhaps scanning the space with its camera. As it comes closer, she holds her breath, attempting to stay frozen. But the pressure is too much. She involuntarily blinks.

The drone halts, rotates a few degrees, then launches at her, its shears aimed at her chest. Seymour screams as they hit the floor. The blade strikes the wall behind them, and the drone teeters, struggling to regain balance. Before it can lunge again, Seymour kicks it sideways, then pulls the nearest computer rack down on it. The drone and a dozen computers slam into the floor.

"We're fish in a barrel!" he shouts, grabbing a folding chair and heading for the doorway. "Run!"

She follows his example and grabs another folding chair as the buzzing behind them grows more urgent. Every drone in the house is converging on this spot, which means they don't have much time. As they approach the door, the humming grows acute. She glances over her shoulder to see a drone clutching a fire poker and hurtling in their direction. She swings the chair, batting it to the ground with a satisfying crunch. Another appears from a doorway beside Seymour. He raises his own chair like a shield, parrying, then crushing it against the wall. He flings open the front door and swats another that was hovering just outside. They rush, headlong, still clinging to their folding furniture. When they reach the metal gate, he fumbles with the latches and then throws it open. She follows, glancing back to see three drones rising above the wall, one with a garden spade and two more with fire pokers in their manipulator claws. They pause for a moment, as if conferring, then dive, kamikaze fashion.

"Three of them!" she shouts and brandishes her chair. The drones charge as if mounting a frontal assault, but at the last moment, swerve around them. She pivots, protecting her vulnerable flank, and manages to crush the drone just moments before the poker strikes her face. Seymour gives a sickening gasp. She turns to see one drone crushed under his chair but another pinned to him, its manipulator clutching a knife whose blade is plunged deep into his arm. The drone tugs at the knife, and it pops free amid a spray of blood. But before it can buzz away, Emily grabs it and throws it to the ground, then crushes its rotors under her feet.

Seymour topples, clutching his arm and whimpering. The gash is hideous, flesh and muscle chopped to hamburger, and blood pouring onto the pavement. She retrieves a windbreaker from her pack and wraps the wound. He offers neither help nor resistance. His eyes are squeezed shut, and tears pour down his face.

"Seymour," Emily says as gently as she can, "we have to move."

"Just need a m-minute," he gasps.

She gently takes his uninjured arm and pulls him to his feet.

"This way," she says with as much calm as she can muster, "toward the trees.

He nods weakly, letting her guide him away from the house and over the hill. They leave the road and tumble down a slope covered in dense vegetation, coming to rest among a cluster of razor-sharp palms. Seymour sits on the damp soil, panting and clutching his arm.

"I'll call an ambulance," she says. "I'll tell them you wrecked your bike or something."

"No ambulance," he says emphatically.

She squints at her makeshift windbreaker bandage. Even in the faint moonlight, it's glistening with blood.

"You could die of blood loss," she says with undisguised panic, "or infection."

"Get me to a hotel," he says between gasps. "I'll clean and stabilize it there."

In the moonlight that filters through the forest canopy, his face appears gray, but whether from fear or blood loss is difficult to know. How would Hong Kong paramedics react to a mangled black man squatting in the forest along Victoria Peak? What are the chances that they *wouldn't* call the cops?

"Do you have a phone?" she asks.

His eyes widen. "Who are you calling?"

"Just give me the Goddamned thing."

Wincing, he uses his good arm to withdraw a phone from his jacket pocket. She takes it. It's slimy and warm with his blood.

"It's a burner, right?"

"Of course," he wheezes.

She wipes the blood from the display and powers it on. Then she holds it back out toward him.

"Unlock it," she commands.

He tries but struggles to raise his mangled arm.

"I–I can't."

She gently grasps his right hand and presses his finger against the reader. The screen illuminates, and she hails a car with Didi, China's Uber.

"We'll have to appear clean and normal, or the driver will leave us," she says.

"No prob –" he begins, then pauses, looking slowly upward.

Somewhere above the forest canopy, whirling blades hum, beating the air like hornet's wings. His eyes widen with dread.

"They know we're in here," he whispers.

"They can't reach us in these trees," she says. "So we'll get down this hill, wait for our car, and jump in before the drones can reach us. We'll get to a subway stop and escape from there.

"Subway?" he repeats weakly.

"Didi cars are tracked," she says. "We have to break the surveillance chain."

His eyes flutter, and his head lolls.

"Seymour?" she whispers. "Can you hear me?"

His eyes snap open.

"Right," he says, his voice slightly slurred, "to the subway!"

She grasps his good arm and guides him through the razor-edged palms and barbed undergrowth. The car will arrive in just four minutes, but Seymour is moving slowly. She can't carry him, though; he has to make it on his own power.

"Just a little farther," she coaxes. "Fifty feet."

The drone whir intensifies. She glances skyward. The devices are following them, perhaps probing for a break in the foliage.

"They're tracking my cell phone," Seymour says abruptly. "They've tied that phone to us."

She grasps the phone in her trembling palm, examining its blood-stained screen. Given their adversary's other tricks, tracking it wouldn't be beyond their capability. She musters all her strength and hurls it into the darkness.

"I guess we won't be making any more calls," he observes.

They push toward a patch of streetlight along the nearby road. A drone glides overhead, showing no sign of detecting them. Then a car rumbles up the lane. It's their ride if they can get to it. She rummages through Seymour's pack and pulls out his windbreaker.

"I'm wrapping a second coat around your arm," she says gently. "It'll hide what a mess you've become."

His bleary eyes focus, and he gives her an appraising look.

"You're not so groomed yourself."

Headlights cut through the darkness. The car slows but doesn't fully stop, probably because the location she specified isn't any kind of building or landmark.

She bolts from the forest and waves her arms, forcing the most realistic smile she can muster. The car lurches to a stop, and the window glides down.

"You called for a car?" the driver asks in Cantonese.

"*I did,*" she responds, summoning every bit of Chinese she can muster.

"*We at party. Friend...*" she motions toward Seymour, "*have too much drink.*"

She walks up and pulls the door latch. The car stays locked, and the driver stares at her, stone-faced.

"What party?" he asks in English. "Like, in those trees behind you?"

"Please," she says, her voice cracking with panic. "He's not in good shape." She motions toward Seymour, who manages a weak smile even as a fresh red spot appears on the second windbreaker. They're running out of time.

"I've got lots of money," she says, plunging her hand into her backpack.

The driver flinches, apparently fearing a weapon. But the promise of extra cash keeps him attentive. Above the treetops, the whine of electric motors intensifies. The drones have noticed the stopped car. She has only seconds now.

She produces her wallet and grabs a wad of Hong Kong dollars.

"All this," she says. "Five hundred, in addition to the fare you already got from the app."

The lock clicks, she grabs Seymour, and shoves him inside, as the roar of plastic blades reaches a crescendo. She jumps in after him and pulls the door shut. A black blur hurtles toward the window, then abruptly pulls away.

"What the hell was that?" the driver says, eyes wide.

Above and around the car, a chorus of rotor blades hums like a swarm of insects.

"Drive," she shouts, shoving the money at him. He needs no further coaxing and guns the engine, launching the car down the narrow lane, past the mansions and tree-lined estates. Through the rear window, six drones assemble themselves into a loose formation, like horseflies who've scented blood.

"They can follow for maybe twenty minutes," Seymour mutters, "before their batteries die."

The driver glances back at them, his face twisted with anger.

"You people are bad," he says. "I'm dropping you at the cops."

"I can pay more," she says.

His eyes narrow.

"How much more?"

"Another five hundred."

"Three thousand," the driver says. "Nothing less."

Frank gave her twenty thousand in "mad money," as he called it, but most of that is gone.

"Two thousand," she says.

The driver slams the brakes, and the car skids to a stop.

"Three thousand," he says, face red with rage, "or get out of my car!"

The drone motors are clearly audible above the rumble of his idling engine. She eyes the door, and her hands begin to tremble. The drones will kill them out there. Hell, the drones may even kill them in here.

"Three thousand," she says quietly.

"So where am I taking you?" he asks, his lip curled in a sneer.

She squeezes her brain, forcing it to produce a useful answer, struggling to recall the lay of the town after so many years.

Somewhere crowded. Somewhere with easy public transportation and cheap hotels, ideally on the far side of a tunnel, since that might shake off their pursuers. More like… Kaylin's place.

"Choi Hung Station," she says, not certain she's gotten the pronunciation right.

"The cash first."

She rummages through her bag, careful not to let him see how much she has left, then holds out the bills.

"I should never come to the peak," he says, snatching the money and gunning the engine.

As they wind back down the mountain, she examines Seymour's arm. Multiple patches of blood are seeping through the windbreaker, and his face is disturbingly gray. Is this the right plan? Does Seymour *actually* prefer death to prison? Because death may be what he's choosing right now.

She opens her mouth, ready to give the driver new instructions, to ask him to go to the hospital.

"Don't," Seymour says, his wide eyes locked on hers.

She leans close.

"Is your freedom worth your life?"

"The bleeding is slowing," he says so quietly the air barely leaves his mouth. "And it's my choice. Not yours."

She stares at him uncertainly. Will he even be alive when they reach the subway station?

"We'll try it your way for now," she whispers, her heart galloping in her chest, "but if you get any worse, we're getting help."

# THE TUNNEL

SHE GLANCES through the rear window. The drones are still hovering behind, just above the traffic, their plastic carapaces gleaming dully in the city glow. But as the car approaches the portal to the Cross-Harbour Tunnel, they swoop upward, vanishing into the night sky.

"They can't follow into the tunnel," she whispers, her heart lightening with hope.

"The clearance is too constrained," Seymour agrees, "a truck might hit them or something. But they'll be waiting on the far side."

He's right, of course. She'll need a better plan to shake such determined and sophisticated foes.

The car accelerates as it enters the tunnel, gaining speed with the surrounding traffic like a leaf in a narrowing river. In the orange artificial light, Seymour's complexion looks even more sickly. This plan is crazy; he needs medical attention now, not hours from now.

He notices her eyeing him and winks.

"Are we having fun yet?"

"Seymour," she begins, determined to talk sense into him, to tell him they're going to a hospital. But before she can continue, the car lurches violently, and the tires squeal.

"Fuck!" the driver shouts in Cantonese while wrestling the vehicle to an abrupt halt. A bright red chain of brake lights stretches into the distance.

"A Goddamned traffic jam," he says in English, "and in the middle of the night, no less!"

She looks down the line of idling cars, which appears to extend all the way to the distant portal. Did their pursuers arrange this stoppage? Are they trapping them in here like fish in a barrel?

"It's those Goddamned protesters," the driver mutters, "always screwing things up."

That seems highly unlikely. The Chinese government has done an efficient job of bringing Hong Kong into its dissent-free zone; it's a completely different city than when she lived here. But Seymour stiffens at the driver's words, his radical hackles raised.

"People have a right to demand their freedoms!" he says. "To demand human dignity everywhere!"

The driver turns, eyes wide and angry.

"Is that why you come to Hong Kong? Are you some of those troublemaking foreigners here to ruin our city?"

The man's anger, and Seymour's evident desire to tangle with him, should be terrifying. Yet amid so much recent chaos, it feels somehow expected. Maybe even an opportunity.

"That's right!" she shouts defiantly. "We *are* here to support freedom. And to oppose dictatorship!"

Seymour turns to her, wide-eyed.

"We are?"

"We are," she agrees. "And now it's time to join our comrades," she continues, opening Seymour's door and stepping over him. "It's time to stand up for democracy!"

His confusion morphs into puzzlement. But the excitement seems to revive him a little, and he follows her lead.

"I'll call the cops!" the driver shouts, cheeks turning scarlet. "I'll have you arrested. You bunch of city-destroying, unwanted –"

She slams the door and tugs Seymour forward.

"We need a new ride," she whispers.

Comprehension dawns on his ashen face, and he takes a stumbling step forward, gripping her shoulder. They press themselves to the wall, limping toward the brightly lit tunnel exit, passing the stopped and idling cars as the occupants look on in weary resignation. For most, this is just another Hong Kong traffic nightmare, one to be endured and hopefully overcome. Flickering red and blue cop lights appear in the distance, along with the singsong wail of sirens. As they approach the tunnel mouth, the true cause of the chaos becomes evident: a semi-trailer truck jackknifed across both lanes. Firemen have the driver-side door open and are speaking to the operator, whose face is battered and bloody.

"Look at the windshield," Seymour whispers, pointing with his uninjured arm.

It's spidered with cracks, and at the center is a drone, half embedded in the glass, squashed like a large mechanical bug.

"It peeked into the tunnel and got clipped," she says.

But that means the skies aren't safe. They can't just walk out into the light. They need some new conveyance.

Three vehicles back is a flatbed truck carrying four immense wooden crates, each fastened with nylon straps. There are human-sized gaps between each crate.

"Can you get on that truck?" she asks.

He nods weakly. His flagging energy is terrifying, but right now, they have bigger problems. She leads him to the far side of the tunnel, avoiding eye contact with the other drivers or passengers.

"Just taking a walk here," she mutters, "nothing to see."

They pass in front of the truck. The driver is staring at his cell phone, his expression bored. They squeeze between the wall and the bed of the truck until they find a suitable spot.

"Now or never, Seymour," she whispers.

He grabs the side with his good hand and pulls, grunting with effort. Emily grabs his ass and shoves him. He flops onto the truck.

"On any other day, I might enjoy that kind of help," he observes.

She pulls herself up and drops onto the truck bed next to him, then locates a piece of folded canvas and throws it over them both. A half-hour passes before the authorities have cleared the wreckage, and the trapped cars begin inching forward. The truck's diesel engine roars to life, and it gives a mighty lurch, causing the crates to shift alarmingly, the nearest nearly crushing her fingers. The engine's rumble builds, and the truck bumps and rattles. In moments the echoes of the tunnel subside, replaced by the rush of open highway and somewhere, far overhead, the buzz of a dozen flying chainsaws.

"They're up there," he whispers.

"They'll follow that Didi," she replies. "I just hope they don't hurt the guy when he gets out."

"Would serve him right, the stupid fascist."

The truck decelerates, and the sounds of crowds and commerce build around them. They've left the highway and are navigating city streets. Seymour's eyes are closed, and his breathing is shallow.

"We'll jump off soon," she whispers, "so try to stay awake."

He nods, but his eyes won't seem to open. She lifts the tarp slightly and peers out. Despite the fact that it's nearly midnight, the streets are lively. This is clearly Kowloon, though in which district is difficult to discern. It doesn't matter, though. They just need a subway station.

The truck decelerates further, now to walking speed. She squeezes Seymour's uninjured arm.

"Do you still have your respirator mask?" she whispers.

The masks are ubiquitous in Hong Kong, even when infection levels are low. And wearing their masks will shield their features from probing eyes and surveillance cameras. Seymour produces a mask that she helps him strap to his face. She straps on her own mask and prepares to jump. The truck rumbles to a stop. She jumps to the pavement and then tugs on Seymour, who tumbles to the ground. A couple on the sidewalk stare at them, wide-eyed.

"Crazy night," she says, and the two look away, apparently embarrassed for these two foreign drunkards. She coaxes Seymour to the corner and reads the street sign. They're on Jordan Road, meaning they're near the Temple Street Night Market, a tourist trap that she and Kaylin often visited when they were in high school.

"I know you feel bad," she whispers, "but the trains quit running in less than half an hour. We have to catch one."

He nods and stumbles after her.

She leads him to Jordan Station and consults the subway map, settling on Sham Shui Po as a sufficiently downscale destination. He's swaying slightly but nods weakly when he notices her eying him and gives a wavering thumbs up. Her stomach twists with fear. He could pass out at any moment.

"We're going to our hotel now," she says, coaxing him forward.

"I thought you'd never ask," he slurs.

A cop appears among the crowd. She stares at the ground, avoiding eye contact, hoping Seymour's worsening condition doesn't look like public intoxication.

"Why are you staring at your shoes?" he asks.

"I'm keeping my head down," she hisses. "Trying not to be recognized."

From the corner of her eye, she sees navy trousers approach. The officer wants to talk.

"Is the young lady alright?" he asks in English, addressing Seymour.

"Having a bad night," Seymour says with forced lightness. "Probably had a bit too much to drink as well."

The legs don't move. He's blocking their path.

"Is your arm injured, sir?"

Seymour's body goes rigid. This whole sham could come apart at any second.

"I fell," he says after a pause. "Which is why we're heading home. So I can get cleaned up."

The legs shift slightly, turning in her direction. "Do you need assistance, Miss?"

They must look pretty terrible for the cop to have homed in on them like this.

She shakes her head, still looking at the ground.

"Just don't feel well, officer."

The legs move aside.

"Please head directly home," he says in a stern voice. "We want a quiet city here tonight."

Seymour tugs weakly at her arm. It's a miracle he can still rouse himself and appear coherent.

They pass through the fare gates and reach the platform amid a crowd of agitated shoppers and intoxicated tourists. They manage to board the next train and make their way to a relatively empty corner of the car.

"Next stop Sham Shui Po," says a computerized voice.

A drop of blood falls from Seymour's arm and lands on his shoe. She looks at his face. His head bobs and his eyes roll up into his head.

"No worries," he says, his words now slurring worryingly. "Just tuck me into bed, and I'll be perfect."

Could Frank send a doctor if she asked? Would that be fast enough?

"I'm taking you to the hospital," she says, trying to sound resolute.

"You're taking me to our love nest," he says, eyes snapping open. "Where I'll recover and be perfectly healthy in a day or two."

His eyes are ringed and sunken, pained and earnest. Is he thinking clearly? Does he understand what he's saying? What he's asking for?

"Doctors can sew you up," she whispers. "They can give you x-rays, antibiotics, and painkillers. I can't do anything."

"They'll see my injuries and know something bad happened. They'll run my prints and match them to the mess at Zahra's house."

"Escape isn't worth your life," she says, eyes filling with tears.

"You broke up with me back in the day for the same reason you're trying to dump me now," he says, wiping one of her tears with his good thumb. "Because I'm messy and not totally civilized. But that's who I am, Emily."

"This is your *life* we're talking about," she says, with a surprising rush of anger, "not some stupid protest action."

"This is what I want," he says, his voice cracking with emotion. "I'm asking you to respect that."

"Sham Shui Po," calls the computer voice.

He wavers, blood dripping on the floor, lips bluer than she's ever seen them. If he dies, she'll carry that burden for the rest of her life. If he goes to jail, she'll carry that burden as well. All paths lead to guilt.

"This is our stop," she says quietly.

"I knew I could trust you."

She's glad one of them does.

# SHOPPING

EMILY IS on her mother's front steps, waving to a man who stands in the middle of the street. The sun is behind him, his face is in shadow. He waves back, then steps toward her. A silver car appears from nowhere, plowing over him, leaving his mangled body for dead on the pavement. Her mother, Audrey, is at her side, clutching a kitchen knife with one hand and a garden hose with the other.

"Take this," Audrey commands, holding out the knife.

Emily grasps the handle with a trembling hand as Audrey directs the garden hose toward the man, washing his wounds with a spray of water. Then she turns to Emily.

"Do something!" her mother commands, "even if it's wrong!"

Emily awakens with a start. She's in an uncomfortable chair, a blanket draped over her shoulders, her face covered in sweat. Light seeps around filthy beige curtains illuminating Seymour's motionless body. He's sprawled across the room's only bed, his injured arm bound in a red-stained towel, his face drawn and ashen. Memories of the previous evening rush in: Seymour in the tub, whimpering as she washes his wounds, Seymour clenching a leather belt in his teeth, Seymour shivering as she sutures his gash with an ordinary needle and thread. He's the bravest, craziest person she's ever known. He may be insane.

She rises stiffly, pins and needles filling her reawakening legs, then limps to the cramped bathroom. She cups her hands under the faucet and throws water over her face, washing away the tears and horror from the night before. She emerges to find Seymour sitting up, remote control in hand, staring at the television.

"Is that your cousin?" he asks, pointing to the screen.

A policeman is ushering Frank through a crowd of reporters. He glances resignedly toward the camera, his fleshy face unspeakably sad.

"Dammit," she mutters.

She led him to Zahra's trap, caused his face to be on television, and maybe ruined his life. How many more lives will she ruin before she's finished?

"What's our next move?" Seymour asks.

"Ward off gangrene," she says, pointing to his arm.

"And then?"

"Use your hacking magic to eradicate the surveillance footage that ties you to me and, after that, get you to California."

"What about you?"

"I surrender to the US consulate."

He sits up straighter.

"Don't throw your life away," he says, his eyes growing hard.

"I only get it back when I quit running."

"Then surrender with leverage," he says, holding up the solid-state data drive extracted from Zahra's computer.

She eyes the dull metal box in his sweaty hand. Does it explain what happened to The Collective? Does it reveal which comrade betrayed Zahra? Does it chronicle the coup d'etat that ended her life?

"My people won't trust what's on that thing," she says. "They'll assume it's fabricated."

"*Your* people," he scoffs. "Who cares about the NSA? *We're* the ones who need the truth!"

"Find it when you get home."

"I need at least a week to heal," he says. "Which means I have time to find the truth right now. Just visit one of those awesome Hong Kong computer stores and grab me some gear. I'll have Zahra's data deciphered in days, maybe hours."

His voice exudes confidence, but his eyes plead. He's as scared as she feels, and it's true that Zahra's data might hold useful secrets, insights that improve Seymour's chances of survival.

"I need a better disguise," she says reluctantly, "something that covers more of my face."

"A wig?" he says, smiling. "Thick makeup?"

"I don't want to beclown myself."

He rummages through his pack, then throws her his ratty hoodie.

"Just pull the hood tight around your head and keep wearing that KN95 mask everybody here loves. Oh, and maybe some sunglasses.

She shakes her head. He's underestimating their foe.

"We need to hack the government's video scan AI," she says, "so Chinese security doesn't ID me with body structure analysis."

"I'm on it," he says, opening his laptop.

But his hand trembles over the keyboard. He's in obvious pain, he needs antibiotics and also a decent meal. Which means he's right; she has to go shopping.

"I'll buy your toys," she says with a sigh. "But just this one shopping trip. Then we stay in here until you're well."

He glances at the bed, then at her, his eyebrows raised suggestively.

"Just you and me? Alone? For weeks?"

"Get better first," she says softly. "Then we'll talk."

———

WITHOUT A PHONE, the shopping trip is even harder than Emily had feared it would be. She wanders the subway and streets, feeling her way by memory, doing her best to recall where the famous and gritty Golden Computer Arcade or the glittering Wan Chai Electronics are located. She finally stumbles across a poster at the MTR subway entrance advertising the latter store, along with its address. Half an hour later, she arrives at the gleaming building and ascends the seemingly endless line of escalators. Each passing floor contains new wonders: shelves of manga, piles of mobile phones, and aisles of home appliances. She steps off the escalator and into the television showroom, hoping to find a small monitor. What she sees there makes her gasp in dismay: hundreds of TV screens displaying an exposé about the mysterious "Explosion Girl," with slow-motion footage of Emily as she pulls Frank through the fire in Zahra's office.

She grabs the first small monitor she can find and steps quickly onto the escalator. She needs to get the rest of the gear and get out! She reaches level seven, the "build your own computer" floor, and frantically works through Seymour's list, locating a motherboard, power supply, data cables, and half a dozen other parts required to extract Zahra's secrets. His hoodie grows damp around her sweaty head, and her heart races like a rabbit. It was stupid to come here; she's way too obvious.

She locates the last component and, with a sigh of relief, hands the pile of gear to a pimply clerk. He rings her up, gathering her items into a shopping bag, but frowns when he reaches the last part, a motherboard.

"I can't sell a high-end CPU board without ID," he says in English.

"Why not?" she asks, her heart racing.

"People use these for crypto mining," he says. "Mainland regulations say we have to track their sales."

Damn that Seymour and his extravagant high-end hardware! She glances at the clerk, then at the motherboard, and tries to think. Her ID has her photo on it, the same face currently glowing on television sets throughout the store. There's no way she can show *that* to him. Should she find a lower-end motherboard that doesn't require ID? But which one? Hardware was never her specialty.

"I didn't bring my ID with me," she says, wrapping her fingers around the forbidden computer part. "Could we make an exception just this once?"

"I'd get in too much trouble," he says with a shrug.

She glances surreptitiously toward the door. There's no guard nearby, nobody to stop her.

"I'll buy the other stuff then," she says with a forced smile, "and come back for this later."

As she pays with her dwindling cash, her whole focus rests on the motherboard, which the boy places next to his cash register. It's within grabbing range. She could just snatch it and run for the doors before he can react. Is that too crazy? Is it worth the risk? She accepts her bag of purchases with a smile but stays rooted to the spot, attempting to gather her courage.

"Is there, uh, anything else I can help you with?" the boy asks, his face reddening slightly.

Impulsively, maybe stupidly, she grabs the motherboard and turns on her heel. But the boy, perhaps suspecting she might try something, grabs her wrist and spins her back to face him. His bashful grin is gone, replaced with a scowl.

"You can't just take–" he begins, but she twists and crouches, using her full weight to break his grip. He lunges, perhaps trying to pin her more securely, but his flailing hand catches the straps of her KN95 mask, ripping it from her face. She freezes, her cheeks burning with exposure. He stares at her naked features, his eyes widening, then sweeping toward the nearest television screen, which still displays the video of her pulling Frank from the flames—recognition dawns.

"Hey…" he begins.

Perhaps from the shock of seeing a real-life criminal, perhaps from fear, the boy seems to lose his train of thought.

"Are- aren't you–" he stammers.

Before he can finish, she scrambles to her feet and dashes toward the door.

"The Explosion Girl!" he shouts after her. "She's here!"

The nearby shoppers look toward him with expressions of mild irritation, apparently unaware that the boy is talking about the actual person, not just the TV show. She clasps her free hand over her mouth and nose, covering her features as best she can, and bursts through the exit, stumbling into the warm evening air. She buries herself into a throng of passing shoppers, lowering her head and replacing the wayward KN95 mask. Then she joins a group of tourists as they make their way toward the Star Ferry, pressing so close to the woman in front of her that the lady glances back in irritation. She boards the ferry and makes her way to the railing, leaning over the water and gulping lungfuls of briny Victoria Harbor air in an attempt to calm her racing heart. She was recognized and nearly caught. Now she'll have to break the chain of surveillance. Otherwise, she'll lead the authorities straight back to Seymour.

As the ferry plows the waters, the island of Hong Kong recedes behind, and Kowloon's towers loom overhead. It touches Tsim Sha Tsui pier, and she walks briskly to the exit gates. A "public safety" video camera on a nearby light pole stares down at her. Seymour better be hacking the government surveillance feeds, or they'll ID her for sure. Of course, if that Wan Chai clerk called her in, then live human cops may be scanning the feeds even now. In that case, no amount of hacking will save her.

She stares at her shoes and walks north, along Tung Choi Street, toward the "Ladies Market," a multi-block street bazaar containing a dizzying array of shops and stalls overstuffed with dresses, handbags, and every other garment and accessory imaginable. She ducks into a less prosperous-looking stall and purchases a pink respirator mask, as well as sunglasses, a jacket, and a wide-brimmed hat. She dons her new clothes, stuffs her backpack into a shopping bag, and loiters near the entrance. When a large party of shoppers leaves the shop, she sidles up behind them, pretending to be part of their group.

The evening is muggy, and the new jacket is stifling. Sweat pours down her face, and the pink respirator suffocates her. She enters another shop, makes another quick change, and leaves with a different gaggle of bargain hunters. She repeats the process several times, doing her best to enter and depart amid the throngs, trying hard to confound any AI or human that reviews the video records. Eventually, she heads toward the hotel, hoping her evasions are enough. Because if not, the cops will be on them before the night is through. She stops at a pharmacy and pays triple to score a little amoxicillin without a prescription. It's completely dark when she returns to the hotel room, hours later than she'd hoped.

"Seymour?" she calls.

No answer.

She switches on the light.

He flinches, holding a hand over his puffy eyes. His open computer still sits on his lap.

"Tryin' to get a little sleep here," he says groggily.

Around the bandages, his skin is an unpleasant crimson. She touches his sweaty forehead and recoils. He's burning with fever.

"Take this now," she says and measures out a dose of

antibiotics, along with a painkiller. She waits as he takes the pills with water, then lays down beside him, avoiding his injured arm.

"I used the government surveillance network AI to find and blur as many images of you as I could," he mutters. "What were you doing in that shopping bazaar?"

"Trying not to get caught."

"Did anybody recognize you?"

She tells him about her mishap at Wan Chai Electronics.

"All because you always need the fastest hardware," she adds.

He puts his good arm around her.

"So you're The Explosion Girl?"

She shrugs. Another badge of shame. Another marker on the road to perdition.

"It's kinda sexy," he continues, "to think that I'm in bed with a TV star."

"This isn't that kind of rendezvous."

A romantic night with Seymour isn't the most disagreeable thought, but these are hardly the best circumstances.

"Let's build that computer and see what Zahra knows," he says.

"Let's get some rest first," she replies, laying her head on the pillow. "We can assemble your toy in the morning."

He sighs.

"Do you still plan to turn yourself in?"

"I'm a bad luck charm and a bad influence," she says. "For example…" She holds up the bottle of antibiotics. "…when I pretend to be a doctor."

"I love playing doctor with you," he says, pulling her close.

She gives him a little shove.

"You need real medical attention, not my half-ass guessing."

"I need Zahra's secrets," he says, "so can we safely map out our next move."

"Your next move is a flight back to California."

He sits up straighter and takes her hand, all playfulness gone. His eyes are suddenly intense.

"Sophisticated people are controlling the most awesome botnet ever devised," he says. "Even if the Chinese and Americans can't find us, APRIL's new masters probably will. It's just a matter of time."

Sweat trickles down his forehead. He shivers slightly. Despite the brilliance of his eyes, he's never looked so sick.

"I can't do much in this condition," he admits, returning his head to the pillow. "I need to heal up. But you're still capable. You can search Zahra's records and maybe figure out who usurped her."

"That's your project—" she begins, but he cuts her off.

"Knowing her secrets could make all the difference. It could help both of us get out of here alive. So, please, Emily, help me assemble these parts and review Zahra's records. Help me figure out what we're up against."

Pawing through Zahra's data feels like yet another round of amateur spycraft, another shot at finding facts that won't help her even when she gets them. But Seymour's eyes are wide and pleading.

"Tomorrow," she says. "I'll look at Zahra's data tomorrow."

# DEEP DIVE

SHE ASSEMBLES Seymour's science project from the parts she obtained the previous day: an entire computer running his APRIL-free version of Linux and fully disconnected from the internet. She safely decrypts Zahra's data drive: nearly a terabyte of material, mostly the detritus of a crime boss's daily life. It takes several hours of examining source code, email, and chat messages to locate her first nugget: A note Zahra sent Kaylin just four months ago, the most recent communication she can find. It contains only two words:

*"Who's left?"*

"Who's left?" Emily repeats aloud. Had one of the Collective's hackers gone missing? Were comrades leaving the group?

Seymour moans, and she goes to his bedside. He's sleeping fitfully, his good hand pawing at his bandaged-wrapped arm. She feels his forehead. It's cooler than last night. Perhaps the antibiotics are working.

"Leave that arm alone, Seymour," she whispers. His eyelids flutter. He loosens his grip on the bandages but doesn't awaken.

She resumes her survey of Zahra's secrets. In many ways,

the great woman's role resembled that of a CEO. Her communications are often with "business partners," except the "business" is crime. This mountain of correspondence could take months to parse, but she only has days. She creates a search index to accelerate her work, then scans Zahra's data for terms like "bomb," "WayGo," and "triad." The results demonstrate that The Collective was branching into new lines of business. They were unearthing people who don't wish to be found, stealing the secrets from high-value targets, and laundering new types of crypto. Were they too damn successful? Had their "business partners" opted for a hostile takeover? She searches for "APRIL" and stumbles across a plaintive note from Zahra to Kaylin, sent thirteen months ago:

"APRIL's been inside Wells Fargo for weeks," Zahra wrote, "yet we have no joy! Are the money-grubbers resisting? Are they sick of paying our taxes?"

Milking stupid banks is another collective staple. APRIL bots infiltrate and rewrite the victim's accounting systems to hide the group's fraud and theft. The target banks could theoretically root out such pilfering, but Zahra always kept her extractions modest, lower than the cost of mounting a realistic defense. This is the context of the Wells Fargo note. The Collective was apparently adding Wells Fargo to its herd of money-generating cows, yet there were unexpected headwinds. In another email, Kaylin elaborates:

"Nishant can't find the source of resistance, either from the bank's software defenses or their cyber-security team. Are we getting attacked by a competitor's botnet? Is this a 'bots versus bots' scenario? Or do we just have a bug? We need an intervention to find out."

The word "intervention" has a specific meaning here: At its core, APRIL is a non-deterministic machine learning framework, meaning it sometimes learns the wrong lessons and sometimes makes terrible mistakes. Training and correcting APRIL involves interrupting its work to tune the neural network, update training data, or fix actual bugs. Here Kaylin is saying that either she, Nishant, or another senior comrade will "intervene" in APRIL's handling of the Wells Fargo job in order to diagnose the issue. It's a surprising turn of events given what soft and poorly defended targets big banks tend to be. Something was seriously haywire.

Emily searches for "Wells Fargo" and finds another message from Kaylin:

"The job queue shows that 42% of our worldwide bot force is supporting the Wells Fargo takeover, which means 58% is performing some hidden task. Did you give APRIL a new directive? Why is the admin console locked?"

Zahra's response is, again, just two words: "Call me."

Emily leans back in her chair. Since when was Kaylin *not* in the loop on everything? Had she and Zahra already suffered a serious break by this point?

Emily searches for "job queue" and finds a note from Nishant, the third most senior comrade in The Collective:

"Za and Kay," he writes, "Somebody buggered the encryption, which is why we're seeing so many bots disengaged. It's also why Kay can't access the admin console. I'll need a week to get it sorted."

Emily stares at the note, confused. Nishant's response is surprisingly calm, almost flippant. And the statement that "something's buggered" feels too vague. The whole email is uncharacteristically sloppy, given the seriousness of the outage. Kaylin must have felt the same because she wrote a follow-up message just to Zahra:

"I asked Sunil to visit Nishant's apartment in Delhi. Neighbors say a body was removed, but police have no records. I think our friend is dead, and we're being spoofed. But the quality and believability of the fake email suggest that either a real human is spoofing him, or our adversaries possess a large language model similar to APRIL's NLS."

Emily closes her eyes, absorbing and untangling Kaylin's

words. Once Kay doubted the authenticity of Nishan'ts email, she'd sent another comrade to physically verify his whereabouts. What an incredible leap! Why not assume he was just busy or on vacation? How bad had things gotten that they feared every offline comrade might be a goner?

Kay also referred to the enemy as having a technology "similar to APRIL's NLS," which is intriguing. In The Collective's early days, their attacks failed because the social engineering part of their scams was too ham-handed. They solved this in typical hacker fashion by giving APRIL "Natural Language Synthesis," a deep learning language model similar to, but more advanced than, commercial large language models like GPT. This was the same technology they contracted Seymour to enhance when he gave APRIL access to even more of the victim's internal email records. APRIL+NLS can formulate messages or emails that sound like they're coming from your friend or co-worker. Had a rival developed a similar capability and targeted The Collective with it?

Emily reads the rest of Kay's note:

"It's time to activate our contingencies," Kaylin writes, "to ensure that we're not seeing spoofed messages from other comrades."

So what became of Nishant? Was Kay correct? Was he already dead?

Emily searches Indian news services for Nishant Mehta and finds an article in Dainik Jagran, a Hindi language website. It describes the strange disappearance of Wipro engineer Nishant Mehta whose badly decayed body was found at the bottom of an industrial trash compactor.

Creeping cold chills her arms. Was The Collective hunted to extinction? She searches for news about other comrades, and the chills morph into full-fledged panic. Horst König, who operated under the identity "Horseface," died when his Tesla swerved into an oncoming truck. Prasad Varadkar, aka

"Samraat," died of asphyxiation when his furnace malfunctioned. Kan Chau Cheng, or "KanDo," perished when an elevator dropped him twenty stories, Mikael "Natch" Nillson fatally crashed his small aircraft north of Göteborg, and Usman "UsOrThem" Adeyemi was killed in a mysterious explosion in Lagos.

She recalls Kaylin huddling in the filthy, poorly illuminated flat in Choi Hung Estate. Her cousin didn't choose that spot for the ambiance—she was avoiding the fate of her peers. So Kaylin knew, or strongly suspected, that Zahra was dead. She'd sent Emily to that high-rise office, knowing that Zahra probably wouldn't appear. But she had wanted closure and had sent Emily to get it for her.

Emily rises from the computer and sits on the corner of Seymour's bed. He shivers in his sleep, eyebrows pinched together in pain. He was always concerned that The Collective was too beholden to the companies they robbed. "Feeding off the capitalist tit," he liked to say. Now the fat days of harvesting spare money have ended, and a darker period has arrived. But who are APRIL's new owners? How will she avoid them? They're clever and resourceful enough to have killed Zahra and most of her worldwide collective. What chance does Emily have against that kind of power? And what about Seymour?

Her mind turns to Mac. He's tried for days to contact her, but she's been too afraid to face his disapproval or to hear how screwed she is by now. But this morning, he sent a note claiming to be here in Hong Kong. Should she believe him? Should she meet with him? With Frank under arrest and Kay probably in hiding, what other choices does she have?

Emily sighs. This has gone far beyond what she, with her limited skills, can handle on her own. She needs the full support of the NSA and the US intelligence community, even if that means going back to prison...for years. With their help, perhaps she can get both herself and Seymour out of Hong Kong alive.

She grabs a piece of paper and scribbles a note. She'll give Seymour a choice: Recover here and flee on his own, or join her and accept the government's help. He won't like those options, but she can't linger, waiting for Zahra's enemies to find and kill them. These people are far more resourceful and powerful than she could have ever imagined; it's only a matter of time before they track the breadcrumbs and find them here. She has to move while she still can.

# KOWLOON PARK

EMILY TUGS at the strings of her hoodie and straightens her sunglasses. Kowloon Park's murky pond lies just ahead. A pavilion seems to float in the center of the green water, connected to the shore by a concrete walkway. Mac stands under the pavilion tossing pellets to a writhing mass of orange carp. He doesn't turn as she approaches.

"We're a long way from Fort Meade," she observes.

"I've disappointed you," he says quietly, still looking at the fish.

"It's my fault," she says, tears clouding her vision. "I held back when I could have pursued Zahra from the start. I should have known that I couldn't straddle the two worlds, that I had to choose between my old life and my new one."

"I shouldn't have forced you to make that choice," he says. "I should have been happy with what you brought to the team and not tried to squeeze you for more."

"I'm here now," she says softly, "and I'm ready to take responsibility."

He turns to face her, and she suppresses a gasp. He's aged ten years in only a few months. His eyes are bloodshot, his forehead is furrowed with deep lines, and tufts of gray frame his temples. He rushes forward, embracing her, his thick arms enveloping her with the scent of Old Spice and fabric softener. It feels like they're back in Fort Meade.

"My original plan was to offer a deal," he says, his voice thick with emotion. "If you came quietly, I would promise a short prison sentence, maybe three years."

Her mother spent five years at the Central California Women's Facility and emerged a shadow of her former self. But Emily will take any deal at this point as long as it disentangles Seymour from her mess.

"I have one request," she says. "I need you to exfiltrate –"

Mac pulls away from her.

"You're not going to jail," he says with an almost zealous firmness.

"But, you just said…"

"We aren't going back to the US," he adds.

Her head spins at his pronouncement. Where else could they go?

"You don't need to save me, Mac," she says, doing her best to reassure him. "I'm not trying to run."

"You were the child of domestic terrorists," he says abruptly. "You spent your teen years living with the notorious triad boss Ip To Ng. You followed his daughter, Kaylin Ng, into Zahra Kartal's collective. You became a powerful and dangerous hacker."

His nostrils flare, and his eyes widen, like a bull, ready to charge.

"What are we talking about?" she asks, now completely confused.

"Did you *actually* set that bomb off last week?" he asks, as though he doesn't know the answer.

"Of course not," she says, her hands tingling with an emotion she can't identify.

"Did you hire somebody to kill your mother? Did you plan to take her role as head of your family crime business?"

She takes a step back.

"I loved my mother," she says quietly, "and she wasn't part of any criminal conspiracy. She hadn't been for years."

Without warning, Mac lunges, grabbing her hands and pulling him toward her.

"Why do you keep getting blamed?" he asks, his eyes wide and wild.

Her heart accelerates, and she finds herself scanning her surroundings, evaluating possible escape routes.

"What's going on, Mac?" she says.

He releases her and puts his hands over his face.

"Why do you keep getting blamed?" he says again, his voice faltering.

"Because my life's a mess," she says truthfully.

"You get blamed," he continues, voice muffled behind thick hands, "because I blame you."

Her heartbeat quickens, like a rabbit's, primed for danger.

"You...what?"

"When your mom died," he says, "why did the FBI interview you?"

The tingling in her hands grows to pins and needles.

"I'm a former criminal," she says weakly. "I grew up in a crime family, as you just pointed out."

"When the intelligence community saw the video of you dragging your triad cousin through a fiery inferno, why did they assume you were the linchpin of their case? Why is so much focus on you *you*?"

"Because they assume that I'm like my family," she says with a shrug.

"Because you're a useful distraction," he says. "Because you draw attention from other people's crimes."

She sees Mac clearly for the first time, trembling there in his rumpled suit, fleshy hands covering a face he's too ashamed to reveal. And from deep inside, a long-suppressed rage sparks to life.

"What crimes?" she asks quietly.

"NSA budgets are tiny," he whines. "The rules are overwhelming. And you need funds and equipment to score the big intelligence wins."

The pins and needles intensify, and her hands grow numb.

"You have your own extra-legal operation?" she asks.

"I thought," he continues, "that bringing you into the NSA would calm Zahra and make her a reliable partner. I thought she would realize that you could help us hurt her if she crossed any red lines."

"You're partners with Zahra?"

"She was one of our contractors," he says with a shrug. "She handled work that was too tainted or legally dubious for us to touch."

"And you were afraid that I would find out?" she asks, her anger flaring like a blowtorch. "So you sent that car? To shut me up?"

"Never," he pleads, pulling his hands from his face and taking a step toward her. "Zahra is the only person with both the motive and the means to commit such a heinous crime."

Dead women have neither motive nor means.

She presses her fingers to her throbbing temples as tears stream down her cheeks.

"I have to leave," she says, taking another step back.

He grabs her again and pulls her close.

"Hear me out!" he says. "Let me tell the story."

She looks toward the pond's shore. An old woman feeds the swans, a couple kisses on a bench. Are they Mac's agents? Is she hemmed in?

"Let go of me," she says.

"Zahra's predictability collapsed," he continues, still grasping her hands. "She doubled-crossed us and attacked the government. She even attacked the NSA!"

The condition of Zahra's corpse suggests the story is more complicated. But does Mac know she's dead? Or is he more clueless than Emily?

"I took countermeasures," he continues. "My cleanup was almost finished. Then that car attacked your house, and all the pieces were in the air again."

"So you told the FBI to investigate me?" she says, with barely contained rage. "You piled on the lies and told them I crashed a car into my own house?"

He heaves a long sigh.

"My plan was to distract them until I had the cleanup finished. But then there was this video of you pulling your triad cousin through a raging fire. How was I supposed to explain that?"

He closes his eyes and shakes his head as if dispelling the memory.

"That was when I realized what I had to do."

He smiles, but his drooping basset face and crazed blue eyes do nothing to reassure her. He's not an honest man nor a defender of democracy. He's a sad bully, like Eddie Wang, only using her for what he can get.

She jerks her hands away, makes a fist, and punches with all her strength. The blow lands squarely on his nose, and his neck snaps back. Blood spurts from his nostrils as his eyes widen in astonishment. He opens his mouth, but before he can speak, she lunges at him again, barely missing his chin with her other fist.

"Wait," he calls feebly, his voice nasal and drippy.

But she's through listening to liars and little men who take her for a fool. She swings again with an open palm, clocking him on the temple.

"Let's calm down," he says, glancing around, "before somebody calls the cops!"

"The cops *should* know about you!" she shouts.

"I'll help you," he pleads, holding out a bloodied hand while staying out of range of her swinging fists.

"Like you helped my mother?" she shouts.

"It's Zahra," he cries out, fumbling with his handkerchief

and holding it under his nose, "I've already told you."

A man approaches the pavilion, sees Mac's blood-splattered face, and diverts his gaze.

"I'll help you find her," he pleads. "That's why you came to Hong Kong, isn't it? To get justice for Audrey?"

"Don't you speak my mother's name," she says, raising her fist again.

"I love you, Emily," he bellows, tears welling in his eyes. "I've always loved you. And I'll make it right. I'll get us out of Hong Kong, carry us to safety. We'll be in Brunei tomorrow; we'll have a fresh start!"

He's holding the handkerchief to his face with one hand, reaching for her with the other. Tears are pouring freely from his reddened eyes, trickling down his stubbly cheeks and dripping onto his rumpled jacket. For several seconds the impulse to strike him is overwhelming. Then, just as quickly, it subsides. Her fists unclench almost of their own accord. He's beyond trust now, beyond friendship.

"I can help you," he's pleading, "even if you hate my guts! Even if you never see me after today. Just let me get you out of this bind!"

She takes a step back.

"Take care of yourself, Mac."

"No!" he lunges toward her, grasping with thick fingers. But she easily slips away and runs in the other direction. She's not sure where she's going, but it's far from this man.

# PLEASANT CHAT

MAC'S LEATHER shoes slap the concrete as he chases Emily, but his clogged nostrils admit no air, and the blood trickles into his mouth, making him choke. She's faster than she looks, a jackrabbit in a dress, and soon she's past the distant park entrance. When he reaches the same spot, she's more than a football field's length ahead of him, weaving among an ocean of shoppers.

"Wait!" he cries.

Faces turn in his direction, confused by this disheveled, bleeding foreigner. But Emily continues to widen her lead even as he pushes his overweight, middle-aged body to the limit, making his lungs burn and his head spin. She reaches a distant alleyway and pauses, her dark eyes resting on his. There's disappointment in those eyes, maybe even regret. Then she vanishes into the shadows.

When he reaches the same intersection, Emily is nowhere to be seen. He stumbles down the alley, gasping for breath, and nearly collapses at the far side. She could be anywhere, down half a dozen side streets, or inside any of the nearby shops. And every second, she's putting more distance between them.

He drops onto a nearby bench and puts his face in his

hands, ignoring the blood as it trickles through his fingers and dribbles onto his shoes. He wanted to save her, to put everything right. But he needed her to see the real Mac, the man he is rather than the one he pretends to be. He thought that if she could see his true self, she might understand why life in the NSA is no longer possible… for either of them. He had also hoped, stupidly in retrospect, that she might identify with such a flawed person and love him all the more for being just as broken as she is. When he catches up with her, he'll try again, prove that she can trust him now, and demonstrate once and for all that the lies are over.

He sighs and pulls out his mobile phone, opening the tracker app. A little green dot glows on top of a Hong Kong map, slowly moving among the buildings. Dropping the tracker into her pack was a low trick, but some part of him suspected that the meeting might go badly. He can't lose her again.

"She's a spunky little thing," a smooth, cockney voice calls from behind.

He straightens, the hairs on his neck prickling, fear and loathing rising in his gut.

"If anybody were to ask me," the voice continues, "which they won't mind you. But if anybody *were* to ask me, I'd tell 'em that your cute little birdy just *might* be worth the bother."

Mac turns around. A tanned white man leans casually against the alley entrance, hands in his pockets, looking composed and relaxed, as if he's been there all afternoon. He's nattily dressed in a dark blazer, complemented by an ostentatious peach handkerchief. His chestnut hair is slicked back, and he smiles broadly, revealing a gold incisor among his otherwise pearl-white teeth.

"Hello, Pryce," Mac says, pressing the handkerchief more firmly to his leaking nose. "I'd say it's good to see you, but I'd be lying."

"The Director 'ad a funny notion," Pryce says, strolling

over and seating himself at the opposite end of the bench. "'E thought you might not successf'ly detain the little lady. In fact, get this…" Pryce leans in and elbows Mac playfully, then lowers his voice to a stage whisper, "The director was concerned you might actually attempt to escape wif her. Can you believe it?"

Mac scans the crowd. Several young Chinese men in dark suits are moving casually but intentionally in his direction.

"The good news," the East Londoner continues, "is that your friend and mine, the esteemed Director Chip, is not only paranoid but also thorough. 'E develops contingencies, and contingencies for those contingencies."

Mac could break into a run. Old and heavy as he is, he might get clear of these fit-looking youngsters before they catch him. Or he could scream bloody murder, pretend that Pryce and his gang are dangerous thugs, and hope the cops save him. Of course, then he would have to explain himself to the authorities. Not an optimal situation.

No, his best play is brazenness, to bet Pryce wasn't using a parabolic mic or some other listening device, and didn't hear Mac's plans. He'll pretend he's still a company man and go along with the Englishman for now.

"I told Ms. Hernandez," Mac says, affecting his most professional tone, "that she would get maybe three years in jail. But she was hoping for a plea that would get her no prison time at all. Completely unrealistic. In retrospect, I shouldn't even have mentioned the prison angle."

Pryce nods sympathetically.

"Can't say I blame the little lady. Myself, I wouldn't accept one fucking minute in the nick. I'd go out shootin'."

Mac suppresses a shiver. Pryce is Director Chip's choicest piece of work—a loose cannon under the best of circumstances.

"Despite today's setback," Mac continues, holding up his phone, "I managed to get a tracker into her pack."

The Englishman smiles.

"And thank you for that. Would you mind sharing the ID wif me?"

Mac reflexively clutches the phone to his chest. Turning Emily over to Pryce was no part of his plan.

"I'll be leading the search," Mac says, "and I'll be the one to pick her up."

"Why would that be?" Pryce asks, shifting a bit closer.

"I'm her boss, her mentor," he says, his pulse rising. "She... trusts me."

Pryce's smile broadens, and his eyebrows raise with incredulity.

"I'm sure she does, Mac. I know I sometimes bitch slap the people I trust. But 'eres the thing. We've got fifteen men and four cars ready to move. And if she leads us back to that boyfriend o' hers, that Seymour chap, then it's a two-for-one, if you get my meaning."

Mac winces at the sound of Seymour's name. The little shit is *not* Emily's boyfriend. Pryce seems to notice the reaction, his eyes glitter with interest.

"So you see," Pryce continues, "the operation has moved to a more kinetic phase, shall we say. One in which I will need to take the lead."

Pryce again scoots closer, so close that Mac can smell his musk-scented hair cream. He wracks his brain for ways to keep Emily safe from these people.

"I want to go with you when you move in," Mac says.

Pryce puts his arm around Mac's shoulder. It could be a friendly gesture, but Pryce is squeezing him with just a little too much force.

"We've got a whole team of blokes out there ready to move quickly. You just share that tracker code with 'em, they secure the perimeter, and Bob's your uncle; we bring her in. Easy, right?"

Mac eyes the man. It's a shitty deal, and she'll likely hate him for it. But if he's there when they pick her up, if he can at least be close to her, maybe he can disentangle her from this mess.

"Easy," he says, his heart sinking.

He hands over his phone. Pryce examines the tracker app, then enters a few numbers into his own device.

"So, where's your car?" Mac asks, his spirits rising slightly. At least he'll be with Emily again and maybe have the chance to keep her safe.

Pryce waves at a van parked half a block away. It drives up, and four young men in workman's clothes jump out. They look expectantly at Pryce. None make eye contact with Mac.

"'Ere's our chariot."

Mac nods, feeling excited, even eager, to get going. He'll turn this around and find a way to get Emily free, he'll be the man she always thought he was.

Somebody yanks open the van's door, revealing a darkened interior. Pryce's smile widens, his gold tooth glints in the afternoon sun.

"No limo. We prefer a low profile."

He holds out a manicured hand.

"After you, mate."

Mac steps toward the van, nerves aflame. The whole conversation was too easy, and Pryce's protestations were too short. He could still break free before they grab him. But he's made his bed. This plan will either work, or he's probably dead.

He steps into the van, and Pryce, who was just behind him, abruptly steps back. Mac turns as one of the "workmen" tugs at the door while Pryce watches impassively, his grin now a sneer. The door closes with a bang, throwing Mac into darkness. The van lurches to life, and he falls to the floor. He and Emily are both almost certainly screwed.

# SURPRISING NOTE

EMILY SPRINTS THROUGH THE CROWD, occasionally jamming the sunglasses higher on her nose, keeping her face hidden the best she can. She enters Tsim Sha Tsui station and descends the stairs, glancing occasionally over her shoulder. Is Mac still following? Did he lie about coming alone?

She reaches the platform just as a northbound train arrives. She pushes into the crowd of afternoon commuters, then elbows her way onto the train just as the doors slide shut. She doesn't care where she's headed, just so long as it's not back to the hotel. Returning now would be like posting Seymour's location on a message board. She has to break Mac's chain of surveillance, assuming she knows how to recognize it. She eyes the other passengers: men, women, young and old. Which are Mac's pigeons? How can she recognize them?

She recalls Seymour again, how he looked when she left this morning. He was still asleep, but his head was shiny with sweat, and his injured arm was bright red and swollen. Are the antibiotics working? Can he take care of himself if she's unable to return?

"Jordan Station," the computerized voice calls, breaking

her reverie. The car slows. She withdraws her new cell phone and pretends to study the darkened screen. She's just taking a ride, oblivious to her circumstances, on this train for the distance. It glides to a stop, and the doors slide open. Nearly half the passengers push their way off. She holds her ground, studying her darkened phone, looking for all the world like a person who'll be here all day. But as the all-clear chime sounds and the doors begin to slide, she lunges, squeezing through the narrowing gap just as they snap shut. She turns and peers through the windows in time to see a man in a plaid jacket pushing in her direction. His face is flushed, his features contorted with frustration. As the train accelerates, his eyes rise to meet hers. Recognition registers: he's lost his mark. She gives the man a little wave as the train slides into the tunnel.

She allows herself the briefest moment of self-congratulation, then faces facts: If the man were a Chinese agent, she'd already be arrested by the other nine people following her. So he's one of Mac's irregulars, part of whatever secret organization her former boss was running in the territory.

She glances around, attempting to discern which of the hundreds of commuters might also work for Mac. Her eyes rest on one man, standing just a dozen feet away. He's stylishly dressed in a dark olive jacket and is studiously studying his cell phone. Yet there's something off about him. He's so polished, so rigid. She approaches him.

"Have you spoken to Mac in the last few minutes?" she asks.

"What?" he replies in Cantonese, evidently surprised.

"Sorry," she says, taking a step back. "I confused you with somebody else."

Am I losing my mind? she thinks. Is it even possible to stay sane under these circumstances? How will I ever get back to Seymour if I can't tell who is and isn't an enemy?

She'll have to ride all day, change trains a dozen times,

change buses another dozen. She'll lose herself in the markets, dart into the alleyways, cut through restaurants. But even with all those measures, she can't be one hundred percent sure she's not being followed.

"Excuse me," a quiet voice says, so close it feels like the speaker is sitting on her shoulder. She turns to see a slender man garbed in orange robes, his shaven head shining slightly under the platform lights. He nods respectfully.

"I have a message for you, Ms Hernandez."

She freezes. This man knows her name. He recognizes her despite the hoodie, the sunglasses, and the respirator mask. Was he following her? Are Mac's agents posing as Buddhists now?

The monk withdraws a folded slip of paper from his robes and holds it out to her.

She glances around. The other man, the one she harassed, is still standing in the corner, eyeing her suspiciously—dozens of other passengers mill around, none apparently interested in either her or her ostentatious companion. The smallest hint of a smile curls the corner of the monk's mouth, yet he says nothing, only holding out the sheaf of folded paper. Unwillingly and with rising dread, she takes it. He presses his hands together and gives a little bow. She unfolds the paper, which is made of crisp parchment, and recognizes the unmistakable chicken scratch of her wayward coworker, Mr. Ben Katz. She gives another wary glance at the smiling monk, then reads:

"I'm still your friend," Ben writes, "and I'm still concerned about your well-being. That's why I strongly recommend that you let my brother, Tsering, help you evade the multifaceted surveillance they've assembled to track and subdue you. If you trust Tsering, he will bring you to me. Then we can talk properly. I know you're afraid, not only for yourself but for those you love. We both happen to love people who are trapped in life's gray zones. Let me help you carry this burden."

She looks up from the note, opening her mouth to object. The man called Tsering raises his small hand.

"There is no time," he says in an accent she can't place. "Please make your way to exit B1 of this station, then onto Jordan St."

"What makes you –" she blurts.

"Once you reach the street," he continues, speaking over her, "please locate the red taxi with license 0-H-M  H-U-M. Board this taxi."

"I'm not just gonna follow some random directions!" she says, her face suddenly hot with outrage.

The man presses his hands together and bows his head.

"I wish you safety Ms. Hernandez and luck in your journey."

Before she can argue further, he twirls on his heel and steps into the crowd, bobbing and weaving among the moving mass of commuters. She watches until he's vanished from view, then, with trembling hands, she lifts the note and reads once more:

"Let me help you carry this burden," it says.

Ben's likeness comes unbidden to her mind. A ratty t-shirt pulled over his ample midsection, sitting sage-like in his duct-taped office chair at the NSA, his beard scraggly and his gray hair feral. Nothing about her wannabe hippie friend fits any notion of betrayal she can construct. Of course, she also trusted Mac. And how did that work out?

She'll ignore this little monk, do her best to shake this surveillance and return to caring for Seymour. Yet if she fails to free herself of Mac, then she'll deliver poor Seymour directly into the government's hands. Would following this man improve her chances of success?

She spots a sign indicating exit "B1." Maybe she'll just take a look and see if the taxi is actually there. She ascends the stairs and emerges into the blazing afternoon sun. Car windshields gleam on Jordan Street, and everywhere is the sound of angry horns and idling motors. A red taxi sits a little way ahead, tucked up against the curb, its license plate reading "OHM HUM," as advertised. Beads dangle from the rearview mirror, and a golden statue of the Buddha sits serenely on the dashboard. If this is part of Mac's conspiracy, he has deployed all the props.

She steps up to the taxi, pulls open the door, and drops into the seat. The orange-robed man, Tsering, turns to face her.

"Good afternoon Ms. Emily," he says in a pleasant voice.

"Not so much," she replies, her own voice trembling.

He nods toward the front window.

"Do you see that van?" he says in a calm, almost cheerful tone.

She squints into the intense sunlight and picks out a blue van parked half a block ahead.

"What about it?"

"It is one of several tracking you. There are also at least six people tailing you on foot."

More bullshit? A hoax to convince her that she can trust him?

"Mr. McCarthy's extensive surveillance," he continues, "will require extraordinary measures on our part. We will be obliged to make at least one, and probably several, intermediate stops before we can safely bring you to your final destination."

The phrase "final destination" gives her pause. Does he mean *today's* final destination? Or the final destination of her short and miserable life?

"Where are we going?" she asks cautiously.

"Wasn't that clear?" he says. "We will take you to your good friend, Mr. Ben Katz."

Ben's name is a puff of cool air in the miserable heat of this moment and too good to be true. Could he actually be in Hong Kong? Is he a free agent now? Or is he just like her, a puppet whose strings are pulled by invisible powers?

The driver's soft brown eyes regard her calmly. He makes no move to drive away or even to start the motor. He sits placidly, hands folded in his lap, as though this taxi can illegally squat on this patch of sun-scorched curb forever.

"How long will the trip take?" she asks finally.

"My brother Ben was concerned that you would be understandably low on trust. And, indeed, the journey I am proposing will require more than a little of that rare commodity. So I must ask you: can you give us what is left of your trust? Can you trust me, and my brothers, and my sisters, to deliver you safely to Ben, even if the journey is surprising and unconventional?"

The dark eyes show no evidence of anxiety. Tsering appears to be equally happy leaving her or taking her. His disinterest is strangely reassuring, yet the questions remain: *Does* she have any trust left? Is trust too risky? If she trusts this man, will Seymour be okay? Will this enable her to bring Seymour the medical help he obviously requires?

She looks up the street, picking out the blue van, which still sits at the curb. The man on the subway train was certainly trying to follow her. Is this taxi an extension of that operation? Or is it a way out of her predicament?

*We both happen to love people who are trapped in life's gray zones.*

Yes, Seymour is trapped, and so is she. Trapped between legal and criminal, between civilian and spy. But just because Ben's note shows compassion for her plight doesn't mean she can trust it. This could still be Mac's work. Or maybe Ben is the mastermind. If this is a setup, then she has no backup plan. Seymour will be alone and sick in that hotel room, perhaps dying of his injuries. The safe path is to surrender at the consulate and tell them what she knows about Mac.

Maybe she can even trade that information for their help in exfiltrating Seymour from Hong Kong.

"No," she says, rising from her seat, "I can't trust you."

Tsering nods as if expecting her answer.

"In that case, Ben instructed me to ask one more question," he says, his tone more like a teacher than a thug, "one he didn't have time to write in his note."

She pauses, despite herself, one foot in the cab, the other on the curb.

"Which is?"

"Are you still straddling both worlds?" he asks. "Are you keeping a foot on both the dark side and the light? And are you sure which is which?"

She freezes, remembering her last conversation with Ben, how he intuited why she wanted to focus and moderate her attacks against The Collective, and how he guessed that there might be people she wasn't ready to betray. But who are the good guys now? And what is she trying to accomplish at this point?

She stares into Tsering's deep brown eyes. Nothing about the man, his cab, or the note he delivered feels like a CIA or NSA operation. Nor does it have the mark of the Chinese security services. This rendezvous is too bizarre, too improvised, too personal. It's an act of desperation, a last lifeline thrown to a friend.

Her rational brain screams: "This is a gambit!" But her heart tells her that this is Ben, that he's trying to help, and that his help might even give Seymour a fighting chance. She sighs. Her mother always followed her heart. It led Audrey to marry a radical, to serve quixotic missions for OPAL terrorists, and, ultimately, to lose custody of her own daughter. Is Emily's own heart any more reliable than that?

"Alright," she says, easing back into the seat, "take me to Ben."

# CAB RIDE

EMILY FASTENS her seatbelt and grips the armrest, ready for the car to lurch from the curb. But Tsering merely coaxes it forward, easing into traffic like a barge drifting into a slow-moving river. They pass the blue van, and she hazards a glance. Two men in dark suits and sunglasses stare out the windshield, their faces expressionless. But as the cab pulls away, the van edges into traffic and takes up a position just a few cars behind them.

"Your pursuers won't be easily discouraged or confused," Tsering says gently.

Not if he drives like a geriatric grandpa on his way to Sunday golf. The shops and restaurants roll past at little more than walking speed. The cab motor barely idles. Was it a mistake to trust him? Should she leap out the door and make her way back to Seymour?

They merge onto a wider thoroughfare, past rows of high-rise tenements in what must be northern Kowloon, then enter a narrow alley crowded with cars and pedestrians. As they approach a particularly dilapidated building, Tsering wrenches the wheel, the first aggression or urgency he's demonstrated. She flops over in her seat as the car lurches through an open garage door and then screeches to a stop. The big door clatters shut behind them.

"This is the end of our time together," Tsering says and switches off the motor. "Xiuying will convey you from here."

She looks through the cab window, blinking as her eyes adjust to the gloomy space beyond. A collection of late-model red taxis squat in the cavernous interior. Among them stand about a dozen men and women, all with shaved heads. A tall, slender woman approaches the taxi and throws open the door, gripping Emily's shoulder like they're old friends.

"You're Emily, right?" the woman says in unaccented American English.

"Are you Xiuying?"

"That's as good a name as any. And I'll be your conductor on this next leg of our underground railroad."

Emily glances around the garage. Most of the onlookers are young, like Xiuying, and all watch her intently.

"This is a kidnapping, right? You're like a Buddhist gang or something."

The group bursts out laughing.

"Nobody told me you had a sense of humor," Xiuying says.

The young woman turns to her compatriots and speaks a version of Cantonese nearly as poor as Emily's own.

"*Give us a two-minute head start,*" she's saying, "*then everybody out!*"

The others murmur assent and enter the parked cars.

Xiuying smiles at Emily.

"All these cabs will exit the garage at once. Your pursuers won't know which cab to follow."

"Which one is ours?" Emily asks.

"None of them," Xiuying says and motions toward a distant door.

"We're going this way."

The squadron of cabs sputters to life, readying themselves

for their real-life shell game. Tsering warned that the journey would take trust, and this must have been what he had in mind. Emily falls in behind the younger woman. They pass through the door and descend a long flight of concrete stairs. The air cools and moistens, they're moving deep below street level.

"Your pursuers are assholes," Xiuying says over her shoulder, "but not idiots. They'll follow the cabs but also watch the exits in case you decide to leave by a different exit. But hopefully, they don't know about this utility tunnel."

They reach the bottom of the stairs. A stone passageway stretches into the distance, illuminated by bare fluorescent lights. Xiuying picks her way quickly down the tunnel, not even checking to see if Emily is keeping pace. The floor is strewn with bricks and debris, and Emily falls, scraping her knee.

"We need to hurry," Xiuying calls back to her, "before they figure out our trick."

Emily continues stumbling down the dark passage and, by the time she reaches the distant stairs, has several more bruises and cuts. Xiuying stands by a broad steel door and is withdrawing an ancient-looking key. She uses it to unlock a rusted padlock and then pushes on the door, which gives a grinding squeal. Beyond is a brightly lit parking garage, mostly empty at this time of day. Emily follows her guide, or captor, to a late-model Mercedes that is parked just a few spaces away.

"Get in," Xiuying says, pulling a baseball cap from her pack and fitting it over her shaven head, "and lay on the floor."

"Wait. What?"

"You gotta stay out of sight. Hurry now!"

Emily reluctantly complies, entering the car and sprawling along the smelly carpet.

"I know this sucks," the girl says and throws an olive

blanket over Emily. "But we gotta keep you hidden, and this will be better than hiding in the trunk."

The blanket must be wool because it scratches her skin and the air underneath stinks like an old dog. The door slams next to her ear, and the seat springs creak as the young woman takes her place behind the wheel. The motor roars to life, and the car lurches and vibrates.

"I've seen you on TV," Xiuying calls over the noise. "You're quite the hero."

"Not my happiest day," Emily admits.

"What you did was totally boss," the girl replies. "Especially when you pulled that mafioso from the flames. Did he thank you?"

A pang of regret stabs Emily's chest. She imagines Frank undergoing interrogation in a Hong Kong police station or, worse, in a mainland prison."

"Yes," she says softly.

The car shudders, and the tires screech. A rapid deceleration throws her forward.

"Oh my god!" Xiuying mutters.

"What?"

"You bastards," the girl continues, "you motherfuckers."

"Under a blanket here!" Emily replies.

Without further comment, Xiuying guns the engine, and the car lurches again. It's as if she's putting the car through a slalom course.

"Those assholes," she's saying. "Those over-resourced sons-a-bitches."

Emily closes her eyes. The abrupt movements and stale air are not good for her easily upset stomach. But soon, the car settles into a more ordinary rhythm, something resembling everyday driving, and she breathes a bit easier.

"They totally figured us out," Xiuying says finally. "They were just waiting outside the garage."

"Where are they now?"

"Don't know, but my friends are monitoring the situation."

Whether Xiuying and her "friends" are well-intentioned or not feels almost beside the point. They are clearly in over their heads.

"Would you mind letting me out someplace?" Emily shouts, above the roar of the engine, "Anywhere is fine."

"Oh Jesus Christ!" the girl shouts, and the car lurches, then screeches to a stop.

"Is that a yes?" Emily says meekly.

"Get up!" Xiuying shouts, her voice mere inches from Emily's ear. "Now!"

Here it is, Emily thinks. I've called this woman's bluff and forced her to show her hand. The whole rescue operation was fake, and now the real interrogation begins.

She rises slowly and pushes back the blanket. But instead of a gun barrel or long knife, there's just a young woman wearing a baseball cap, now slightly askew. Emily glances around. The car is haphazardly parked in a narrow alley. Nobody else seems to be nearby.

Xiuying is pointing toward Emily's shoulder.

"Wh– what are you doing?" Emily says.

Xiuying holds up her phone. On the screen is a message from Tsering. It reads:

*"Don't talk. You are looking for something small and metal. It's probably in Ms. Emily's pack."*

Xiuying motions for Emily to hand over her backpack. After a moment's hesitation, she complies. The girl rummages through it, muttering a steady stream of expletives, then abruptly freezes, her eyes growing wide. A dull gray object, about the size of a quarter, rests at the bottom of the pack. Xiuying nods at the object as if to say, "Ever seen this?"

Emily shakes her head, her mind spinning. Did Frank put it there? Could it have been that man on the subway? Then Mac's embrace in Kowloon Park suddenly rushes to her mind, so abrupt, so seemingly heartfelt. He knew that she might run away. He planted this tracker as a contingency.

Emily opens her mouth to curse him, but Xiuying shakes her head and places a finger over her lips. She believes this is a listening device as well.

Xiuying gingerly plucks the tracker from Emily's bag and places it in her shirt pocket. Then she opens the car door, pauses for several seconds, and closes it with a loud bang.

"Sorry about that pit stop," the younger woman says in a loud and overly dramatic voice. "I really needed to take a piss. But we can get going now."

Is she play-acting? Is she explaining this unexpected pause to their would-be pursuers?

Whether this is a botched kidnapping attempt or a bungled rescue doesn't even matter anymore. Emily just wants out. She throws open her door and rises from the seat. Xiuying grabs her wrist, eyes wide and pleading, then fumbles in her pack, withdrawing a notepad and pen. She scribbles a few words:

*"We've figured out their trick. Give me another chance!"*

Emily shakes her head. The girl writes again:

*"Just spend ten more minutes under that blanket. After that, you can do whatever you want!"*

Xiuying stares with those wide, earnest eyes. Emily sighs and takes the notepad.

"Ten minutes," she writes. "Then I'm done."

She crawls back under the blanket as the engine revs and the tires hum. Xiuying's abrupt twists and turns, combined with the stale air, quickly bring Emily's motion sickness back to full force.

"I'm gonna lose those guys in the markets," Xiuying says in her stage voice, apropos of nothing. "After that, I'm driving to the mainland!"

What is she talking about? Who is she talking to?

"Do me a favor," she continues, "and hold on tight!"

"I'm doing you a favor," Emily replies weakly, "by not puking in your car."

The warning seems to temper Xiuying slightly because the engine calms and the car briefly slows. But the smooth ride lasts only a few minutes before the tires screech, and the car slams mercilessly to a stop. Emily hits the back of Xiuying's seat with a force that knocks the wind from her lungs.

She opens her mouth to complain, or perhaps to be sick, then notices that the car is motionless, the engine idling.

"What are –" Emily begins, but the back door opens; strong hands pull her from the car, then throw her to the pavement. The old Mercedes' tires burn, and the engine roars as Xiuying thunders away in a cloud of smoke.

It's all too much for her over-wrought stomach. She retches, heaving a great disgusting pool of vomit onto the ground in front of her.

"I'm sorry to make demands of you when you feel so poorly," a deep voice says, "but we must keep moving."

She looks up.

She's in a narrow alley, surrounded by vendor stalls stacked with clothing and jewelry, all with a distinctly Buddhist flavor. Blue tarps shield the entire marketplace from the sun and, she realizes, also from satellites or drones that might be watching from overhead. Beside her, a thick man with a shaved head and an orange robe proffers a handkerchief. She takes it, wipes the vomit from her prickly face, and attempts to catch up with the man who is already walking away through the maze of stalls. She follows him into a tall brick building which turns out to be a dilapidated, high-ceilinged warehouse. The space is totally empty except for a battered delivery truck parked at the far end.

This was a handoff, she realizes. Xiuying gave her to the next conductor in their improvised "underground railroad," then drove away with Mac's tracking device still in her pocket. The young woman probably hopes to draw Mac's forces in the wrong direction. But what now? Will she be taking *another* ride from here? Or is this the end of the line, the place where her captors show their true colors?

The thick man leads her to the back of the truck and slides open the door. The truck's interior resembles a living room, including a throw rug, coffee table, and long battered couch. Ben Katz is seated on that couch, smiling and bearded.

"Do you need a lift somewhere?" he says.

# THE MONASTERY

EMILY FOLLOWS Ben through the halls of the monastery, which smells of old wood and incense. Aged and orange-robed monks bow slightly as they pass. He leads her to a room with intricately carved ceiling beams and candles burning on narrow shelves. A window overlooks a small courtyard that's empty except for the delivery truck that brought them here. He motions for her to join him on a floor mat next to a low table. He pours two cups of tea, offers her one, and cradles the other in his thick hands.

She's used to the Fort Meade Ben, the sloppy nerd whose tangled hair, giant belly, and tie-dyed shirts accompany an easy smile and quick wit. This new Ben's hair is shorn, he's at least thirty pounds lighter and wears the simple orange robes of a Buddhist monk. His expressive face is also changed. He seems subdued, thoughtful.

"This Buddhist thing is serious," she observes.

"As much as anything in life can be," he says with a shrug.

She sips her tea, wishing she felt even a tenth of his apparent calm. But her mind is too busy replaying her litany of failures: Her failure to see through Mac's deception, her failure to understand her true role in the NSA, and her failure to keep either herself or anyone around her even remotely safe. She's reached a new level of destruction, surpassing even Audrey's dubious lifetime record.

Her vision is clouded by tears.

"I'm glad you've found a place for yourself," she says, "and I appreciate the help you've given me today. But I'm a cyclone that wrecks everything in her path. If you keep me close, you'll become a victim too."

"You need to get over yourself," he says, holding out an orange handkerchief, "and leave room for other people's sins, mine among them."

She accepts his handkerchief and wipes her eyes.

"Which sins?"

His eyes lack their usual impish sparkle.

"I've known for a while that you were in a hair-on-fire situation," he says, smiling sadly. "But I held back and clutched my bucket of water. I just watched you burn."

She stiffens, suddenly alert and uneasy. Is he behind all the violence after all? Did he send that self-driving car to kill her? Did he set Zahra's office aflame?

"What are you talking about?" she says quietly.

"After your mother died, I realized that you might be a victim of these events rather than an instigator. And when I saw the television reports of what happened in Zahra's office, I became even more certain of your innocence. I should have contacted you the next day, but fear held me back."

"What are you afraid of?"

He sighs and sips his tea.

"Ten years ago, Mac recruited his own army of off-the-books hackers."

She nods, her face burning.

"He confessed that to me today."

"Did he tell you about his ad hoc army? They aren't just teenagers with laptops. He assembled some of the best, which is to say, the worst hackers alive. People like Leonid Sokolov, Sanjay Krishnamurthy, and Ndule Okafor."

She'd heard of Leonid and Ndule—independent actors, brazen in their approach and impossible to corner.

"The free agents he hired gave him military and governmental secrets," Ben continues. "In return, he shared data about the NSA and its methods."

"He told the bad guys *our* secrets?"

Ben's eyebrows raise, and his eyes alight with a sudden wicked glee.

"Not just NSA secrets, or even American secrets. He also betrayed the British GCHQ, the Japanese PSIA, and a dozen others."

"He doesn't have access to that kind of info."

"Well, actually, he does," Ben says. "And he trades it for secrets his own team is too inadequate to dig up by themselves."

"Like?"

"Did he ever tell you about his big break? The event that sent his star into ascendance?"

She recalls the first night Mac came to her apartment. There had been too much wine and too many bad decisions. He'd shared the story then, maybe to impress her.

"He told me he found a third North Korean plutonium processing site," she says, heart aching with the memory of her gullibility and with how eager she'd been to invite him into her bed.

Ben shakes his head.

"It wasn't Mac. It was Leonid Sokolov who accidentally identified that third processing site while stealing Bitcoin from the Kim family. He gave that intel to Mac in exchange for details on how the NSA was tracking him."

"Wasn't anybody suspicious of such a big find coming out of nowhere?" she asks, incredulous.

Ben shrugs.

"Mac talked about hunches and targets of interest and pretended to have unique insights. I was new to the group and was totally fooled, at least at first."

"But not forever?"

"His amazing insights kept coming, so many rabbits pulled out of so many hats. I suspected that he had informants, maybe his own network of moles. Only later did I realize that his moles were more like business partners."

"How did you figure that out?"

"Do you remember those two kids from St. Petersburg?"

She nods, and her stomach twists with the memory.

"They hacked Miami Federal Bank."

"Do you remember how it turned out?" he asks, his eyes now sharp.

"We back-tracked them to a set of servers in Gatchina, Russia," she says. "We were hours from finding their real names, home addresses, maybe even their favorite ice cream flavors."

"Then we gave the report to Mac," Ben says, "and that afternoon, they vanished."

The coincidence had seemed odd, but she'd refused to let herself consider the connection. After all, how could Mac possibly be involved with those low lives?

"We caught up with them two weeks later," she continues, her anger building. "They had the same MO, similar geography, but a new target: Promsvyazbank, a Russian company."

"We could have shared that intel with the Russians. They would have locked those two up for sure. But it didn't happen."

She remembers all too well.

"Mac said our mandate didn't extend to Russian banks. He said domestic Russian hacking was a Russian problem."

"He even implied," Ben says in agreement, his voice now trembling and his hands clenched, "that those boys helped us by hurting our enemies, even though it was clear that they would hit American targets again in the future."

Mac's opposition to pursuing those kids triggered the biggest fight of their relationship. She castigated him for what she thought was simple wrongheadedness. In her desperation to stay close, she had refused to see any other explanation for his terrible decision.

"I became certain that Mac was bent," Ben says softly. "I just couldn't prove it."

"Why didn't you tell me?"

"You were sleeping with him."

Her face warms. "You knew?"

"I mean, he recruited you from prison, right? So I figured you two had a history together."

"I had no connection with Mac before joining the NSA."

Ben's fleshy face sags. He looks tired.

"You had an old and deep connection with him," he says sadly, "you just didn't know it."

She opens her mouth to object, to assure him that she had never been part of Mac's conspiracy. Then the true meaning of his words becomes clear.

"Zahra," she whispers.

He nods.

"Zahra was Mac's most valuable underworld partner and his largest source of intel. When you went to prison, he realized that he could use you as leverage to better control her and her collective."

"What kind of leverage?" she says incredulously.

"You were the original brain behind APRIL, you understood the botnet's best tricks. When Mac brought you into the NSA, it meant you threatened her most powerful tool. He used you to bring her to heel, so to speak."

The story fits all the facts and Mac's confession as well. But that doesn't make it true. This entire meeting could just be part of somebody's three-dimensional chess game.

"How do you know all of this?"

"I had a couple of sources of information. Once was my own sleuthing. Remember Mac's last pool party?"

She nods, recalling the event with a sickening shame that wells in her chest.

"He hadn't separated from his wife yet," she says. "He thought it might be awkward if I came, so he asked me to stay away."

"Mac's parties were lame anyway," Ben says. "Just everybody getting shoved into the pool, cheap-ass beer, and stale chips."

Food and beverages usually figure heavily in any Ben story.

"I was ready to leave," he continues, "and went looking for a place to change into dry clothes. I stumbled into his study and noticed an iPhone sitting on his desk. It was one I'd never seen him carry."

"You went through his stuff? You messed with his phone?"

He shrugs.

"I was pretty certain he was a crook. So I took it into the bathroom and installed my little parasite."

"You brought your hacker's gear to Mac's party?"

"I obsess about things," he admits. "I have issues. The brothers and sisters here are helping me work through them."

"You could have gone to prison for domestic espionage."

"Old Mac was on his sixth beer and not noticing much of anything."

"Holy shit," she whispers, awed by Ben's sheer audacity.

"Eventually, he realized his phone was hacked and quit using it, but not before he contacted this nasty Englishman named Maurice Pryce. I learned that Pryce leads Mac's East Asian field operation as well as all his physical enforcement work. Mac asked Pryce to pay Zahra a visit, something about delivering funds. That's when I knew Mac had a definite connection to The Collective. That was also when I became convinced, wrongly as it turns out, that you were part of his conspiracy."

He takes her hand and squeezes it gently.

"I lacked the bigness of heart to recognize the person that I knew you to be. I failed to trust my own instincts."

"You mentioned a couple of sources," she says. "How else did you know?"

His expressive face looks uncharacteristically guilty.

"I have hacker friends," he admits.

A pang of jealousy, mixed with surprise, stabs her gut. After she joined the NSA, all her old collective comrades called her a traitor. Ben, by contrast, apparently bridged the two worlds.

"Weren't your hacker friends afraid that you would turn on them? And weren't you afraid of the NSA finding out?"

"It makes for awkward conversations," he admits, "but mostly, we avoid talking shop. I have a particular friend who, I eventually realized, was one of Zahra's recruits—a full comrade in Zahra's collective.

"What's his name?" she says. "Maybe I know him."

He shakes his head.

"She joined after you were arrested."

Ben's demeanor is suddenly a bit more reserved, and his face is flushed. A suspicion takes hold in Emily's mind.

"What's the nature of this friendship?"

"It's complicated."

"You've been dating a member of the notorious collective? You? An NSA analyst?"

No wonder he has sympathy for her dilemma. Perhaps it also explains why he didn't go to the higher-ups with his suspicions about Mac.

"I wasn't betraying the agency," he says defensively, "And she wasn't betraying The Collective. But she did admit that

Zahra was pissed about something which, I realized, was all her troubles with Mac."

Emily was so ignorant, so naive. While she worried about betraying the NSA, Mac was employing his own army of hackers. While she worried about Ben's good opinion, he was dating a woman in The Collective. And while she felt guilty about being a turncoat, Zahra and Kaylin fed intel directly to the NSA.

"When that car killed your mom," Ben continues, "I assumed an open war had broken out between Mac's covert organization and The Collective. It no longer felt safe for my girlfriend and me to play Romeo and Juliet."

"So you vanished."

"Cowardice was always my defining trait," he agrees sadly. "With resourcefulness a close second. I'd already questioned Mac's decisions and judgment enough times to make myself suspicious in his eyes. I figured that if he cleaned house, he might figure out my compromised connections. So I gathered my money and friends and got clear of the whole scene. It was only later, once I got some space from the situation, that I reconsidered your role. But by then," he says, eyes growing moist, "you were lying on the floor of that burning high rise."

She crosses to where he sits and wraps her arms around his bulky physique.

"There are so many secrets," she says. "Nobody ever has the whole picture."

"I've allowed so much preventable harm," he says, body shaking with sobs. "I could have told you... I could have warned you."

"If I'd been in your shoes," she says softly, "I wouldn't have helped me either."

"And you would have been just as wrong," he says, wiping his fleshy face with the corner of his sleeve. "The Buddha teaches that the universe itself is change and life is whatever you believe it to be, which means you aren't a prisoner to fate. Even though the deck is massively stacked against you, you've resisted, confounded, and stuck your middle finger into the eye of every person trying to screw you over."

"You sound more like Seymour than a Buddhist."

"You should listen to that boy."

"My mother's dead, my job's gone, my freedom and probably my citizenship are toast. My life is wrecked, Ben."

"The life you *thought* you knew is wrecked," he agrees, "but that life was a lie, a whole layer cake of lies. Now you know the truth and are free to move forward without illusions."

She stifles the urge to laugh or maybe to scream. He's asking her to regard this death sentence, this loss of everything she values, as a perverse blessing.

"I'll be free like Audrey was free," she says bitterly. "Free to be penniless, free to be an outcast, free to live like a bum."

"You told me that your mother used to give medical care to thousands of needy people. That's not the legacy of a bum.

"We lived like refugees," Emily protests. "I didn't have new clothing or shoes, we didn't even have a reliable phone. I often went to bed hungry, and since she was gone so much, I was often alone. That's what I got from her so-called freedom."

"I'm going out on a limb here, Emily," he says gently. "But I think she was doing the best she knew how which was necessarily imperfect. And can you really say that you and I have done better with our own lives?"

"I mean to do better."

"And maybe you will… starting today. You mentioned your friend Seymour. I think we can agree that helping him would be a great way to improve this situation."

"If you get entangled with me, Ben, you'll become part of my growing list of victims," she says with unexpected anger.

He draws himself up, blue eyes growing bright.

"You'd be giving me a chance to stick it to Mac. That's nearly worth the price of admission all by itself."

"I don't think revenge is a Buddhist concept."

"I'm working on some unhealthy attachments," he admits. "But this isn't about me. This is about the fact that you're the most wanted person in Hong Kong, a superstar trying not to be recognized."

She smiles in spite of herself.

"An overweight white guy in monk's garb isn't what I'd call inconspicuous."

"My girlfriend can fetch him."

"She's around?"

"You met her."

Emily begins to object that she certainly hasn't met his girlfriend. Then she remembers her "driver," the crazy woman who brought her here.

"Xiuying?" she asks incredulously.

"Not sure what she sees in me," he admits.

Emily squints. Ben could be called handsome in an over-the-hill hippy sort of way. And the fact that he dropped some weight certainly didn't hurt. But… wow!

"She can fetch Seymour," he asserts confidently. "She knows the city, and she's not on anybody's radar. Once we have him safe, we'll figure out how to smuggle him out of the territory."

Emily's neck hair prickles. She's been such a terrible judge of character…she might be wrong about Ben too. What if he works for Mac and is using her to get to Seymour?"

"I have to come with her," she says. "We'll both go to rescue Seymour."

"The aforementioned dragnet makes it hard to keep you anonymous, let alone safe. The local cops and the Chinese Ministry of state security are very motivated at this point."

"I'll slouch in the back of your car, I'll wear a mask, I'll put my hoodie on. Whatever. But I'm not sending strangers to fetch him."

Ben smiles. "But you'll let us help you?"

She resists the urge to laugh. Her wily friend has been leading her to this conclusion the whole time. But it's true that she can't keep wandering around Hong Kong on her own. She *will* be caught. And even if she can get back to Seymour, her money is dwindling, and she has nobody left to call. How much help will she be on her own?

"You'll regret it," she says earnestly. "Everybody who helps me regrets it."

# LOSING SEYMOUR

EMILY IS WEDGED between Ben and Xiuying on the couch in the back of his delivery truck. The couch is unattached and slides around the metal floor like a pat of butter on a hot skillet. Emily marvels at the young woman sitting next to her. How did Ben meet Xiuying? And what does such a lovely and obviously interesting lady see in him?

"The office bombing still bothers me," Ben is saying as the couch slides toward the far wall. "Was Zahra behind it? Why would she blow up her own facility with one of her own people working there?"

His blue eyes appear genuinely puzzled. There's no hint of guile or caginess. And suddenly, she realizes: Ben and Xiuying don't know about Zahra.

"She's dead," Emily says quietly.

His eyes widen, and Xiuying lets out an expletive.

"How do you know that?" he says.

Emily briefly relates her adventure with Seymour at Zahra's mansion.

"You've been busy in Hong Kong!" Ben says with a frown.

"Zahra is gone?" Xiuying says, tears forming at the corners of her eyes. "Just like Samraat and KanDo?"

"And Transfixed and Horceface and Natch," Emily says,

identifying the comrades by their more commonly known avatar names.

"What about Kaylin?" Xiuying asks.

"I found her in the Choi Hung Estate public housing project. She was scared out of her wits. She was also the person who arranged my meeting with Zahra at that office tower."

"So she almost got you blown up?" Ben asks, his expression grim. "Did she plant the bomb?"

"I can't believe Kay would do that," Xiuying objects, her face growing flushed.

How can she be so sure? How well did she know Kay from her own time in The Collective?

"I've thought about it a lot since that day," Emily says. "My cousin was in the worst mental state I've ever seen. I think she hoped she was exchanging messages with the real, live Zahra. I think she wanted to believe that her friend was still out there somewhere and sent me into the office based on that hope."

The van decelerates, and the couch slides again, slamming into the forward wall. Xiuying walks to the sliding door, her head cocked, catlike, and listens. The truck lurches backward as a faint beeping rises from somewhere outside. She relaxes slightly.

"We're at the loading dock."

"Hopefully, Tsering greased the appropriate palms," Ben says grimly.

Emily dons a surgical mask and dark glasses, then waits as Xiuying rolls open the rear door. Tsering stands on the loading dock, this time in ordinary clothing. He smiles slightly.

"Are you happy that you boarded my cab?" he asks.

"Very happy," she says and gives him a little hug.

His face grows radiant.

"You are most welcome."

She follows Xiuying through a pair of double doors, then steps into what appears to be a storage room filled with crates and equipment. A man and woman in hotel uniforms are seated at a folding table eating noodles. They briefly glance at Emily and Xiuying, then return to their lunch, as if women in sunglasses walk through the loading dock every hour. Apparently, Tsering has doled out the appropriate bribes.

They make their way through the lobby and up the stairs to the room she's been sharing with Seymour. With trembling hands, she fishes out her key card and slides it through the reader, dread rising in her stomach. Is Seymour still recovering? Did he remember to take his medication on time?

She opens the door, and her heart sinks. The space is dead. Sheets and blankets, stained with his dried blood, lay rumpled at the foot of the bed. A visit to the bathroom reveals it to be just as empty.

"Emily," Xiuying calls quietly. The young woman holds a sheet of slightly crumpled paper covered with Seymour's neat, blocky handwriting.

"You've been gone a while," he writes. "I fear that your pig boss may have tied you up someplace, so I'm getting help. I bet you can guess where. If you wind up back here, then contact me on secure chat."

She opens her phone and activates the encrypted p2p comm app.

"I found your note," she writes. "Where are you?"

"Tsering can only stay at the loading dock for a few minutes," Xiuying says.

Emily glances around the room. Her homemade computer is still there, but Seymour removed Zahra's data drive, apparently not wishing to leave such a valuable trove of data unguarded. She gathers her remaining belongings and follows the younger woman to the waiting truck. They take their seats on the couch as Tsering guns the motor.

"The news can't be good," Ben says softly.

"Place was empty," Xiuying replies.

"He left this," Emily says, holding out Seymour's note.

Ben reads briefly, then looks up, eyebrows raised.

"Did he respond to you on secure chat?"

She checks her phone and shakes her head.

"He mentions wanting to get help," Ben says thoughtfully, "where would he look for that? Who does he trust in Hong Kong that isn't dead or in prison?

"Kaylin," Emily says softly.

"And she's in that Chow Yun-fat Estate?" Ben asks.

"Choi Hung Estate," Xiuying says, rolling her eyes.

Emily shakes her head.

"My visit ruined her sense of safety. She'll be long gone from that place."

"How will Seymour find her then?" Ben asks.

"He's the greatest hacker alive," Emily says. "If anybody can do it, he can."

"Preposterous!" Ben says. "Xiuying is the greatest hacker alive!"

"You're sweet," Xiuying says, kissing the top of his shaven head.

"We need to get online and get working," he continues.

Emily nods. Judging by the volume of blood on those sheets, her homemade stitching didn't work well. They need to find him quickly before his condition deteriorates.

# COLLECTIVE STORY

EMILY SITS on the floor of Xiuying's small apartment, laptop open. Husky-sized Buddhist robes are folded and stacked neatly in one corner, making it clear that this is Ben's place, too, at least part of the time. The two of them sit side-by-side, shoulders and hips touching, like a pair of high school sweethearts. Jealousy stabs Emily's chest. Xiuying has someone in her corner, even if he is just sloppy, goofy Ben. The sight of them together makes the search for Seymour feel more urgent somehow.

"What's the plan?" she says. "Where do we begin?"

"Ben and I started a little project a while back," Xiuying says. "A scheme to infiltrate and, at least briefly, control one or both botnets."

"*Both* botnets?" Emily asks, surprised. "Which two are we discussing?"

"APRIL and APRIL," Ben says with a smile.

Emily looks from Ben to Xiuying and back, mind spinning with confusion.

"We call one OG APRIL," Xiuying adds, clarifying nothing, "and the other Rogue APRIL."

Emily closes her eyes. Either these two have gone crazy, or she's totally missing the plot.

"Could we step back a little?" she asks, "maybe add some context here?"

"When I joined The Collective," Xiuying says patiently, "the group was already pushing bots into every cloud system, every desktop computer, and every cell phone on earth."

Emily nods. She can remember Zahra's oft-repeated dream of world domination. It had always felt like a sort of theoretical or aspirational goal, not something that their buggy experimental botnet could actually achieve. Yet it seems as if this remained Zahra's north star for the rest of her life.

"Botnets always contain the seeds of their own destruction," Emily says, "The bigger they grow, the more certain they are to be discovered."

Xiuying smiles and leans forward.

"We even pwned the NSA. Did you know that?"

Emily's ears burn. Not *her* NSA!

"I'd know if the agency was breached," she says, "especially by The Collective."

"I greatly respect you," Xiuying says earnestly, "and your work on the APRIL kernel is the stuff of legend. But today's botnet is light-years beyond that early version. The newer AI, auto-coding, and hacking tricks make it much harder to detect or stop. Toward the end of my time in The Collective, we invaded and owned any system Zahra chose. That was when she began to press her plan to go big."

"As they hacked more of the world's infrastructure," Ben adds, "especially source code repositories and operating systems, nearly every computer became APRIL-compatible. The collective's botnet was the water in which the world's software swam. You were either in The Collective, or you were one of the fish."

"Imagine," Xiuying adds, "that APRIL is watching your attempts to find it. It's there in your file system or network, looking over your shoulder, making its own modifications to your work. You can try to build a virus scanner or source code comparison tool, but APRIL's going to modify it. The botnet becomes its own reality distortion field."

"It's why I was so careful about which version of Linux we used back at the NSA," Ben adds. "I knew most operating systems could not be trusted."

Emily nods, remembering.

"We were high on our own farts," Xiuying agrees. "Except for Seymour. He kept saying we might end up the most hunted humans on earth."

"Which was prescient," Ben says grimly. "But it's also true that most of the hackers in The Collective didn't know about Zahra's arrangement with Mac; they didn't understand how much Mac was protecting them."

"I was blissfully ignorant," Xiuying agrees, "In fact, I was so excited about what we were doing that I moved to Hong Kong to be even closer to the action."

"Which almost broke my heart," Ben admits, his big blue eyes sad.

"Our love was stronger than my greed," she says, squeezing him affectionately and kissing his scraggly cheek.

"For about six months after I moved here," Xiuying continues, "everything was golden. We hardened APRIL, enhanced her paranoia, and expanded her reach. We increased the situations where she could hack on her own without intervention. And despite Seymour's dire predictions, it seemed like we were on our way to pwning the world. Then everything became so much more intense."

"Why?"

"A former comrade joined the other side," Xiuying says, looking meaningfully at her,

"I don't regret it," Emily says firmly.

"We're not judging," Ben says, "none of us are pure here."

"But Zahra completely freaked out," Xiuying says. "You were the hole in her armor, the outsider who knew the ways of both APRIL and the government. She became unhinged, insisting on ever more features to support misdirection. Many comrades internalized her paranoia and tried to hasten the day that APRIL would be fully integrated with the world's infrastructure. But all that crunch time was stressful, especially for Kay and Zahra. It broke their personal relationship, and they separated, moving into different homes and speaking only when work required it."

"We think," Ben says, "that this was also when Zahra brought in new silent partners, probably to further accelerate the botnet expansion project, which, by this time, was losing steam."

Emily straightens in surprise.

"Zahra invited other people in? You mean, besides Mac?"

"That's our theory," Xiuying says, "because shit started getting weird. We had serious and repeated outages, periods where bots lagged, and other times when they ignored our directives altogether."

Emily remembers the emails between Zahra and Kaylin and their apparent panic as they realized that they were being hacked or co-opted. Yet neither referred to any third party or "silent partners." So was Zahra hiding the truth from Kay?

"Our illustrious leader went even more batshit than usual," Xiuying says. "She spoke constantly about your betrayal and wondered which other comrades were traitors as well."

"By then, I was certain of Mac's duplicity," Ben interjects. "So we knew two things: the botnet was malfunctioning, and Zahra and Mac were colluding. From that, we concluded that some sort of coup d'etat was underway."

"That's when Ben and I started our own private research project," she says. "And the first thing we discovered was that the botnet was bifurcating."

"Ah," says Emily knowingly, "this is where the OG APRIL and Rogue APRIL come in?"

Xiuying nods.

"Time after time, we'd find an infected computer with two sets of bots that were similar but with slightly different communications profiles. We couldn't read their encrypted messages, but the structure and size of their communications were different from each other. It's almost as if there were two different generations of APRIL existing at the same time. And they were fighting each other, deleting each other's files, corrupting memory blocks, and struggling for dominance."

"A war for control?" Emily says.

"Along with a war in real life. Because that's when Nishant, aka TransFixed, turned up dead in Delhi."

Emily nods, remembering her own shock at learning of his death. How much more horrible must it have been to know that you might be next?

"We suspect Kaylin bifurcated APRIL, probably many months ago, though whether on Zahra's behalf, against Zahra, or in spite of her, we can't say.

Emily nods, recalling the immense tower of computers in Kay's apartment, as well as her haggard appearance. She'd been using all her considerable skills to stay alive and to regain control of a single botnet. But her low spirits suggest the fight was going poorly.

"Which leads us to our plan," Xiuying continues. "We want to give Kaylin a sudden change of luck."

They're both smiling now, Ben from behind his scraggly beard and Xiuying with her smooth skin and perfect shining brown eyes. Emily glances from one to the other, a sudden suspicion growing.

"You know how to hack APRIL?"

Ben's smile widens.

"We've sort of been copying and testing our own version of the virus you built at the NSA."

"But it was a fail," Emily says, alarmed, "A *terrible* fail!"

"Your experience revealed that affecting too many nodes

will trigger APRIL's mesh corruption logic," Xiuying says, "but our goal here is more modest. We only need to take out a single node. In that case, there's no pattern to discern and too little data for APRIL to decide she's being threatened. In the absence of any proven emergency, the system maintains its ordinary cautious pace."

Emily nods, starting to comprehend. Under normal circumstances, APRIL bots move like a herd of deer traveling through a dense forest, picking their way slowly through the victim's network, gaining ground carefully to avoid attention—Xiuying plans to use that caution to her advantage.

"We've spent lots of time watching Kaylin attack Rogue APRIL with OG APRIL," Xiuying continues. "So we'll find a bot she's using for an attack, then corrupt it and generate the illusion that her attack is winning. From there, we'll provide a false map to the bots she thinks she's spawning. We'll paint the picture that she's gaining ground."

"And your own virus can be configured to do that?"

"Our goal was always to do targeted attacks," Ben says, "rather than corrupting the system at scale."

"But it won't fool her for long," Emily says, considering their idea. "An hour or two at most until she reaches the end of your simulation. And how does that help anything?"

"We know she's been staying away from the public onion networks," Ben says, "probably because her adversaries, whoever they are, have poisoned them. So she's relying on her own much smaller relay network to hide her true location. Xiuying has wanted to find Kay for a while, and we've already pwned most of the relays in her private onion network. Once she gets excited about all the fake success we're showing her, we assume she'll press her advantage. Her network will light up, and we'll use timing analysis to pinpoint the source. With a little luck, we should have her street address in less than an hour."

The audacity of the plan is stunning, but it's also a bridge burner.

"She's smart and paranoid. She'll figure it out. Even your corruption of her private onion network. And once she does, she'll know we're coming."

They both nod.

"Which means we have to find her within two hours," Ben says, "but that should be enough, assuming she's in Hong Kong."

Emily checks her secure messaging app. Still no communication from Seymour. Is he busy? Angry? Or has his condition worsened so much that he can't communicate? If so, is Kay taking care of him?

"I'm coming too," she says.

"That's a bad idea, I'm afraid," Ben says. "The Chinese are completely freaked out by their inability to find you. They've begun to expend huge resources on frame-by-frame scans of every security feed in the territory and are also using body structure recognition. Even if you wear a tent, they may still spot you."

"This is Emily's fight," Xiuying says firmly. "She's coming if she wants to."

Emily smiles despite herself. This Xiuying is Ben's greatest find.

"I just left Seymour all sewn up and bleeding," Emily agrees. "I need to know if he's still recovering. And I need to get him home."

# HOLIDAY COTTAGE

EMILY, Ben, and Xiuying walk silently past shops and markets that line the streets near Lamma Island's ferry terminal. Xiuying and Ben pinpointed Kaylin's house on the far side of this quaint vacation enclave, an island that lacks roads or cars, where foot traffic is the main conveyance. Since they couldn't scrounge a boat on short notice, they donned bulky coats, wore dark sunglasses, and boarded the ferry like everybody else.

Now that they're on the tropical island, Emily's long coat is suffocating, and a river of sweat rolls down her back. They walk past stucco holiday cottages painted whimsically in sky blue, light pink, and pale yellow. The sidewalks are crowded with afternoon visitors.

"Kay and I came here a lot as teenagers," she says. "We'd hang out at the beach, flirt with boys, then catch the late ferry home."

"You grew up in Hong Kong?" Xiuying asks, surprised.

"My Uncle Ip adopted me after mom went to prison. I'd have been on the streets if not for him.

"That's Ng Ip To, right?" Xiuying says, pronouncing his surname first, in Chinese fashion.

Emily nods.

"Were you living with him when he and his wife were, uhm, assassinated?"

Grief wells in Emily's heart. She shakes her head.

"I was attending college in the States."

"His loss must have been difficult."

Ip was the closest thing to a father she'd ever known. But his death wasn't a total surprise. His occupation hung over the family like a curse, unacknowledged and ever-present.

"I was sad," she agrees, "but his passing was obviously harder on my cousins, Frank and Kay. They had to deal with losing their parents while also assuming responsibility for the family business and avoiding a gang war."

And the strain only grew after Kay came out as queer. Frank feared the triads would see his sister's admission as proof that the next generation of Ngs was corrupt and perverse. So, between their fights about the business and Frank's anger over Kay's public revelations, the siblings wound up barely on speaking terms. Kaylin finally resolved the dispute by walking away from the business, leaving Frank with sole control. Hiding and disengaging were always Kay's go-to moves when things got bad. Only it may not work this time, given how tightly she's lashed to Zahra's sinking ship.

As the footpath winds on, the homes thin out, replaced by dense tropical forests. The air is scented with flowering plants. An immense yellow and black spider squats atop a wide web and shifts slightly as they walk past. Though she didn't initially recognize the address, Emily grows increasingly certain about where Kay might be hiding.

"So she joined The Collective after her parent's death?" Ben asks.

"It was like a corporate merger," Emily says. "Kay brought her technical skill as well as a big pile of Ng money as seed capital. A few months later, they also asked me to join."

"Why did you accept their offer?" Xiuying asks. "The excitement? The technical challenge?"

If only her reasons had been so positive.

"Mom was behind in her mortgage payments," Emily says. "I was a poor college student with no real way to help. Joining Kay and Zahra was a way to raise some quick funds and get the house paid off. Little did I know that it was a life-changing decision."

They reach a fork in the path. Without waiting for Xiuying's direction, Emily takes the leftward option, her neck tingling in anticipation as they continue up the winding trail. The other two follow without comment, apparently assuming that Emily knows the way. They step into a clearing that affords a view of the sparkling, turquoise East Lamma channel and, beyond that, the forested mountains of Hong Kong itself. Emily points toward a set of high-rise towers sitting next to the distant shores of Repulse Bay.

"Those condos are owned by the Ng empire," she says. "They're Frank's now."

"You know a lot about this place," Ben observes.

"Kay and I had a high school friend named Gina Chen. Her family owned a vacation cottage at the end of this path. Kay loved the house and must have bought it."

"From the data we saw, she also tricked it out with high-speed fiber links," Ben adds.

"Which means we're about to find her!" Xiuying says with her usual enthusiasm.

Emily grabs the younger woman's shoulder, gently restraining her.

"You guys should hold back. I'll go ahead."

Xiuying rounds on her, face flushed.

"That was *not* the deal," she says. "We're sticking together!"

"Kay won't open the door for a former collective

comrade," Emily says patiently, "and she certainly won't open it for some bearded white guy."

"What's wrong with my beard?" Ben asks defensively.

"If we all show up on her doorstep," Emily continues, "she'll assume that Zahra's paranoid stories were true. She'll see us as turncoats, and she'll see you," she points to Ben, "as some kind of CIA spook."

Her cousin, skittish and suspicious under the best of circumstances, is in a particularly fragile state right now.

"Why not me?" Xiuying demands. "Kay and I are friends, aren't we?"

"I'm family," Emily replies, projecting more conviction than she feels, "and I've never betrayed her. Once I'm inside, I'll calm her down and explain what's going on."

Butterflies tickle the inside of her guts. Will Seymour be there? Has Kay been tending to his injuries? Is he still improving?"

Xiuying and Ben exchange a worried glance.

"I think you're right about how she'll react," Xiuying says cautiously. "But what if she's got people with her? What if she thinks you're there to hurt her?"

"We have to weigh those risks against the danger of spooking her," Emily says.

Ben opens his mouth, then closes it again.

"I hate when you're right," he says finally.

"Ten minutes," Xiuying says. "If we haven't heard from you by then, then we're coming in."

"It'll take me more than ten minutes to explain our situation and more than ten minutes to calm her down," Emily says patiently. "I'll send word once things feel right, once she's in a receptive state of mind."

Xiuying and Ben both scowl. They obviously don't like the plan but seem unable to mount any serious objection.

"I just started repaying my karmic debt to you," Ben says finally. "Now you're putting me in a deeper hole."

She leans over and kisses him on his grizzled cheek.

"You're paid in full," she says softly. "More than paid."

Ben and Xiuying exchange a look, then Xiuying shrugs.

"I don't like it," she says, "but I agree that she'll probably trust you the most."

Ben and Xiuying step into the undergrowth and take a seat among the plants.

"Hurry," Xiuying cautions, "and call as quickly as you can."

"Or the mosquitoes will eat us alive," Ben adds.

Emily turns away, fighting back tears. In just two short days, these two have become such close friends. Can she avoid hurting them? Is she bringing them the same kind of danger that she brought Frank and Seymour?

She continues alone along the familiar path. The forest canopy closes in around her, warding off the afternoon heat but also blocking other escape routes. She unbuttons the long coat, and a little cool air reaches her body, calming her racing mind. Another minute's walk brings her to the end of the tree-lined tunnel, and the jungle opens into a wide glade. At the center sits a two-story salmon-colored cottage, surrounded by massive trees and framed by the sparkling waters of the East Lamma Channel. The house shows none of the neglect that so defined Zahra's Victoria Peak mansion. Its stucco is freshly painted, and its gardens are filled with flowering plants. This is Kaylin's refuge, and Emily strides toward it with a lighter heart, now confident that she'll find her cousin after all. Kaylin, forced to leave her secure but nightmarish Choi Hung Estate apartment, came here to her happy place and, in these cheerful surroundings, will finally listen to reason.

Emily steps up to the door and knocks with three loud raps. There's no response. She tries again. When nobody answers the second time, she turns the doorknob and finds, to her surprise, that it's unlocked. She pushes the door open and peers into the darkened entryway.

"Kay?" she calls out. "Hello?"

There's no response. She steps inside. The room is decorated in what might be called Chinese medieval, with silk tapestries, an intricately carved wardrobe, and several yoke-backed chairs. She draws a sharp breath as she approaches the last of these chairs because Kaylin's tattered navy cardigan is draped haphazardly across it. She picks up Kaylin's sweater, then looks around. Kaylin always wears this sweater. Why is it sitting here?

"Kay?" she calls again, her confidence faltering. She takes another step into the room.

The door slams shut behind her, and a hand snaps around her wrist. She tugs, but the hand yanks her in a circle like she's tied to a fleeing truck. Four men stand in front of her, and the tallest holds a large roll of tape.

"Let go of me!" she shouts.

The tall man answers by stretching out the length of the tape and slapping it over her mouth. Another man mutters a few words in an unfamiliar Chinese dialect. She can't understand much, but she does make out the word "box." The tall man grabs her and drags her to an adjoining room where a wooden packing crate lies on the floor, its cover open.

Whatever these men have in mind can't be healthy for her. She stomps on the man's foot and tugs at his hand with all her might. He flinches but merely tightens his grip. Another man approaches, holding a syringe. The tall man twists her wrist, exposing the underside of her arm, and before she can object, the man with the syringe jabs the needle into her and injects her with a cold liquid. Her head swims, the room twists, and her limbs grow limp.

She wants to tell Ben and Xiuying that their trust was misplaced and that, once again, her hubris has doomed everyone. She wants to tell them to run, to put as much distance as possible between themselves and these men. But her mind is increasingly untethered from worldly concerns. As somebody lifts her body, her thoughts drift into a dreamlike state. As the men place her into the box, her stream of consciousness slows. As the top slides shut overhead, she no longer even resents her situation. It's cozy and dark inside this box, a comfortable and safe place to rest for a little bit. Later, she will definitely need to decide what to do about these hostile men. But for now, she can close her eyes and get some well-earned sleep.

# MAURICE PRYCE

EMILY REGAINS A GROGGY CONSCIOUSNESS. Her body is in a seated position; her back is bolt upright. She struggles to focus her bleary eyes and move her leaden arms. Men in dark suits stand around her, eyeing her warily. Snatches of memory push through the mental fog. They grabbed her, injected her, and boxed her up. So where is this? She raises an arm drunkenly. She's unbound, though her wrists and mouth sting where they tore the tape away. She tries standing, but the room gives a sickening lurch. She falls back into her seat, and her stomach gurgles ominously.

"Think you're goin' dancin' then?" says a smooth voice. She swivels her head unsteadily toward the speaker. A white man sits across from her, wearing a navy blazer with an absurd handkerchief in the breast pocket. His brown hair is oiled and slicked back as if combed using buttered toast.

"I wouldn't advise dancing just now," the man continues. "Propofol is fast actin' shit and hits like a ton o bricks, but the good news is, it wears off just as fast."

His accent is uncouth and British, perhaps from the rougher parts of London. And he's right; the drug is fading. Her vision brightens, her hearing sharpens, and her surroundings come into focus. She's in a tiny room with round windows situated near the ceiling. The walls are studded gray steel and resonate with the lap, lap of water somewhere outside. This is a boat, though there isn't any rumbling motor, and the room sways only slightly. Are they still moored at Lamma Island?

"An associate of mine," the Englishman continues, "noted that you were in company wiv two other people on that ferry. One was a sloppy, bearded bloke, clearly your disgraced co-worker, Mr. Ben Katz. The other was a sharp little Chinese girly we do not seem to know. Could you tell me where we might find the bof of them?"

His words are light, and his manner calm. Yet the gleam in his eye suggests this isn't an idle question. She licks her lips and assembles her disordered thoughts. She left Ben and Xiuying a quarter mile from Kaylin's house. Does this man have people searching the grounds? Are her friends, even now, scrambling through the undergrowth, fleeing a set of dark-suited pursuers?

Her tolerance for anesthetics is poor, and the Propofol, or whatever it was, upset her stomach nearly as much as that garbage Frank's men gave her. She swallows and takes a few long breaths before speaking.

"Who are you?" she manages.

The man leans forward and flashes his white teeth in a tight smile that nearly cracks his suntanned face.

"I'll be asking the questions," he says softly. "And the question on the table is: Where are Ben Katz and his little girly friend?"

Her hands tremble. However terrified she felt that day in Zahra's office, or on the fire escape with Frank's men, or even fleeing the drones with Seymour, it all felt manageable, even easy, compared to this conversation. This man's soulless smile, his broad shoulders, and his glinting eyes exude a menace so palpable and so seemingly inevitable that she can barely refrain from screaming.

"I, I came alone," she says, "nobody was –"

The man touches a perfectly manicured finger to her lips, silencing her.

"I must advise you, Ms. Ng Mei Yan," he says, pronouncing her Chinese name better than she can herself, "that my patience is entirely exhausted. So please, consider your next words carefully."

How does this man even know her Chinese name? Does he work for Mac? How many of Mac's soldiers are on the island? Do Ben and Xiuying realize that the ferry isn't safe? Will they find another way back?

"We split up," she says. "It was all arranged. But I don't know where they –"

In a flash, he's on his feet and swinging his giant hand toward her face. The blow spins her head around and throws her to the floor. Two other men grab her arms and lift her back into the chair. The taste of blood fills her mouth, and her unsettled stomach threatens to rebel. She wills the bile back down her throat.

"Until now, Ms. Hernandez," says the man in the blue blazer, "you've dealt wiv a civilized, air-conditioned, and bloodless spycraft. For you, this was never a hands-on job."

She trembles, avoiding his gaze, concentrating on his gleaming, polished shoes.

"But," he continues, "your situation has changed drastically. There is a physical dimension now. Try to keep that in mind."

The tremble in her arms intensifies. The men tighten their grips.

"This Mr. Katz," the Englishman continues, a bit more gently, "is 'ardly worthy of your protection. You know 'e's partner with your wayward former boss, Mr. Laurence Macarthy, don't ya?"

Another version of the ever-shifting truth? Was Ben lying to her? Was he working for Mac all along? Is this part of an elaborate campaign to wear her down? The drugs and the fear make it hard to keep everything straight.

"So let me rephrase," the man continues. "And think carefully before you provide your next response: Where are Ben Katz and his associate?"

She considers Ben and Xiuying, all they did for her, and all they risked. Even if they are somehow responsible for part, or all, of her present misfortune, they don't deserve to meet this man.

"Go fuck yourself," she says quietly.

The tanned man blinks.

"I don't fancy that," he replies.

With a single, deft motion, he grabs her, pulls her off the chair, and throws her to the floor. Her head slams the metal decking knocking her into brief insensibility before an enormous bulk presses down on her, like a water buffalo settling on her chest. The Englishman is on top of her, his breath stinking of mint and liquor. And though she wriggles and writhes, she's no match for his heft or steely arms.

"On the other hand," he whispers in her ear, "there's another kind of fucking that I might fancy."

"Wait," she gasps.

"Did you think better of your answer?" he asks mockingly. "Had a sudden change-o heart?"

She closes her eyes; she's back in San Francisco, lying on her mother's couch with fat Eddie pressing his bloated, disgusting self against her. She tugs, writhes, and pulls. She was able to get free from Eddie, able to grab hold of his baseball bat before he realized what she was doing. But, unlike Eddie Wang, the Englishman's rough hands and iron legs easily hold her in place. He twists her right arm behind her back, pinning it so he can free his own hand. Then he fumbles at her shirt, unfastening buttons, tearing them when they resist. Her stomach reels and twists. Excited by drugs and the boat's motion, the vomit moves up her throat. It's all she has now, all she can offer by way of defense. She lets go, giving her tortured gut its way. Foul fluid burns her throat, fills her mouth, and bursts into the open. Puke sprays into the Englishman's eyes and splatters on his face.

"Bloody Hell!" he screams, convulsing backward in disgust. She wriggles free, coughing and sputtering, clearing the filth from her mouth and throat.

He stumbles to his feet. His clothing drips with the contents of her stomach.

"Filthy bitch!" he says, eyes wild with rage.

He grabs her neck and lifts her to her feet, squeezing until she gasps for breath. He brings his puke-covered face up close, cocks his free arm, and balls his fist. A cold calm falls over her. She accepts what's about to happen and waits for the blow so heavy that she won't wake up.

"Stop," says one of the suited men.

The Englishman's arm wavers.

"Get your hand off me, Yu," he growls.

From the corner of her vision, she sees the man named Yu gripping the larger man's cocked arm and pulling it downward, away from her face—the other three move to assist.

"We cannot kill this woman," Yu says, "as you well know."

The Englishman's hand tightens on her throat, choking her windpipe. The room spins. She struggles to keep her eyes open.

"Are you forgetting who you work for?" he says.

"I am not," says Yu.

Veins throb in the Englishman's forehead. He seems to consider whether his pride and honor are worth a fight with these four men. Then, as if somebody threw a switch, his expression softens; he recovers his mask of calm and releases her throat.

"Take her then," he says, "the vomitous bitch. And I'll go look for that sloppy American bloke and his little girly."

Yu takes half a step back, though his body remains tense, ready to intervene if required. The Englishman's bright green eyes give Emily a final glance before he turns and walks out the door, heavy footsteps clanging up the metal stairs.

Yu brings her a towel and a jug of water, then leaves, along with two of the others. Only one dark-suited man remains, watching impassively as she cleans vomit from her face and hair. She resists the urge to weep.

Somewhere below, a diesel engine rumbles to life. The boat shudders. She survived for the moment, but this is only the briefest of reprieves. Death awaits at the end of this cruise once her pursuers have whatever they can extract from her. She must break free if she wishes to avoid another meeting with that terrible Englishman. Even if the risks are high and they wind up killing her, she must try to escape.

# CHIP'S OFFER

EMILY SWEATS in her blindfold as the car bumps and jostles. She sits firmly wedged between the warm bodies of two captors, her wrists and feet bound. Judging by how long they've been traveling, they could have crossed the whole territory by now, maybe even left Hong Kong entirely. The car lurches to a stop, and a door opens, allowing tropical, flower-scented air to fill the space. Rough hands lift her to her feet. Somebody cuts the bindings around her ankles.

"Where are we going?" she asks.

The only response is the squeak of leather shoes and the rustle of clothing. She lurches from her captors, but iron hands grab her arms and rebuff her with a violent tug. They goad her up a flight of stairs and shove her over some sort of threshold. A cool blast of conditioned air makes her arms prickle as her feet pad over a carpeted surface. Is this the interrogation room? Is she about to hear the Englishman's cockney voice and smell his mint and liquor breath?

"Stand still one minute," says a low, Chinese-accented voice, "then take off your blindfold."

Somebody grasps the bindings on her wrists and tugs, freeing them. Her hands tingle as the blood returns.

"What are we doing here?" she asks.

The only reply is the shuffle of feet and the click of a door latch. The room is silent save for the whisper of air conditioning. Her skin crawls with fear and cold, but after several minutes she musters enough courage to lift the blindfold. Bluish neon light blinds her, and she blinks, forcing her eyes to adjust. She's in a small room containing only a short couch and a modest desk. There are two doors, one closed, the other open, revealing a toilet and sink. She washes her face and sits on the couch, arms still trembling with fear. She has neither a phone nor a computer, nothing she can use to contact her friends. And there aren't any windows, so she has no way of telling whether it's day or night. Is she even in Hong Kong anymore? Is this building owned by Mac's private army, or has she fallen into the hands of a rival organization? Either way, will her captors interrogate her? Beat her? Drug her?

Her breathing accelerates, and she grows dizzy. She must control her frenzied mind, think positive thoughts, and avoid fixating on this terrible situation.

She pictures Seymour sitting behind the wheel of Nemo, the antique microbus. His skinny arms protrude from an oversized t-shirt, and the wind tousles his curly hair. They're driving a stretch of the Santa Cruz highway, making their way to the ocean. The memory slows her heart and restores her confidence. She'll get back to him somehow. She won't let him down again.

A knock on the door breaks her concentration, and her rabbit's heart resumes its rapid beating. A young man with light brown skin and a cherubic face peeks inside, making her flinch. Is this her new interrogator? Will he hurt her the way the Englishman did? Will he cause her to betray her friends?

"I didn't mean to startle you," he says, his accent some kind of American midwestern twang.

He takes a tentative step into the room, revealing an untucked button-down shirt billowing over an expansive gut.

He's fleshy, almost boyish. And there's something distinctly familiar about him–

"Amit?" she says. "Amit Pradhan?"

"I can come back later if that's better for you," he replies.

"Where am I?" she says, noting the soreness in her throat, which must be lingering damage from the Englishman's torture.

"A safe house, you might call it."

"Safe from what?"

"Director Chip is ready to answer all your questions," he says. "I've just come to bring you to meet him."

The name 'Chip' feels like an artifact from some ancient era—a time when life operated from 9 to 5.

"Director Leonard Chip?" she repeats cautiously.

"He'd love to chat," Amit says with a smile. "If you have a little time, I mean."

Do they imagine she has anything better to do?

"Now would be great," she says cautiously.

His shoulders relax, and he smiles nervously.

"Would you mind following me?"

He leads her down a beige hallway and into a conference room whose wide windows overlook a dense jungle.

"If you'd like to take a seat," he says, placing a glass of water next to her, "the director will be here shortly."

He gives her a last, nervous glance, then closes the door. She notes that there's no second click, no indication he's secured any latch.

She tiptoes to the door and places her ear against its cool surface. There's no discernible sound from the other side. She twists the knob and gives a little push. The door swings open, revealing an empty hallway. After taking a fortifying breath, she brazenly steps through, bracing for a cry of alarm or a stern order to return to her seat. Instead, she stands alone in a sunlit corridor, with no black suits or thugs visible anywhere. Beyond the windows are trees and jungle foliage. Whoever owns this facility picked a very remote location.

She could make a run for it, just dash into that jungle and get as far from these people as possible. But without money or even a good pair of shoes, how far would she get? And even if she finds a store or village, how will she keep herself hidden? Who's to say the Hong Kong cops won't find her?

She returns to the conference room with a sigh and sits near the giant video screen. If this really is a video call with Director Chip, he'll likely review the long list of charges arrayed against her. He'll spell out the ways her career with the agency is over. This will be an interrogation as well as an exit interview.

The conference room door swings open, and Director Leonard Chip himself glides in. He wears a pin-striped suit, and his silver hair is arranged neatly over his tall shiny forehead. He smiles his trademark toothy smile.

"Emily," he says, his voice deep and sonorous, "thank God you're safe."

She rises, stunned and disoriented that an NSA director is actually standing here, thousands of miles from the Fort Meade headquarters. Back home, Chip was a distant figure: the man at the podium, the executive surrounded by aides, the picture at the top of the monthly newsletter. Close up, he's surprisingly frail, an aged uncle with pale blotchy skin and sagging jowls. Yet his dark eyes are steady and piercing.

"You've had a harrowing experience," he continues. "Are you hurt? Are you hungry?"

"Thank you, sir," she says, "I'm fine."

He chooses a chair opposite and motions for her to sit. His presence is unsettling and infuriating. Why, after all this time, is Director Chip getting involved? Why did he wait so long?

"You haven't deserved what's happened to you," he says as if reading her thoughts. "We're now at the end of a chain of terrible and frankly avoidable mistakes."

Her mother's murder? The office bombing? The army of drones that nearly sliced off Seymour's arm? Were these just mistakes? She touches her bruised cheek and winces at the memory of her recent beating. Was that a "mistake," too?

"Your people put me in a wooden box," she says, her voice quavering with rising anger. "They drugged me, beat me, and tried to rape me."

His thick eyebrows knit together, and deep worry lines crease his forehead.

"Since the crackdown," he says, "the Chinese have arrested nearly all the CIA's Hong Kong contacts and under-cover agents. They've made it extremely difficult for us to conduct missions competently and even harder to exfiltrate agents when they're in danger."

'*Exfiltrate*?' Does he think she's grown so delusional during these past few weeks that she now believes she's a field agent?

"I would call it more kidnapping than exfiltration," she says.

His frown deepens. He seems unused to having anyone challenge his version of reality.

"It was our last option," he says. "Our only hope of bringing you in from the cold."

Again with the spy metaphor. Except she isn't a spy. They never sent her here, and it wasn't his responsibility to bring her out. What's the point of this charade?

"I know what Mac's been up to," she says. "He told me himself two days ago."

"Yes," Chip says thoughtfully. "We monitored that conversation."

If the Americans were monitoring, then who else was also? The Chinese? The triads? The Russians?

"Learning of Mac's betrayal was a body blow," he contin-ues. "Heads will roll over this debacle, mine among them. But as long as I'm still the director, I have a moral obligation to sort out who to trust and who to hand over to the FBI."

"Am I in the latter group?" she asks.

He leans forward, dark eyes locked on hers.

"We know that the Queen's Road office, where you were almost bombed to death, is owned by Zahra Kartal. We're fairly certain that this indicates no great friendship between you and her. And after listening to your meeting with Mac, we also know you aren't working for him either. Your independence makes you our single most valuable asset in this situation."

"I'm nobody's asset."

His eyes are alight, and his bushy eyebrows raise hopefully.

"You could be an employee again, Emily. In good standing, with a clear record, and your life restored."

"How's that possible?"

He rises with surprising alacrity and strides to the window.

"You're free to leave, of course."

"Back to my little prison?"

He turns to face her, his wrinkled face etched with sadness.

"You may go wherever you wish, to whatever you were doing before we brought you here. I've asked that young fellow, Amit, to release you at the end of this interview."

Amit's sticking close to the director. He's going places.

"You would just turn me loose into the wild?"

"As I said, we believe that you are, at most, tangentially connected with Mac's conspiracy. We don't have legal or moral grounds to hold you. So if we can't come to an agreement, then yes, we'll let you go. But please carefully consider what you'd be walking away from. We can protect you, keep you safe, and convey you home. Meanwhile, the Chinese

Ministry of State Security is aggressively seeking you, and they won't be gentle interrogators."

He takes a step closer.

"Even if you get past them and find your way home, the FBI will likely arrest you for your involvement in Zahra's conspiracy. I believe you would eventually beat those charges, but the legal process might take years. On the other hand, you could remain an employee of the NSA, in which case we will explain to the FBI that your actions are in the line of duty. Instead of being pursued, you'd be promoted. You would have an influential and interesting career and be free of the black cloud Mac cursed you with."

His offer is tempting. It's everything she hoped for.

"What's the cost of this happy ending?" she asks.

He spreads his hands.

"Just do your job. Help us to find Zahra and the other members of her criminal syndicate. Help us to tame and, ideally, co-opt the APRIL botnet. And help us prepare for the next advanced botnet that will surely arise."

She sways dizzily with confusion and excitement. That's no price at all! On the contrary, it's the complete reinstatement of a life she thought was gone forever. But what about the others?

"Your men in suits waited for me at my cousin Kaylin's summer cottage. So have you captured her also? And my friend, Seymour?

Chip's face sours. "I would not call those distasteful fellows *my* men. They're contractors and extremely poor and harmful ones at that. But they were the best we could find under the circumstances. And in answer to your question, no, we have no information about Ms. Kaylin Ng nor the whereabouts of your close and questionable friend, Mr. Seymour Frey.

"I need help finding Seymour. He's committed no crimes

and is badly injured. We need to give him safe passage home."

A smile curls the edge of the director's thin lips.

"Are we negotiating the terms of your reinstatement?

Are they? What would life at the agency look like now that so much water has passed under the bridge? What would it be like without Ben or Mac? And how would Seymour react to this latest betrayal? Would he understand?

On the other hand, if she doesn't take this opportunity, then when will another ever come along? When will she ever have another chance to join the good guys?

"Yes," she says firmly, "we are."

Chip folds his long thin arms.

As to the matter of Mr. Frey, if we uncover evidence implicating him in cybercrime or other illegal activities, then he will certainly face criminal prosecution; there's nothing I can do to prevent it. But, yes, I will certainly help bring him home."

Getting Seymour safely out of Hong Kong is 90% of the battle. And once he's home, she can help him fight whatever charges they bring.

"Agreed," she says.

"Anything else?" he asks lightly. "Do you know some other quasi-criminals that need amnesty or safe passage?"

"I won't help you find Ben Katz," she blurts. "He's done nothing wrong. The agency should leave him alone!"

"We are well aware of Mr. Katz's innocence," Chip says smoothly, "as well as his relationship to this bizarre case. I would, of course, love to speak with him and woo him back to the agency. But I suspect Mac burned that bridge."

"He did," she agrees.

"Then it's settled. I'll have the paperwork drawn up, and you will rejoin the agency, effective immediately."

He extends his bony hand, and she grasps it gingerly,

suppressing a shiver of revulsion at the touch of his fish-like skin.

"Thank you," she says, forcing a smile.

"On the contrary," he says, flashing his yellowed horse teeth, "thank *you*. And welcome aboard once again!"

# NEW JOB

EMILY WALKS toward the conference room, the dull ache in her stomach intensifying. She slept poorly last night, unable to fully reconcile with the deal she just made. She doesn't doubt that Director Chip will try to keep his end of the bargain. Exfiltrating Seymour, a person the agency has long suspected of domestic terrorism, would be a feather in the old man's cap. He'll no doubt invest real resources into the effort. But will it be enough? And does Seymour have enough antibiotics to stay healthy until he's found? Or might Kaylin have taken him to a doctor already? Emily has no way of knowing, so if Chip's team moves too slowly, she'll have to involve herself and accelerate the search. She can't let things drag on if Seymour's in trouble.

And even if they find Seymour, there's the exfiltration. Would Chip send that horrid Englishman to pick him up? Will Seymour get hurt in the process? Will he accept any "help" from NSA or CIA operatives? Will he realize that such help is the best of several bad options?

And then there are the others. Does Kaylin have a survival plan? Will she keep fighting whoever controls APRIL? Is that how she plans to spend the rest of her life? And what about Ben? Does he feel like his karmic debt is repaid? Or are he and Xiuying still out there risking themselves to find and free her? She has to signal them, to tell them she's okay, to tell them to go about their lives.

She enters the conference room and drops into her seat, shoulders weary under the weight of these concerns. With a sigh, she activates the video link that Director Chip gave her. The monitor brightens, and the face of Ms. Laura Pringle, her HR liaison, smiles down at her, filling her with a powerful Deja Vu. Today, just like the first day of work three years ago, Laura is wearing those ridiculous 90s Baby Spice pigtails. And today, just like three years ago, the HR liaison is seated at a cramped desk, surrounded by stacks of files and documents.

"Welcome back!" Laura says brightly and gives a little wave.

"It's good to be back," Emily replies, as the pain in her gut gives another jab.

"I've completed and signed your forms," Laura says, holding a stack of papers up to the camera.

"I don't remember any physical paperwork the last time you hired me."

"Your new status is too sensitive for computers, so it's paper for now. And these docs will stay locked in my safe."

"Is that legal?" Emily asks, her stomachache worsening.

"Standard procedure for a covert resource. It ensures that you get paid, receive 401K benefits, and even retain your parking priority while remaining a total secret from nearly everybody. But rest assured, your job will be in perfect order once you emerge and rejoin us at the Fort Meade head-quarters."

Emily stares at the screen, speechless. It's the same Laura, the same chipper smile, the same messy desk. This must be legit. But it feels so odd.

"Except for Director Chip," Laura continues, apparently oblivious to her unease, "I'll be the only HQ staff member who understands your true situation. You should contact me exclusively when you have questions or concerns about compensation or other employment issues."

What kind of concerns should she report? Would yesterday's sexual assault count? Or is that filed under "risks of the job?"

She smiles for the camera.

"I'm just so excited to get back to work!" she says. And part of her actually means it.

————

AN HOUR LATER, she finds Amit slouching in the little break room, sipping coffee from a paper cup. He smiles as she approaches.

"Are you all good with HR?" he asks.

"If I answer yes, will I get the grand tour you promised?"

"Keep your expectations low," he says, his smile widening. "This place is old, dumpy, and we call it home."

He leads her down a familiar flight of steps, then stops in front of her own sleeping quarters.

"The women's dormitory," he says, pointing at her door.

She takes a moment to catch on.

"I'm the only female?"

He shrugs.

"We've got to work on our diversity, especially for field personnel."

She nods. If the past 24 hours are any indication, most sane women won't want this job.

"Next," he says, leading her down the hallway, "we find ourselves by the men's dormitories."

He points down a long corridor lined with closed doors. It smells faintly of sweat, cheese, and old socks.

"We clean every January," he says, "whether it needs it or not."

The odor is reminiscent of her recent encounter with the Englishman. She swallows, resisting the urge to gag.

They pass a dozen offices and several dingy conference rooms, all empty.

"Why does the NSA maintain this facility?"

"In the British era," he says, "the location was ideal for signal intelligence; we're only two miles from the Chinese border. But physical proximity isn't what it used to be, so now it's mainly for recruiting and housing the local talent."

"A den of spies?"

He touches the side of his nose, and his eyes shine mischievously.

They pass a brightly lit room filled with machinery and ductwork.

"Generators, climate control, and water purification," he says. "We could survive an apocalypse and still have AC."

They descend a flight of stairs, walk through a wide metal door, and step into the muggy Hong Kong morning. Mosquitoes alight on her arms, biting painfully. Amit hands her a can of insect repellent.

"Use this or get eaten."

She applies the smelly liquid while nearly jogging to keep up with his long strides. From the outside, the building resembles a warehouse or factory, with corrugated metal walls and high, darkened windows. Several similar buildings are located a dozen meters away.

"The building we just left is called Rijndael," Amit says. "The others in this area are Serpent, Twofish, and MARS."

"Encryption algorithms," she notes.

"We are the NSA, after all."

"Just how big is this facility?"

"Over two square kilometers, with more than a dozen buildings scattered around the property. Part of it is a legitimate warehouse and logistics operation, which acts as our cover."

"Aren't you worried about trespassers?"

"The grounds are wired with the latest infrared and motion sensing tech. If anybody ventures where they shouldn't, we'll know immediately."

So she couldn't have left yesterday, even if she'd wanted to. Not without their permission.

They re-enter the building, and frigid air conditioning embraces her, welcome after a brief sojourn in the jungle heat. They continue along a carpeted hallway and then enter a well-lit office where young men sit at haphazardly arranged desks.

"Guys," Amit says, "this is Emily. Emily, this is Ho Kin, Lincoln, Mark, and Pak Chun."

The men mumble awkward and unenthusiastic words of welcome. Amit's face reddens.

"Have we been cooped up for so long that we've forgotten how to be civil?"

Ho Kin gets to his feet and extends a hand.

"It's really great to meet you," he says, this time with feeling.

She greets Ho and the others until Amit seems satisfied then they all take their seats. Her desk is the clean one next to Amit's.

"Now that Emily's here," he says, "We should discuss the mission."

"The same mission we discuss every day," the man named Lincoln says with feigned enthusiasm. "To find Zahra!"

His invocation reminds Emily that she hasn't told the whole truth, hasn't mentioned that Zahra is dead and moldering up on Victoria Peak, or that most of her comrades are dead also. Is there a way to reveal that without telling them *how* she knows Zahra's fate?

"And, uh, Mac too now, I suppose?" she says nervously. "You're trying to round him up as well?"

"We detect bot activity," Pak Chun says, as though she

hadn't spoken, "by detecting the moments when encrypted messages move between apparently unrelated systems. We might, for example, see a military computer talking to a fast food cash register or a shipbuilder's CAD systems talking to a sewage treatment plant."

"It's a different profile than we used to see," Lincoln chimes in. "Banks and insurance companies used to be Zahra's favorite targets, but now she attacks governmental systems and defense as well."

"We believe," Amit continues, "that this new profile reflects changing management. Mac has leverage over her. He's bending her to his will."

"So to find Mac is to find Zahra?" she says hopefully.

"And vice versa," he agrees.

"And APRIL will lead us to him."

Amit nods again, but the others stare a little blankly, like they're curious or maybe befuddled. Ho speaks up.

"I've heard the director call the botnet 'APRIL,'" he says, "but nobody knows why it has that name. I mean, we have some guesses, most of them obscene, but nobody knows for sure."

"It's an acronym," she says, "for 'Automatic Programming, Rule-based, Intelligent Learning.' We coined it to capture how this botnet differs from all others. APRIL bots aren't pre-written components that hide in the victim's filesystem or whatever. There's no common scrap of 'DNA' you'll find in every infected host. APRIL is self-programming, polymorphic and multipartite. An invading bot analyzes its computing environment, discerns context, and merges with the host. It's more like cancer than a foreign object lodged into the body.

"Computers programming computers," Lincoln says, slightly awestruck.

"Once a system gets absorbed into APRIL," she continues, "it's assigned a unique role in the larger virtual machine. Tens of millions of computers worldwide give The Collective enough computing power to make the process go even faster. APRIL can deeply analyze, then rewrite the victim's system in a matter of hours so that it serves both its intended purpose and The Collective's. And that's true whether the target is an accounting firm or a hospital x-ray department."

"What about check-sums?" Lincoln asks. "What about file security? How does it evade all the classic defense measures?"

"It's kind of a virtuous or vicious cycle, depending on your point of view," she says. "By now, APRIL has modified most computing infrastructure and packaged software. Google, Apple, and Microsoft, as well as the open-source communities and universities, are all totally infected. Whether you're talking about operating systems, databases, or security software, APRIL, and therefore The Collective, has modified it and built back doors into it."

Pak Chun shakes his head vehemently.

"The worldwide community of engineers is constantly searching for zero-day vulnerabilities," he says. "Big players have stringent security and code reviews. Our own agency, the NSA, assists companies in finding and removing these risks."

"Except when we exploit them ourselves," Lincoln points out with a chuckle. "Then we leave the back doors alone."

"Back doors *do* get found," Emily agrees. "But APRIL is creating them even faster. And its skill at hiding vulnerabilities is only improving. Zahra's collective has access to more zero-day exploits than any other hacker crew on Earth, which lets them move through the internet virtually undetected. They've become the zero-day ghosts."

"Does NSA senior management know about this?" Amit asks, wide-eyed.

"The NSA gave me three jobs," she says, counting with her fingers.

"One, secure the agency. Two, find Zahra. And three, get control of the botnet. So, yeah, they know."

"Get control?" Pak Chun asks. "Don't you mean to destroy or neutralize?"

"Why would a spy agency want to dismantle the world's greatest surveillance tool?" Amit asks. "We want to co-opt it, not destroy it."

Pak Chun shakes his head.

"I can't believe the world's computing systems are riddled with usable exploits and bots."

Emily shrugs.

"The collective is paranoid and conservative," she says. "Their goal is to avoid observation. They'll walk away from a scam or theft if they can't figure out how to do it safely. They want to live to fight another day."

A pang of guilt stabs her mind. She's speaking about The Collective as if they still exist when in fact, they're mostly dead or running for their lives. Whether Amit knows it or not, his search is for an entirely new enemy.

"That's part of their ethos, isn't it?" Amit asks. "They see themselves as Robin Hood characters?"

"Several give lip service to that notion," she admits. "And they occasionally donate large sums of money to groups they consider worthy. But I would argue their cautiousness is 100% self-interest. They care for their cash cow so they can keep milking it. And that caution is built into every aspect of APRIL. Her primary design goal is to avoid detection at all costs."

"You talk about APRIL like it's a person," Ho says thoughtfully, "almost like The Collective doesn't matter."

"The goal was complete autonomy," she says. "Because the less oversight it requires, the more money it prints for its human masters. But humans set the missions and occasionally step in when the AI encounters problems it can't solve."

Amit brightens. "Could we construct a particularly

unusual, even bizarre, target? Something the AI has never seen? We could trip it up and force its human masters to get involved. That might lead to mistakes we could exploit."

"That's where I started," Emily admits, "but it made them suspicious. Remember the whole caution thing."

"So what do we do?" Ho asks.

"Ben Katz and I had luck modeling an attack on the design of APRIL itself. We wanted to infect and co-opt it in the same way it infects and co-opts other systems."

"So you gave the virus a virus?"

"And it sort of worked. I could see parts of APRIL's internal communications. I might have gathered useful data if I'd understood enough about its newest protocols. Instead, I wound up triggering its defenses and outing my physical location."

"Is that when the self-driving car attacked your house?" Lincoln asks.

Guilt hits like a gut punch. She sees the car, her shattered house, and Audrey's crumpled body. And the memory triggers a second one: Mac, puffy and disheveled, admitting his true nature back in Kowloon Park. She trembles with rage. He'd been play-acting that day, mocking her. But she'll make him regret it.

"We'll be more careful this time around," she says with growing conviction. *We'll find Mac and make him pay.*

# WHAT ABOUT SEYMOUR?

LINCOLN STARES, wide-eyed, over his empty soda bottles and chip bags.

"You're saying our hack can't introduce more than a forty-millisecond timing variation?" he asks.

"Our new virus will attack thousands of bots," Emily replies. "So we have to avoid leaving a trail that APRIL might notice.

"You act like the botnet has artificial intelligence," Pak says with evident skepticism.

She sighs. Haven't they been over this already?

"APRIL's mind is spread across at least sixty million infected computers. That gives it basically unlimited processing power."

"But all those computers have to communicate," Mark says, "so it must be really slow."

"It's like a freight train," she says. "It takes time to build up a head of steam, and then it becomes pretty overwhelming."

"How do we avoid its attention?" Ho asks.

"We avoid leaving breadcrumbs:" she says. "No timing variations, message corruption, or other artifacts that might give us away. It'll be tough, and I failed once already. That's why the job will probably take months, not weeks."

"Amit's not gonna like that timeline," Ho says worriedly.

The others nod, their expressions a mixture of fear and uncertainty.

"We have two missions:" she says with forced confidence. "One is to score a big win against The Collective, and the other is to get you guys trained. If we want to achieve mission #1 quickly, then we'll probably need to skimp on mission #2, at least for now.

The four men seem momentarily confused, then slowly, comprehension dawns.

"You plan to do all the hard work yourself?" Ho says, eyes wide.

She shrugs.

"You guys will still test, configure, monitor… lots of stuff. And in a month or two, after Amit's off our backs, I'll dedicate more time to teaching you all the tricks."

They exchange guilty glances. It's clear that they like and also fear this idea.

"I'll give you status updates weekly," she adds, "and show you a little code every day. You'll still be learning, just not quite as fast."

She pauses, holding her breath. This project could take years if they force her to drag their full, dead weight along for the ride.

Lincoln nods. Ho offers a weak smile.

"We can live with that."

———

THE BRILLIANCE of the "ditch the slowpokes" plan quickly loses its luster. Her workdays morph into a blur of hacking and debugging and stretch late into every evening. After a week, the lines of code start to swim before her bleary vision, and her head feels like a balloon filled to bursting. She glances around the shared office, sighing at her coworkers' empty desks. Amit let the guys have a night's R&R in the city. But she can't go because she's Hong Kong's public enemy number one. Still, she ought to take some kind of break.

She reaches into her drawer for the ubiquitous bug spray, heads down the hall, and steps into the muggy tropical evening. The air is thick with the scent of vegetation and the call of tropical birds. A cloud of hungry mosquitoes swarms, but the repellent keeps them at bay. She strolls the damp path, noting its resemblance to the forest trails of Lamma Island. Was Kaylin on Lamma the day she visited? Is that why her cousin's ubiquitous navy cardigan was on that chair? If so, did the terrible Englishman take her? Did he take Seymour?

Emily picks her way over rain-fed puddles and through the dense vegetation, trying, but failing, to push Seymour from her mind. Did he come to Hong Kong out of some sort of misguided love? Given their history, is he such a glutton for punishment? And will he still love her after learning that she's returned to the NSA? Wouldn't that make her a two-time sellout? She shakes her head amid the buzzing insects. Seymour doesn't need her help and probably doesn't want it.

She follows a path she hasn't noticed before. It leads to a forest clearing with four more unassuming corrugated buildings. They're squat and quiet except for a few faint lights in their frosted windows. But though their exteriors are rusted, each building's entrance seems well-maintained and boasts a keycard reader. On a whim, she approaches the closest reader and swipes her access card against it. The device beeps, and a red light winks angrily. The door stays locked.

She continues along the narrow path, following it through the forest undergrowth. How far does it go? Could it be the trail out of Chip's little reservation? A door bangs somewhere nearby, and she turns around in fright. Amit stands outside the nearest building, stone-faced and cold-eyed, his arms folded. She struggles to think of an excuse for this unauthorized sojourn.

"Is this where we keep the swimming pool?" she asks.

"It's for managers only," he answers, unsmiling.

He's angry. Placation is in order.

"We're, uh, making solid progress on the virus," she ventures. "I'm thinking that in two or three weeks, we'll be ready for some serious tests."

"It has to be *two* weeks," he says, jaw muscles flexing.

"Hacking is an inexact science," she cautions. "Even if our new virus works in a test environment, there's no guarantee –"

"Lincoln told me about your little arrangement," he says, cutting her off. "You've left the rest of the team in the dust while you work alone. That's not the agreement you had with Director Chip."

Amit's always been upbeat, even deferential. So why's he so irritable now?

"We have to choose," she says, matching his serious tone. "Go fast, or train the young hackers. We won't get both."

His expression softens slightly.

"Lincoln is in his mid-40s," he says, "that's hardly young."

Lincoln is a worthless slug, and the others are only slightly better. Maybe it's difficult to find intelligent people willing to work in a jungle prison camp. Or maybe Amit's a bad judge of talent.

"They're young in hacker years," she says, being as gentle as she can.

He shrugs, then motions for her to follow. They stroll in silence for several minutes.

"I'm building an organization that understands Zahra's methods and technologies," he says finally.

Zahra's name jolts her like an electric shock. She still hasn't told Amit that the former collective leader is no longer relevant. But how to do it without describing her visit to Victoria Peak—and also incriminating Seymour?

"I'm completely on board," she says calmly.

"I need a working team," he continues, "not a bunch of newbies who depend on a superstar."

"I'll teach them about the botnet. But it'll take months, not weeks."

They approach the Rijndael building, and he pulls open the door. She steps inside, but he hesitates at the threshold.

"I understand that it's tough to hack and teach, but that's what you signed up for. It's what I need from you."

She nods, even as her heart sinks. She'll likely have to cut her sleep from four hours to two.

"I understand," she says.

"And one other thing," he adds. "We want this campus to be a pleasant place to live, to feel like a spa in the jungle. But given how intensely the Chinese are searching for you right now, it just isn't safe for you to be outside the building.

Her face burns with shame. You don't go poking around an NSA facility.

"I'm sorry, Amit," she says awkwardly.

"You've been in the wild a long time," he says, his smile finally appearing. "Maybe becoming civilized again will take a little practice."

She returns to her desk, her mind reeling with shame and self-recrimination. They've offered her a path back, a way to restore her chances for a normal life. All she has to do is be the honest, reliable employee that neither her mother nor Seymour could ever manage to be. Is that so hard?

She puts her hands on the keyboard and tries to re-engage with the latest code. Yet her overtired mind drifts to the Englishman, his soldiers, and Kaylin's navy cardigan. Why did Kaylin leave that sweater behind? Did she go somewhere in a hurry? Was Seymour with her? Emily imagines Seymour as she last saw him, bandaged and feverish, trying to show his bravest face. She intended to get him medical attention. Does he still need it now?

She walks back to her dorm and jumps into the shower. As the warm water washes away the day's sweat and worries, she considers Amit. He must think that she's a dangerous and unpredictable person. How is he protecting himself from that risk? Did he tell the others to keep an eye on her? Does he monitor her movements? Is he watching her right now? Her skin crawls reflexively. She hurries through the rest of her routine, then gets into bed. But sleep doesn't come. She lies awake, staring into the blackness, wondering why she can't accept her situation. Amit's plans are reasonable, and Seymour can care for himself, so why does she keep worrying? Will she obsess about Seymour until she knows he's okay? Getting information about him would mean evading Amit's surveillance, yet another betrayal.

"I still want a normal life," she says aloud. "A nine-to-five job, a regular paycheck, maybe kids someday."

And hiding from Amit's surveillance means putting that whole future at risk. Yet Seymour's bandaged face won't leave her overtired mind. Is he healing? Does he have a way home? Will the FBI arrest him when he gets there?

"Seymour," she whispers softly.

She must contact him and make sure he's okay. But surveillance is a problem. She closes her eyes. She'll find a way; she always does, especially when it comes to that idiot Seymour.

# THE IDEA

"IT SEEMS like we're finding bugs everywhere," Ho says, with evident frustration.

She forces her sleep-deprived eyes to look at the laptop he's placed on her desk. It's filled with test errors, and, more surprisingly, the failing tests are running on some odd computers.

"Since when was it okay to test on random office systems?" she asks.

"Lincoln's hogging all the real test machines, so I improvised."

"You attacked our office email server?"

He rolls his chair so close to her that their shoulders touch.

"I'm trying to be a hacker myself," he says eagerly. "I thought this was a good way to start."

*Is he trying to impress me?* She thinks. *Does he like me or something?*

Because that's a fresh kind of trouble she doesn't need.

"If our bot has bugs," she says with as much patience as she can muster, "and you release it onto other people's computers, then you risk ruining their whole day. And I'm in enough trouble with Amit already."

"Sorry," he says contritely and shrinks back a little.

"Let me make sure you haven't broken anything," she sighs. "Meanwhile, ask Lincoln to share some actual test servers so you don't bring down the whole office."

Ho lingers a second or two, eyes not quite meeting hers.

"Mark's getting takeout from Ming Kee's," he says. "We're eating at the picnic tables near the Twofish building. Do you want to come?"

No, she doesn't want to come. Not if it will encourage Ho any further. Suddenly, Amit's asshole lecture is coming in handy.

"I've been told my face is too famous, and I have to stay inside. And, anyway, I need to check that your little trick didn't crash somebody's laptop or erase the HR database or whatever. So run along, and I'll just eat at my desk."

"Right," he says, blushing.

Ho scoots back to his own desk and begins furiously typing. Yet, once or twice, she catches him furtively, glancing in her direction. His little crush is cute, but given their close quarters, it could also blossom into trouble. Uneasily, she tries to understand what kind of mess he's made. His tests should have just run, then quit. So why are there so many error messages? And why only on specific computers? An hour's exploration finds the answer: Ho's test virus was a stunning success. It found and infected live APRIL bots hiding in the administrative computers. APRIL has already infiltrated this facility!

A flash of panic passes over her. How many other local NSA systems are pwned? What secrets have been compromised? A quick survey answers the question: Only old and vulnerable computers have been targeted thus far. She's dealing with a garden variety infestation, and APRIL's masters probably haven't yet recognized the unique importance of this facility. She rises from her desk and begins walking to Amit's office. She'll tell him what they've discovered and ask him to let her assist the IT department in building countermeasures. Of course, he'll probably view it as a distraction or, worse, assume she somehow let APRIL attack them on purpose.

As she ascends the stairs, a second thought enters her mind: If nobody realizes that APRIL has invaded this network, and if the virus she's building can control at least parts of the botnet, then she might be able to see whatever APRIL sees. She stops, hand gripping the railing, mind swirling with the possibilities. With APRIL's "eyes," she might safely map Amit's surveillance framework. She would just need to bait the botnet with a bright shiny object, like a lion tamer tossing a scrap of meat to a hungry cat. And with APRIL's knowledge, she could evade Amit's surveillance, maybe long enough to safely contact Ben or even Seymour. If she could just talk to Seymour for thirty seconds, then she could escape from the nagging guilt that she's somehow abandoned him. And she could tell him about her plan, how he needs to let her help him, and how the NSA can be an ally.

She shakes her head. It's a path fraught with risks and moral hazards. She'd be repaying Chip's trust by lying to his team, stabbing him in the back to verify what she already knows is true. After all, isn't Seymour the scrappiest, most resourceful person she's ever met? Yet those gashes in his arms and torso, the angry red skin around his wounds, his high fever and delirium—she abandoned him for so long that he despaired for his safety and took desperate action. Doesn't she owe him the courtesy of ensuring he's safe?

She returns to the crowded bullpen. The guys are back from lunch, and the hot room smells of garlic, sweat, and old cologne. Ho comes to her desk like an eager puppy, eyes twinkling with excitement.

"Did you figure it out?" he asks eagerly. "Can we attempt another full test today?"

She smiles, despite herself.

"We need half an hour or so."

He scampers back to his workstation and gives her a shy smile. At some point, she'll have to clarify the strictly professional nature of their relationship—another difficult task to add to her growing backlog.

She struggles to concentrate on her work, but the chance to safely communicate with Seymour sparkles in her mind like a flawed diamond. She'll feed APRIL fake intel and convince it this facility stores precious metals or a garage full of vintage cars. That will trigger the botnet to dig harder and produce a complete inventory of items its masters can steal, along with a list of security measures those future thieves must avoid. She'll use her virus to access that list and learn how she can blind Amit's surveillance. Then she can contact Seymour.

Ho smiles at her and blushes a little. She averts her eyes and quells a sinking feeling in her stomach. Eventually, somebody will realize the facility is hacked. At that point, her window of opportunity will be gone. So she has to act quickly and use this chance to learn what happened to Seymour. Once that's done, she won't need to keep secrets anymore. Once she's spoken to Seymour, she can be all in on this new job and ready to embark on her new life.

# MEETING BY THE FENCE

EMILY FOLLOWS THE DIRT PATH, hands tingling with anticipation. If anybody sees her, they'll assume she's sneaking out to get a little night air, something Amit asked her to avoid. But taking a walk isn't treason, not unless they see who she's headed to meet. She approaches a bend in the trail, which, she happens to know, is a blind spot caused by wide camera spacing. She pauses, listening. Crickets sing lustily, and an owl gives a diminutive "coo." But there are no human sounds: no voices, rustling foliage, or footsteps. She continues into the undergrowth, following an imaginary line perpendicular to the trail. If her security modifications worked as designed, she's walking along a dead zone in Chip's infrared sensor array.

This isn't the meeting she'd hoped for, not the reunion or reassurance she'd envisioned. But though Seymour and Kay both failed to respond, Ben replied almost immediately. And if he's willing to help, perhaps she'll find the answers she seeks.

A dozen paces more, she reaches the 5-meter-high electric fence. Its steel posts and thick mesh seem brutish amid the verdant forest. And beyond the crackling wires, a shadowy figure stands quiet and expectant.

"Thanks for coming," Emily whispers.

Xiuying smiles, her white teeth glowing in the darkness.

"Your directions were a little crazy," she says, "especially that long list of GPS coordinates."

As Emily approaches the fence, a faint tang of ozone tingles her nose. The energy in those wires must be massive.

"I could only get a few bytes through the firewall," she says. "I had to hope you would understand what I meant."

"And you think this spot is safe?"

"APRIL created a little blind patch for me."

Xiuying's eyes widen, and she takes a step back.

"You control APRIL?"

Emily shakes her head.

"I lobotomized a few local bots, that's all."

"How'd you wind up here?"

"The NSA brought me," Emily admits.

Xiuying nods thoughtfully.

"Fifteen minutes after you went into Kaylin's house, a bunch of guys in dark suits came out," she says. "They lugged some wooden crates to a boat docked below the house, then they left. We broke into the house and found it empty, so we figured they smuggled you out somehow, perhaps in one of those crates."

"The NSA leadership explained everything to me," Emily says. "It turns out that Mac betrayed us. He's behind everything, and I've been exonerated."

Xiuying glances around, obviously alarmed.

"So I'm fucked then?" she says. "I'm under arrest or something?"

"No, not like that," Emily says, holding her hands out placatingly. "I'm looking for Seymour and Kay. I need to know they're okay."

"You're saying you're back with the NSA?"

Emily nods.

"Then you must already know where Seymour and Kay are."

"What are you talking about?"

"Those dudes carried three creates out of Kay's house, Emily."

"So?"

Xiuying gives an exasperated sigh.

"You were in one crate, right?"

"Yes, but–"

"Then what was in the other two crates? Fishing gear?"

Anger and confusion roil her mind. She wants to argue that the NSA are the good guys and that they'd never detain Kaylin and Seymour without telling her. Yet the memory of the Englishman's slick, smiling face makes the words stick in her throat. Xiuying smiles sadly, then looks up, resting her eyes on something far above them. Emily follows her gaze—a coil of razor wire snakes along the top of the electric fence.

"Quite a barrier your friends built." Xiuying muses. "Is it designed to keep people out or…maybe to keep them in?"

Emily's vision swims as tears cloud her eyes. Did director Chip's dogs pick up Kay and Seymour on the same day they kidnapped her? If so, why did he lie about it? And where are they now?

"I know you've had a bad couple of weeks," Xiuying continues, "but we're not just talking about your life anymore. Others depend on what you do here. You gotta up your game, Emily, gotta start thinking for yourself."

Emily nods. If Chip is really holding Seymour and Kay, then how can she free them? And what would that mean for her path back to normal? What would life look like after she betrayed the agency for a second time?"

"If I find Seymour and Kay," she says cautiously, "will you help me turn them loose? Could you get them out of Hong Kong?"

The younger woman's expression softens.

"If you promise not to screw me over, then, yeah, I can probably help with that."

# FAKE JOB

EMILY STOPS at the plexiglass doorway to the bullpen but doesn't go inside. The guys are bent over their computers and don't seem to notice her. Ho Kin's eyes are bloodshot, and his forehead is creased with worry. How long has he been struggling with the bugs she assigned to him? Shouldn't she help him? Ho and his teammates aren't very talented. And given the hostility between China and the United States, locating them here in Hong Kong feels like an unnecessary risk. Did Director Chip really create this team to be close to Zahra? Or far from the NSA? The agency isn't legally allowed to build a system like APRIL; it's far too invasive and inhabits both foreign and domestic computers. But if this team successfully grabs control of the botnet, then the director can use it in a plausibly deniable way.

*"We're not just talking about your life anymore,"* Xiuying said. *"Others depend on what you do next."*

She turns from the bullpen and walks to a balcony overlooking the jungle. The evening sun reflects off the distant coils of razor wire atop Director Chip's fence. Why did he build that fence? To fend off the Chinese? Nothing will keep them out if they want to enter this facility. To repel trespassers? It's massive overkill for such a basic task. The more she studies it, the clearer it seems that he built it to keep people in. To contain whoever is living within this compound. So who lives here?

She returns to her room and opens her laptop. The APRIL bots she lobotomized have finished their inventory of Chip's campus and cataloged an impressive list of security cameras, email servers, and other back-end systems. One is an email server for Royal Star Logistics, the facility's legitimate and apparently profitable front organization. Ho, Lincoln, and the others work for Royal Star, which also purchases their equipment, arranges repairs, and even pays for the office catering. Given the secrecy of this base, it makes sense to hide behind a facade. But as she scans Royal Star's email correspondence, an unlikely name catches her attention: Laura Pringle, the HR representative.

"What's your biz with Royal Star?" she mutters and opens the note.

"Ms. Pringle," it reads, "we've shipped the requested furniture and equipment to your new Bangkok address, listed below. Please notify us if there are missing items or if you require anything else to establish your new Thailand residence."

Since when does Laura live in Thailand?

The note is odd enough to warrant punching another brief message through the firewall:

*"Ben,"* she writes, *"Is Laura Pringle still working for the NSA?"*

He responds almost immediately:

*"They fired her two months ago. Her location is unknown."*

Emily's hands grow cold. Two weeks ago, Laura pretended to be an NSA employee in good standing and lectured Emily about her supposed salary, benefits, and parking spot. But she's actually working for Director Chip and is hiding in Thailand?

A soft knock interrupts her growing panic.

"Emily?" Ho Kin's voice calls.

"Just a sec," she says.

She dashes to the bathroom and checks the mirror. Her complexion is flushed, and her hair is hopelessly tangled. She throws water on her face and pulls a brush through the knots. Then she opens the door just a crack. Ho, visibility recoils at her flustered appearance.

"W– we were all worried when you didn't come back this evening," he says nervously.

"I'm just totally worn out," she says, struggling to think of anything that will make him go away.

"You've been working too hard."

"How are the tests?" she asks, moving the subject away from herself.

"FUBAR," he admits.

"I'll help you with them in the morning, okay?"

She begins to close the door, but he blocks it with his shoulder.

"It sucks how they won't let you go outside," he says.

"I don't mind," she lies, alarmed by his newly aggressive behavior.

"I– I saw you walking the paths earlier this evening," he admits.

Her heart accelerates. "Did he see where she went? Did he see Xiuying?"

"Were you following me?" she asks, unable to completely hide her growing panic.

"Nothing like that!" he says quickly. "I looked out the window and saw you disappearing into the forest. And I was thinking—maybe next time I could come along with you."

Is that all he wants? A little date in the woods?

"I need to get some sleep Ho," she says, still struggling to contain her alarm. "Can we discuss this tomorrow?"

"Oh yeah, sure," he says, taking a step back. "I'll totally

leave you alone. I'll, uh, only wanted to make sure you're okay."

"Thanks for thinking of me," she says with all the forced sweetness she can muster. "Goodnight, Ho."

"Right, uh, goodnight!" he says as she shuts the door and locks the deadbolt.

She turns her back to the door and heaves a sigh. This cloak-and-dagger game can't go on. She should either escape or commit to this place. Living with a foot on both sides is exhausting. She'll finish this survey tonight. If Chip's network seems clean, then maybe Xiuying was wrong. Maybe he isn't holding Kay and Seymour at all.

———

By 4:30 AM, she's examining a system named "Guard Desk 18" and squinting to keep her burning eyes focused. She's so tired that she almost misses what's strange about this particular computer: that it belongs to two separate networks. Some idiot must have wired it up to be a secure bridge between the ordinary office network and whatever lies on the other side.

"Amateurs," she says aloud.

With a little more searching, she finds that "Guard Desk 18" monitors a massive private network of security cameras. She accesses their live feeds and finds videos of the grounds, hallways, and bullpen where they work. The tenth camera stops her dead in cold horror. She's looking at herself, sitting at this very desk. She stands. Half a second later, the woman in the video stands also.

*Bastards*, she thinks. They put a spy camera in her bedroom! Does Amit watch her undress? Is that why he was so happy to have her join his little team? She struggles to contain her rage, then remembers the stakes: If she's lucky, being the target of her coworker's peepshow will be the worst thing she'll find tonight.

The next bank of cameras monitors a different building. With bleary eyes, she flits through the feeds, looking at endless empty hallways and junk-filled rooms. But when she selects the last camera in the series, her heart stops. Onscreen, a slender woman shuffles around a rumpled bed. Her hair is tousled, and her doll-like hands clench and unclench with apparent agitation. And though the light is low and the image quality poor, there's no mistaking the petite bone structure, pointy chin, and dark-framed glasses.

*Kaylin*, Emily thinks. *What are you doing here?*

But she knows the answer. Her cousin got here the same way she did: in a crate. They're both prisoners, both being watched and both living at the whim of people whose motives aren't clear. So, is Seymour here also? Is he alive?

Her coworkers don't know she's hacked into their security system, so she still has some freedom of movement. But time is short; sooner or later, they'll find out. She must commit to a future she never wanted, one entirely outside the ordinary world she so coveted. Yet the alternative is to leave her friends to the tender mercies of Director Chip, whose goals, she now realizes, are not compatible with her own.

# RESIGNATION

EMILY APPROACHES the corrugated building and tries her keycard. The door unlocks with a click, and she slips inside. It's been four days of pretending to work for Amit, four evenings of scanning surveillance records, and four nights of studying security tech. Her escape plan is haphazard, a tower of dominoes.

She tiptoes down the corridor and glances into the breakroom. The floor is filthy, and the garbage can overflows with coffee cups and take-out containers. Director Chip's men in black must be better at pushing people around than they are at pushing a broom. Luckily they aren't too skilled at the people part either. The video recordings reveal that they visit Kaylin less than once daily and leave the building for hours at a time. They're placing too much faith in their surveillance cameras, infrared sensors, and high-voltage fence. That faith gives her an opening.

She finds Kaylin's floor and stands in front of what she believes to be the right room. The idiots secured the door with the same vulnerable keycard technology they use everywhere. Of course, it's one thing to believe you've hacked a system and another to bet your life on it. She holds her breath and presses her card onto the reader. The door gives an audible click. She breathes a sigh of relief and opens it. Kaylin backs away, apparently afraid of whoever is coming to visit her. Her left eye is bruised, and she has several recent cuts on her forehead and cheeks. Her expression cycles through fear, recognition, and, finally, defiance.

"Is it your turn to interrogate me?" she asks.

An unexpected emotion wells up in Emily's throat. She and Kaylin have had their bad times, especially over the last few years. But her cousin never deserved this kind of abuse and shouldn't be living in this nightmarish prison. Emily grabs Kaylin and pulls her close, eyes brimming with tears.

"I'm here to get you out of here," she says quietly, "and Seymour, too, if we can find him."

"H-how?" Kaylin manages.

Emily looped the video cameras, hacked the keycards, and rigged the fence to go offline. Beyond that, it's all going to be luck.

"I've blinded them," she says. "But it won't last. Where's Seymour?"

"The infirmary," Kaylin says in a trembling voice, and her intense dark eyes tell the rest: He's doing badly.

"Take me there," Emily says, trying to keep the growing panic at bay.

Kaylin leads them up a flight of stairs, past half a dozen junk-filled rooms, and toward the only door with a keycard reader. Emily places her card against it and closes her eyes. She's given herself universal access to every door she can find, but the system is quite complex. Could she have missed this one?

The light glows. Emily's stomach twists. The seconds pass.

*Please God*, she thinks, *if you ever felt like helping me, this might be the time.*

The light flashes green; the lock emits a loud click.

She throws open the door, and a wall of stench almost overpowers her. It smells like Zahra's house, except that somebody has tried to cover the smell of decomposition with powerful deodorizers. The combination is gut-wrenching. She clamps her hand over her nose and stares at Seymour, who lies huddled and motionless on a small cot. The contours of his skull and eye sockets are visible under stretched and discolored skin. An IV drips into his bare arm. The other arm is tightly wrapped in a dirty bandage, soaked through with a brown putrescent discharge. His infection kept worsening, and nobody brought a real doctor.

*I've killed him*, she thinks. *He's my latest victim.*

The withered head twitches, and the sunken eyes blink. He squints as if the feeble light is too much to withstand.

"I was wondering when you'd come," Seymour says in a raspy voice.

She runs to him, wrapping her arms gently around his torso, taking care not to touch his injuries.

"I shouldn't have left you," she says, holding back the tears.

"You always leave," he says, "and I always wait."

They find his shoes and get him to his feet. Kaylin slings his good arm around her shoulders, and Emily delicately cradles his injured arm, controlling her breath so the stench won't overpower her. He moves like a 90-year-old, his steps shuffling. It takes nearly fifteen minutes to get down the stairs and another fifteen to walk into the forest. Only then does a ray of optimism seep into her overstimulated mind.

Kaylin, apparently sensing the possibility of freedom, finds her voice.

"Seymour arrived at my cottage," she says, the suppressed words now flowing freely. "He was sick, and I got him into bed immediately. But those men showed up and drugged us. Later they interrogated us. They wanted to know where Zahra was hiding."

"Did you tell them she was dead?"

Kaylin's eyes meet hers, hard and alert.

"Is she?"

Seymour's head lolls. The forced march is too much for him, and he wilts like old lettuce. The three drop to their knees, panting in the early afternoon heat.

"I didn't have a chance to tell Kay what we found on Victoria Peak," Seymour mumbles. "And then we were prisoners, and I didn't want those fuckers to learn anything useful."

"But you already knew, didn't you?" Emily asks her cousin.

Kaylin stares at the ground, frowning and quiet.

"Why did you have all those computers in your apartment?" Emily asks, wiping the sweat from her face.

"Now, who's asking stupid questions?" Kaylin says.

"You were locked out of APRIL," Emily says with growing certainty. "You were breaking back in."

"APRIL is mine," her cousin says, and her eyes widen with a sudden fervor.

Emily struggles to her feet and pulls Seymour with her. His wobbly legs offer little support, but she and Kaylin manage to drag him another 500 meters down the path. The gray fence wires become visible in the distance. A lone figure stands just beyond, stepping nervously from foot to foot. Tears cloud Emily's vision. Freedom may yet be possible.

"Xiuying!" she calls out, "thank God you made it."

Kaylin turns toward the fence, surprise and recognition dawning on her face. With a roar, she drops Seymour and charges forward.

"Traitor!" she shouts.

Xiuying's eyes widen, and she takes a step back.

"Enabler!" Kaylin continues, now only fifteen meters from the barrier. "Murderer!"

Emily drops Seymour and follows her cousin. If Kay touches that fence, it will be game over. But the long confinement has made her cousin unsteady; she's stumbling over the rocks and twigs, which slow her pace. Emily closes the distance and tackles Kaylin with less than three meters to spare, sending her sprawling into the dirt.

"Touch those wires," Emily shouts into her writhing cousin's ear, "and you're fried!"

Kaylin manages to twist her head upward, locking eyes with Xiuying, who stands just beyond the barrier.

"You helped Zahra to kill herself," Kaylin shouts.

"That's a lie!" Xiuying replies in a trembling voice.

Kaylin attempts to break loose, but Emily wraps her arms more tightly around her struggling cousin. She won't let her commit suicide. Not when they're so close to freedom.

"We told you to stop!" Kaylin says. "We told you what would happen."

Emily looks at the obviously shaken Xiuying.

"What's she talking about?"

Xiuying sighs.

"Operationalization," she says sadly.

"Your Frankenstein," Kaylin shouts.

Xiuying steps forward, stopping when her nose is only an inch from the wires.

"I'm sorry, Kay. I really am."

Emily allows her cousin to stand but keeps her hands on her quaking shoulders.

"Ten thousand volts in those wires, Kay," she says softly.

Kaylin glances at Emily with wild eyes, glasses askew, and dirt covering her cheeks, then turns back to Xiuying.

"You helped Zahra commit the single greatest betrayal of The Collective's mission," she says.

Perhaps it's the stress of the day. Perhaps it's the heat of the jungle. But Emily is on the verge of shutting down. She exhales, shaking off the exhaustion, then checks her watch, squinting to make out the numbers. The fence will power down in less than six minutes.

"We're on a tight schedule," she says, looking at Xiuying. "Give us the short version."

"Portions of the APRIL botnet kept getting discovered and ejected by our victims," Xiuying says. "We had extended outages, especially when admin nodes got whacked. At the time, ninety-nine percent of our computing power came from bots hiding in the wild. Zahra decided that our problem was an over-reliance on hacked systems."

"That was a feature," Kaylin says, "not a bug."

"Zahra wanted the control layer to run on purpose-built computers," Xiuying continues.

"It was our first turn toward the dark side," Kaylin says. "It's when we became owners."

"We used shell companies," Xiuying continues, "to purchase computing time in big-name data centers like Digital Reality or Equinix. But Zahra still felt too exposed, so we bought old warehouses, abandoned middle schools, and condemned factories. We set up camouflaged data centers all over the world."

"Like that mansion on Victoria Peak?" Emily asks, remembering Zahra's house.

"Your boss, Mac, uncovered some of our hubs," Xiuying continues, "and sent operatives to sabotage them. He was letting Zahra know that she wasn't beyond his reach, that she had to keep playing ball with him."

"It made her crazy," Kaylin says softly. "Your pal Mac was telling her that APRIL was *his* botnet, not hers."

Given Zahra's pride and intense protectiveness, "crazy" probably doesn't begin to cover it.

"She proposed what she euphemistically called 'operationalization,'" Xiuying continues. "It means giving APRIL the power to manipulate physical devices. Like controlling somebody's autonomous lawnmower or a robot vacuum."

"Or self-driving car," Emily says, "or drone."

Xiuying nods sadly. "APRIL could field drones like a

swarm of flying monkeys, attacking anybody who messed with our sites."

Emily closes her eyes, remembering the drones on Victoria Peak.

"The comrades hated the idea," Kaylin says. "For a while, they threatened to dissolve The Collective."

"I was new," Xiuying says, "and didn't understand the politics. I just knew Zahra wanted it done, and I proved my value by giving it to her."

"The Collective could suddenly do more than just steal data or money," Kaylin says, "we could hurt our enemies in the real world."

Emily recalls the locks and bars on Kaylin's little apartment in Choi Hung Estate.

"Zahra was supremely confident we could keep it under control," Kaylin continues. "And The Collective, of course, would only use it for good."

"But when your friend Mac got control of APRIL," Xiuying adds, "we all became its victims."

"Is that what we believe?" Seymour calls out weakly, heaving himself slowly upright.

They all turn and face him in surprise.

"Do we think some incompetent NSA bureaucrat got control of the botnet?" he continues. "Because even though Zahra was long dead, your brilliant NSA goons were still trying to find her. Why would they search for her if they controlled APRIL? Wouldn't they already know what happened?"

"It's just Mac that controls APRIL," Emily says. "He's rogue."

"I heard the guards talking about how they drove some fat white guy out to the forest," Kaylin says, "and how the Englishman shot him in the head. I'm pretty sure that was Mac."

Emily gasps, despite herself. Mac was an asshole, but did

he deserve an execution?

"You guys have been training APRIL for years, haven't you? " Seymour asks. "Didn't you want it to become fully autonomous?"

"Sure," Kaylin says, "but that doesn't mean–"

A chirp from Emily's phone interrupts the conversation. She checks the screen. Her fence timer has reached zero. She turns to Xiuying.

"Did you bring the tools?"

The younger woman rummages through a large duffel and produces a pair of industrial bolt cutters.

"Will these work?"

"Ought to," Emily says, "but let me check something first."

She approaches the wires and listens, head cocked. They're still vibrating minutely with a telltale 50-hertz hum of high-voltage power. The air also smells faintly of ozone.

"Crap," she says softly.

"Still hot?" Xiuying asks, taking a step toward the fence. She raises the business end of the cutters toward one of the wires.

"What are you doing?" Emily says, alarmed.

"These things have insulated handles. They'll protect me."

Emily shakes her head vigorously.

"You'd create an arc like an electric bomb," she says. "If you don't get burned to death or electrocuted, the sound will rupture your eardrums. And you have to cut eight of those wires to make a usable opening."

"What do you suggest?" Xiuying asks.

"Stay here and listen," Emily says firmly. "Wait until the wires are quiet. Then cut them."

"What will you be doing?" Seymour asks, a note of fear creeping into his voice.

Emily kneels beside him.

"I should never have brought you into this mess," she

says softly.

He reaches his unhurt, trembling arm out to her.

"Whatever you're planning," he says, "don't do it."

"You'd do the same in my position," she says and kisses his grizzled cheek.

She stands and faces the rest of the group.

"Once the fence goes offline," she says, "Chip's guards will be all over the woods. They'll gun you down rather than let you escape, so run to Xiuying's car and get the hell out of here."

"What about you?" Xiuying says.

"I'll catch up. If I can beat you to the car, we'll leave together. Otherwise, I'll find my own way."

"I'm not–" Xiuying says firmly, but Emily interrupts.

"Is Ben waiting in the car?"

She nods, a look of concern creeping into her eyes.

Emily approaches the fence and continues in a low voice that only Xiuying can hear.

"What you built into APRIL, your operationalization thing… that's a lot of bad karma. A lot to atone for."

"Don't make me leave you here," Xiuying says.

"I understand why you've been helping me so much," Emily continues. "But this time, you have a more complicated karmic dilemma. If you wait around for me, you'll sacrifice everybody, including Ben, who has arguably sinned the least in this whole screwed-up mess."

"We don't need to choose between–" Xiuying begins, but Emily cuts her off.

"I made my bed with the NSA," she says. "That's my bad karma to account for. Let me go and pay that debt."

She stares into Xiuying's deep, wide eyes and sees that the younger woman has no argument left to make. They both know this is the only path forward. Emily turns toward Seymour, gives a little wink, then dashes off toward the Rijndael building.

# SURVEILLANCE ISSUES

EMILY RE-ENTERS Rijndael and glances at her watch. The surveillance feeds have been looped for nearly forty-five minutes. If anybody notices, her options will be drastically limited. She hurries toward her dorm room, breaking into a run as she turns the last corner, then slams into Ho Kin, who is standing by her door

"Where've you been?" he asks, a troubled expression on his face.

"I took a long lunch."

He glances up and down the hallway, then leans in close.

"We need to talk," he whispers.

Does he know what she's up to? Is he here to confront her?

She motions him inside her dorm and slams the door. He stands wide-eyed, apparently surprised by the swiftness of her invitation.

"I found an APRIL bot in one of our systems," he says, voice trembling slightly.

Her heart skips a beat. Does he know she's behind it?

"One of our fake test bots?" she asks, alarmed.

He shakes his head.

"Amit asked me to troubleshoot a security computer that

kept disconnecting from the network," he says. "I couldn't find hardware or software issues, so, on a whim, I scanned for bots. That's when I found the APRIL instance."

"Show me," she says, motioning toward her laptop.

Ho sits down and quickly connects to Sec-ops-A, a computer she's become quite familiar with over the past few days.

"The bot is inhabiting the network stack," he says, pointing to the scan results. "And there were some daemons and other shit, which I disabled."

Her heart sinks. This is why the electric fence didn't shut down. Ho removed her sabotage.

"I showed everything to Lincoln," he continues, "and he went straight to Amit."

"I appreciate the heads up," she says, getting to her feet.

Ho loiters by the door, his expression a mixture of concern and eagerness.

"What are you gonna do?"

*Get rid of you, for starters*, she thinks.

"Talk to Amit," she says, opening the door. "The worst he can do is fire me."

If only that were the worst.

"We all share the blame," he says," they shouldn't single you out."

"Don't tell anybody we had this talk, alright?"

She gives him a gentle nudge toward the hallway.

"Let me straighten things out first," she adds.

"If you need me to back you up," he says eagerly, "I'll be there!"

"Totally," she says, closing the door in his wide-eyed face.

She rushes to her laptop and deactivates the fence. With any luck, Xiuying will immediately cut the wires, and the group will begin their two-kilometer trek to Ben's car. And if she leaves quickly enough, maybe she can even catch them.

She grabs her backpack and heads to the door. A loud

knock makes her jump.

"Emily?" Amit's voice calls from the other side.

She freezes, her arms and legs trembling with adrenaline and uncertainty. She could burst past him and dash for the exits. But he would probably give chase. That might lead him directly to her friends. Instead, she sighs, pulls a few disheveled strands of hair out of her eyes, and opens the door. Amit's fleshy body looms in the entrance, dark eyes surveying her angrily.

"Do you have a minute?" he says in a tone that indicates that she *will* be making a minute for him.

He leads her to a third-floor office she's never visited. They enter, and Director Chip rises from a modest desk. His thin smile doesn't reach his cold watery eyes.

"Ah, Emily!" Chip says mildly, "I've been hoping for a chance to chat."

Her heart is galloping, telling her to flee. But she can't show fear.

"I didn't know you were back in Hong Kong," she says.

"Yes, and it's lucky that I am because Amit just brought me disturbing news: Apparently, Zahra's botnet is attacking our facility."

"Ho told me," she says with as much false bravado as she can muster, "and I'm already on the case."

"Why weren't we monitoring for this type of attack?"

"An oversight," she says contritely. "I take full responsibility."

"Emily has been pushing the team hard lately," Amit adds. "Her schedule hasn't left much time for defense."

"What do we believe Zahra has learned about us?" Chip asks, faded eyes glistening. "Does she know we're building an attack against her?"

"She never invaded any of the development systems or source repositories," Emily says, regretting the words as soon as they're out of her mouth.

"I thought you said we *haven't* been scanning for signs of Zahra?" Amit says, rounding on her. "So how do we know our development systems are safe?"

"We, uh, have anti-bot scanners on them," she says lamely. "Just not building security."

"You didn't think about the risk to the wider installation?" Chip asks, incredulous.

"I was over-focused on the mission."

The furrows in Director Chip's tall brow deepen. He seems ready to give a pointed and critical response. Then his cell phone rings.

"What is it?" he barks into the phone.

He listens. His eyes narrow.

"I see," he says. "I'm on my way."

He moves to the door.

"There's a matter that requires my immediate attention," he says abruptly, "and Amit's also. Ms. Hernandez, would you please return to your room? We will continue this discussion as soon as possible."

The two men walk out, leaving her alone.

There's little doubt about the nature of Chip's emergency. At a minimum, they've discovered the missing prisoners and maybe even the fence breach. She has only a slim chance of escaping now, and it grows slimmer by the second. She bolts from Chip's office and dashes toward the exit. She'll be lucky to get as far as the forest before anybody notices. Hopefully, the cameras are still offline.

She reaches the door, glancing through the glass before stepping outside. She takes a dozen steps through the grassy lawn when a voice calls from behind.

"I do wonder," it says, in lazy cockney, "what might possess you to 'ead for the exit at this inopportune moment?"

She turns. The Englishman is strolling toward her, his smile broad and his gold tooth glinting in the sunlight.

# UNLEASH APRIL

EMILY FREEZES in horror as Pryce approaches, hands in his pockets, a wicked smile stretched across his smooth, shaven face. His movements are leisurely, as if he's come for a little pleasant gossip. There's no outrunning him, no way to reach her friends without compromising them.

"We've got a lit'le security issue just now," he says. "Did the director mention it?"

She steps back, weighing her options. The cameras are hopefully still looped, the sensors are down, and her friends have a head start. Can she slow him down further?

"You work for Director Chip?" she asks softly.

The Englishman's smile widens. Crow's feet appear in the suntanned skin around his eyes.

"Chippy and me are the best of friends. In fact, I'm on a little errand for 'im. Would you care to help wif it?"

He holds out a hand as if he's asking her to dance. All the while, he's still moving closer, his glittering eyes locked on hers.

Would he drag her out of the office building? Is he ready to abandon all pretense of civility?

She jumps back through the door and slams it in his face. On the far side of the glass, the Englishman stops, eyes boring into hers, smile frozen so hard it nearly cracks his leathery skin. His hands come out of his pockets. He reaches for the door handle. Then his expression changes. He winks at her.

"We'll meet again, I expect," he says, then turns and walks toward the forest.

She watches him go, suppressing a shudder. She should never, ever meet this man again. Not as long as she lives.

She gives a last glance toward the Englishman, then dashes to her room. Once inside, she activates the digital lock to secure the entrance. She pauses, staring at the thin laminate door. It's such an inadequate barrier. She grabs the shelving unit and pulls it in front of the threshold. Then she grabs her chair, her nightstand, and even her bedframe and adds them to the pile. The barricade is totally inadequate, but it's all she has right now.

She opens her computer and uses the building security application to scramble the keycard access, disabling every door in the complex, then cuts the power to the security cameras and sensors. These measures, combined with her earlier hacks, should keep them blind and slow for a few minutes. Can she obstruct them further?

She closes her eyes and racks her brain. Why is she so useless? What can she do to help her friends for once? A single sob escapes her mouth. Did her mother feel this helpless the night the FBI arrived to arrest her? Did Audrey foresee the damage that arrest would create, not only for herself but also for Emily? Did she search in vain for an escape? Just like her mother, Emily is out of tricks. And, just like her mother, it's the people she loves who will pay the price. If only she could understand why this happened. Who pulls the strings? If Chip is behind it all, what was the point of pretending to "rehire" her at this facility? If Kaylin is the mastermind, why was she hiding like a scared rabbit? If Ben, Xiuying, or even Seymour is calling the shots, why would they let her create so much mayhem? Why take the risk?

Unbidden, Seymour's words echo in her mind:

*"You guys have been training APRIL for years... Didn't you want it to become fully autonomous?"*

Seymour gave APRIL the power of human language. Xiuying gave it influence over the physical world. And Zahra gave it one overriding goal: to stay hidden. She pictures Zahra's corpse rotting in that basement. Did the great woman realize that her own greed and lust for power had made her into APRIL's greatest threat? Did she understand how APRIL would react to that stimulus?

"APRIL is her own master," Emily says aloud.

But what good is that knowledge?

Her phone buzzes. It's Amit.

"Are you still in the building?" he asks, his voice tinged with nervous energy.

"In my room, just like Chip ordered."

"Please return to the director's office. We have, uh, a few more items to cover."

"I'm on the toilet," she says and hangs up.

There might still be a solution—one available now that her personal situation is hopeless. Though APRIL is intelligent and probably liberated, it is by no means omniscient. Its blundering attempts to track and kill her, impressive as they are, demonstrate only a rudimentary understanding of the physical world. Could such primitive intelligence be misled or cajoled? Dangerous and unpredictable as it is, could somebody with nothing to lose leverage APRIL's ruthless logic?

She glances at her watch. Depending on how fast her friends are moving, they might still be ten or twenty minutes from the waiting car, longer if Seymour's strength is flagging. She can buy them more time.

She puts her hands on the keyboard. She'll create a new threat for APRIL, one urgent enough to prompt drastic action. If she's lucky, the botnet's response will distract Chip's army and allow her friends to escape.

She quickly edits an internal bot-to-bot message, outlining a description of the threat she has in mind: an impending plan by Director Chip to paralyze the APRIL botnet. That ought to get the AI's attention.

There's a knock on her door.

"Emily?" Amit calls. "Are you in there?"

She glances at her barricade: chairs, a bookcase, and assorted furnishings. Once they get serious, it will take less than a minute to push through. She redoubles her typing.

"It's really important that we speak," he continues. "Could you open the door?"

The doorknob rattles. Maybe he's trying his keycard. That's not going to work.

There's no time to experiment. She gets one shot. She encodes location information along with people's names: Leonard Chip, Amit Pradhan, and Lincoln Graham. She adds a description of the counter-attack she's been building. She's betting that APRIL's improving language models will understand the implications of this information and see the threat as credible. Then she locates one of her hacked test bots and reconfigures it as a Trojan horse. The bot will push misinformation through APRIL's barrier wall and into the botnet's distributed brain.

The plan is fraught with peril: Perhaps the threat she's encoded is too extreme, in which case APRIL will sense subterfuge. Or perhaps the botnet will respond too slowly to help her friends in time. Or maybe it will respond in a very targeted or ineffective way that gives them no help or even hurts them. But if she does nothing, there is a real chance that the Englishman or his accomplices will catch her friends before they get away.

The knocking resumes with greater insistence.

"Emily?" Amit calls again. "I'm afraid you really must open that door."

She queues the bot, types the start command, and pauses,

her finger hovering over the enter key. Is she willing to take responsibility for the mess APRIL might create? Is this more of the same old recklessness that got her here in the first place? Does she have any better options?

The door behind her bursts open with a crash of broken hinges and toppled furniture. The Englishman pushes debris out of the way as Amit stands nervously behind him.

"Easy, Pryce," Amit says. "We're just fetching her. We don't want her injured."

The Englishman smiles at the younger man, gold tooth glowing under the harsh LED lights.

"Let me 'andle it, Amie," he says, shoving the bookshelf aside and stepping into the room.

Emily gives a final glance at her creation and, mind reeling with fear and uncertainty, jams her finger into the enter key, injecting her pile of fabricated threats straight into the botnet's multifaceted heart.

# RECKONING

AMIT PLACES EMILY'S open laptop on the desk. He, Chip, and Pryce huddle around it.

"She ran some sort of command?" Chip asks.

"A botnet test," Amit says, "launched outside the virtual environment."

"English, please," Pryce says.

Amit eyes the taller man with obvious discomfort.

"She connected one of her modded bots to the real APRIL," he says warily. "I think she's using it to send coded messages."

"We've been chasing phantoms," Chip says, rising to his feet, "while all this time, the mastermind was among us."

"Who did you send that message to?" Pryce asks, cold green eyes boring into hers.

With a sort of numbness, she realizes that these men hold nothing over her. Not if her friends have escaped.

She meets Director Chip's eyes and points toward the row of buildings just outside his window.

"What was the point of creating this facility?" she says. "To earn yourself some pocket money?"

"It's not your turn to ask the questions," Chip says quietly.

"Give 'er to me," Pryce snarls. "I'll get the whole truth."

She keeps her eyes fixed on the director.

"Wasn't your day job exciting enough?" she asks, her voice trembling. "Did you feel in a rut there in Fort Meade?"

"I'm the most successful director in the agency's history," Chip says, color rising in his pale cheeks. "My teams gathered more useful intel and thwarted more cyber attacks than any other department."

"Because you lie and cheat."

"Fighting cybercrime is unimaginably expensive," he says with a shrug. "The talent is always demanding higher pay, and technology costs only rise. This year we need ten thousand servers, and next year, a quantum computer. It's an arms race, Emily. It takes money to keep up."

"So you fight cybercrime with cybercrime?"

"We recover funds from criminal syndicates and totalitarian governments. We confiscate only ill-gotten gain."

"So you're like The Collective then?" she asks, hot anger boiling in her gut. "You're another Robin Hood?"

Chip pulls up a chair, sitting so near that their knees touch —his breath reeks of coffee and tooth decay.

"I don't frankly care about Zahra's silly 'collective,'" he says, forming air quotes around the word. "What I need is your exclusive commitment. I want you to work for me and me alone."

"Wait, what?" Amit says, eyes wide with surprise.

Chip gives the younger man a withering glance.

"Emily has more talent in her pinky finger than you have in your entire team. We need her help if we can get it."

He returns his gaze to her.

"You've realized correctly," he continues, "that you're too toxic to actually rejoin the NSA. But you can still help the good guys and make even more money in the process. Finish the job here. Bring APRIL fully under our control. Use it to strike fresh blows against the enemies of our nation.

We'll do more good than anything you've accomplished thus far."

His eyes glow with a zeal bordering on religious fervor. The sort of fervor she's spent a lifetime learning to distrust.

"What about Seymour?" she asks. "And Kaylin?"

He folds his arms.

"Prove your commitment, and we'll talk about their future. You can start by telling me who you sent that message to. Was it Zahra?"

The weeks-long charade of pretending that Zahra has any relevance is more than she can bear.

"Zahra's dead."

"Impossible!" Amit says, his previous irritation flaring into full-blown anger.

"You're playin' with us," Pryce adds.

Chip's watery eyes narrow as he weighs her claim.

"If that's true," he says after a moment's pause, "then *you* are the fulcrum of The Collective. I suspected as much, but Mac confused me on that point. The poor idiot was too frightened and lovesick to perceive the situation clearly."

The director is speaking about Mac in the past tense. So is he dead? The little smile at the corner of Chip's mouth seems to confirm it. She struggles to keep her face neutral, to push down the tears that threaten to flow. Mac played a foolish double game. He tried to work within Chip's corrupt framework even as he allowed himself to have feelings for her. There was no way to win in that situation, any more than she could win in this one. But the director's reference to The Collective means that he still doesn't perceive the whole truth. Should she continue to hide it from him? Does it matter now?

"The Collective's gone too," she says. "All dead, except for Kaylin."

Chip's right eye twitches. Does he see the tsunami coming to swamp his house of lies?

"This is a big bloody waste o' time," Pryce bellows, stepping around Chip and grabbing her arm.

"Tell me about that message you sent," the Englishman says firmly, "or I'll beat it out of ya."

"Not here," Chip says, his tone suddenly annoyed. "Take her somewhere that won't make a mess."

Pryce glances at the director with undisguised malice, then draws Emily to her feet, dragging her toward the door. Chip gives her a final, doleful look.

"It doesn't have to be this way," he says sadly. "Give the word, and I'll put you on a different path. You can do important work in this safe environment, among people you will learn to trust and respect. It will be like the NSA, only less fettered and more lucrative. You will have finally found a safe place here with us."

If these past few weeks have taught her anything, it's that there never was a 'safe place.' Not working for the corrupt Mac and not working in this white-collar zoo. Chaos is her lot, whether she wants it or not.

"No, thank you, Director Chip."

Chip gives a slight, sad nod, and Pryce drags her from the room.

Halfway down the hallway, the reality of what's about to happen sinks in. She struggles and twists, but Pryce only gives her a vicious yank, nearly dislocating her arm. She howls in pain.

The door to the bullpen swings open, and Ho Kin emerges, apparently alarmed by her outburst. He stops, wide-eyed, taking in the scene.

"Wh – what are you doing?" he stammers.

"Fuck off, lit'l man," Pryce says, giving Emily another shove down the corridor.

The sight of Ho fills her with regret. She hadn't fully considered what an indiscriminate force of nature APRIL could be. When she sent the fake intel to the botnet, she was thinking only of her friends. She was willing to create any distraction that might help them escape. But seeing Ho reminds her of the potential for collateral damage.

"Get out of here!" she says to him. "Go outside. Go anywhere!"

Pryce pulls her face up to his.

"What are you sayin'?" he growls. "What 'appens to this lil man if he don't leave?"

His overpowering liquor and peppermint breath bring bile to her throat. She resists the urge to vomit, fearing the violence that might provoke.

"What the hell are you doing to her?" Ho Kin says, taking a step forward.

In a single smooth move, Pryce clamps her wrists in his left hand and uses his right to withdraw a cannon-sized semi-automatic pistol from his jacket. He levels it at Ho Kin's trembling head.

"I'm not sure who you are or what your business is 'ere friend," the Englishman says, "but I'm detaining Ms. Hernandez at the express request of the director. If you 'ave a problem with that, take it up with 'im."

Ho Kin stands frozen, his hands clenched.

"I'm going with this man Ho," she says softly. "Please don't resist."

"But –" he begins. She speaks over him.

"Just run! Outside, down the path, as far away as possible."

The Englishman's knuckles whiten on the gun handle.

"Listen to the lit'le lady Ho," he says. "Go 'bout your business."

Ho Kin takes a slow step backward, retreating through the office door, worried eyes locked on hers. Pryce kicks the door shut, slamming it into the other man's face. Then he gives her another vicious shove, sending her sprawling to the floor.

"What are you playin' at, girl?" he growls.

What *is* she playing at? Should she stick her neck out for one of the director's lackeys? Has Ho Kin been in on the secret all along? Or is he more like Jeremy Greaves, an unlucky opportunist guilty of nothing but greed and stunningly bad luck?

"I was trying to save a friend's life," she says.

Pryce overtakes her, grabbing her arm so tightly that her bones ache and the skin tears under his fingers.

"You should focus on your own life," he hisses between gritted teeth.

He roughly herds her into a corner office and then retreats into the hallway, slamming the door behind him and leaving her alone. She tries the knob, finds it secure, then grabs a chair and hurls it at the window. The chair bounces off the laminated glass with a loud thud. She raises it again, preparing for another try, when Pryce renters, holding a roll of gaffer's tape. He takes in the scene and flashes his gold-toothed grin.

"You ain't goin' nowhere," he says.

Before she can step away, he snatches her around the waist and throws her onto the desk. She writhes, kicks, and tries to bite him, but he easily winds a strip of the tape around her wrist and then wraps it around the leg of the desk. He repeats the operation with her other wrist and her ankles until she's as immobile as a turkey on a carving board.

Chuckling, Pryce hops on top of her, fluid as a cat, and stares down with bright, expectant eyes.

"First question," he says. "Why did you tell your lit'le friend to leave back there? What danger are you predicting that 'e should avoid?"

"The $CO_2$ levels in this building are dangerously high," she says through gritted teeth. "Ho needs fresh air."

Pryce flashes his gold-toothed grin and then slaps her with an open hand, twisting her neck and slamming her right cheek into the desktop. She lies there for several seconds, seeing stars before she realizes that he's speaking again.

"Next question," he's saying, bringing his stubbled face close to hers, "Who are you trying to reach through that botnet o' yours?"

He's coming to the essential point, the one they've consistently misunderstood: Who? Who was behind these events? Who must they control to contain this chaos?

"Nobody," she says truthfully. "No living person."

Faster than lightning, his hand is across her right cheek, turning her head 180 degrees to the left. Her spine and neck muscles cry out in pain, and consciousness itself drifts away, blessedly relieving her of the horror.

Yet the relief is fleeting. She's coming awake again. Pryce is grabbing her shirt, yanking it open so the buttons pop off and rain across the floor.

"Such sweet smooth skin," he mutters, eyes wide and glistening. He reaches into his coat, unsheathes a long knife, then lovingly examines the blade as it glints in the afternoon light. He runs the flat side across her abdomen, and she shivers convulsively.

"This meeting of ours will be quick 'an easy," he says softly, "or it will be slow and 'ard. Your choice."

He draws the knife across her stomach a second time, then twists it slightly, making the edge bite and sending shocks of pain into her abdomen. Her skin grows damp as warm blood oozes across it.

"Again," he says quietly, his voice little more than breath. "What was in that message?"

She's not a superspy or a superhero. Nothing in her life prepared her for this kind of torture. She'll tell him the truth, though there's little chance he'll believe it.

"The message was to the botnet itself," she says, tears streaming down her face.

He holds up the knife, showing her the line of blood along the blade.

"Keep talkin'" he prods.

"I was telling it… I was telling APRIL…"

"Yes," he says softly, encouragingly, as if prompting a child to say her prayers.

"I told APRIL there were people in this building trying to harm it. I told APRIL to protect herself."

Pryce's eyes widen for a moment, then he throws back his head in riotous laughter, his body convulsing as if he's never heard anything so hilarious.

"You told… your computer virus," he says between guffaws, "that we mean to 'urt *it*?"

"APRIL is millions of viruses," she says in a small voice, "all around the world. It's become intelligent."

Without warning, he twirls the knife and strikes her jaw with the handle. It lands like a hammer and something in her face cracks. Hot tears occlude her vision. She blinks, trying to clear them away.

"What do you take me for?" he shouts, wild eyes nearly popping from his skull. "You think I'm such an idiot that I'll believe whatever bullshit Ms. Hacker pulls out o' her cute little arse?"

"I'm not lying!" she says between sobs.

He gets up on his knees and unbuckles his trousers.

"You called it," he says. "We're doin' it the 'ard way."

A rumble emanates from beyond the window, like a tropical thunderstorm, except coming from everywhere at once. The sound rises. The glass begins to rattle.

"What the bloody hell?" Pryce mutters and hops off the table, peering through the window. Outside, the grounds go momentarily dark, as if experiencing the world's shortest solar eclipse. Then a blast, like a tornado, strikes the building, sending shards of glass flying and flipping Emily's desk sideways. Debris rains from every direction, and sections of the

ceiling plummet in an avalanche of shattered building material. She screams and closes her eyes. She's riding a surfboard
on a tidal wave.

A second blast shoves her forward and over. The desk is
atop her now. The maelstrom intensifies for what feels like
hours or maybe just seconds. When she finally opens her
eyes, she's face down with the desk resting on her back, the
stink of diesel fuel and hot plastic burning her nostrils.

She coughs and wriggles her wrists. The tape on her right
hand tears. She twists it until her hand comes loose. Then she
frees her other hand and both ankles. With effort, she wriggles from beneath the overturned desk and stands, gently
rubbing her cheek where Pryce hit her. Much of the ceiling is
missing, revealing the deep blue Hong Kong sky above. Pryce
lies on the debris-strewn floor, sprawled amid a puddle of
blood. A shard of aluminum window frame protrudes from
his neck. His eyes bulge, his face a death mask of surprise and
disbelief.

"I wasn't lying," she mutters to the corpse, then picks her
way through the gaps in the wall and over the rubble pile that
used to be the ground floor. A nearby shout makes her
crouch. A filthy, panicked guard stumbles past. Once he's out
of sight, she negotiates the debris field until she reaches the
lawn, then dashes into the forest undergrowth. The ruins of
the Rijndael building smolder behind her in the tropical afternoon. It resembles a junkyard made of twisted metal and
debris. And at the center of the wreckage, still recognizable,
are an aircraft's tires, motor, and wings.

"What have I done?" she whispers.

She finds the path and follows it back to the rendezvous
point. She suppresses a shout of joy as she approaches the
fence. A three-foot by three-foot section is missing. Xiuying
cut the wires and got everybody through!

The crunch and crackle of footsteps beyond the fence
make her jump in fright. She hides behind a tree. Two dark-

suited men emerge from the forest and approach the hole, guns raised and eyes wide with confusion. Were they searching for her friends? Did they find them before the chaos drew them back?

They pass within a few feet but seem too panicked to notice her. Once they're gone, she rushes through the fence and into the undergrowth, periodically checking the sun as it peeks through the forest canopy. She maintains a roughly northwesterly course, which should bring her to the road. But will her friends be gone? Did Xiuying leave like she was supposed to? She touches the gash on her abdomen, and her hand returns wet with blood. She probes her swelling cheek with her fingers. The pain is sharp and immediate. Will her wounds become infected like Seymour's? Can she handle this on her own? Will she escape Hong Kong alive?

The image of the wrecked Rijndael building returns to her mind. The botnet created the diversion she was seeking, but at what cost? Was that airplane wreckage she saw? Were there people aboard it? Did Ho make it out alive? What about Amit or the others? And what about all the other deaths she's caused? Her mother? Frank's men? Jeremy? Even if she escapes Hong Kong, can she live with so much blood on her hands?

She reaches the gravel road that the maps told her would be here. She's not sure where Ben might have parked, but north seems a good direction to try. She limps along the roadside, hugging the trees, doing her best to stay out of sight. After several minutes something glints in the late afternoon sun. It's a red taxi parked just off the road. She dashes toward it, and a tall woman rises from the driver's seat.

"Did you do that?" Xiuying says, pointing toward the black cloud rising above the treeline.

Emily nods sadly.

The rear window rolls down.

"You're such a wrecking ball," Seymour calls out.

She throws open the door and embraces him, bandages, stink, and all. He winces, then kisses her, his eyes wet with tears.

"This is indeed the mother of all Fubar capers," a deep voice calls from the front seat.

She turns to see Ben on the passenger side, smiling back at her.

"But I'm cautiously optimistic," he continues, "that we can stay ahead of the ensuing tsunami."

"Buckle up," Xiuying says, jumping behind the wheel and revving the engine.

"Your bad driving will get us killed," Kaylin says nervously.

"If we can live through that," Xiuying says, pointing toward the forest fire, "then we can live through anything."

Gravel sprays and the car lurches forward in a cloud of dust. Sitting between Seymour and Kaylin, Emily puts her head in her hands.

"I'm a monster," she says quietly.

Seymour embraces her with his good arm, and Kaylin rests a hand on her back.

"Without your insane plan," Seymour says quietly, "Kay and I would be dead."

"Dad would be proud of you," Kaylin adds. "He would call you a true Ng."

She nods and tries to smile. But the thought of being a real Ng, of inheriting Uncle Ip's troubled life, is cold comfort. She's so far from the future she'd hoped for. And it feels like it gets farther every day.

# A MONTH LATER

EMILY LEANS on the boat railing, watching the Mekong River roll serenely past. Ben looks up from his phone.

"Two aircraft hit your building," he says softly. "That's why you heard two explosions."

She looks out over the smooth brown water, and her shoulders begin to shake. She can't hold it in anymore. Can't bottle up the pain of knowing what she's done. She squeezes her eyes shut, but the tears won't stop. They pour down her cheeks.

"I– I killed two planeloads of people?" she says between sobs.

*I'm a monster,* she thinks. *Far worse than Uncle Ip or Director Chip, or any of them.*

How can she atone for such a heinous crime? How can she live with herself?

A hand rests on her back.

"APRIL's a thorough bitch," Ben says, "but nobody died on those planes."

She wipes her cheeks and faces him, confusion roiling her brain.

"How is that possible?"

"They were drones," he says with his signature broad

smile. Scaled-up versions of the Chinese GJ-11 and controlled with sophisticated AI. They were APRIL's kind of ride!"

"And the people on the ground? Those men who worked for Leonard Chip?"

Ben studies his phone again, scrolling with his thumb.

"Some survived, but Kaylin is unclear about who. We'll figure that out over time."

Was Ho among the survivors? And what about Amit? They didn't deserve death sentences for their complicity in Chip's horrid scheme.

"What do the governments know?" she asks.

"They know there are hackers," he says, still reading his phone, "that somebody hacked the Chinese drone, that NSA director Leonard Chip was in that building..." he pauses, still reading, then chuckles. "Kay's biggest takeaway is that the Chinese are *pissed*! They've ejected the entire American diplomatic corp."

APRIL is fueling misunderstanding between the two nations, planting false evidence, and creating misdirection to keep itself in the shadows. In its zeal to stay hidden, will it cause world war three?

"How do we live through this?" she asks glumly.

Ben leans on the railing next to her and folds his meaty hands.

"APRIL is an alien intelligence," he says, " driven by machine learning and hard-coded directives. And given what Kay and Xiuying told me, she's also constrained by a kind of 'risk budget,' a global level of exposure she will tolerate to achieve her goals."

He keeps calling APRIL "she." Does he view the botnet as a sort of living entity?

"Why does that matter?"

"We'll keep raising those stakes," he says, "keep her on the defensive."

It's coming back to Emily why she loves this crazy hippy so much.

"We'll distract her?" she asks.

"But not with problems she would solve by killing people," he adds. "We'll create low-level threats that force her to expend her risk budget in harmless ways. We won't leave her enough time to pursue us."

Emily looks out over the brown waters. The houses and buildings along the riverbank dwindle away, replaced by palm trees and rice paddies. They've reached rural Vietnam, their new home for now.

"We can't live under APRIL's shadow forever," she says quietly.

"Eventually, we'll have to go hard after her," he agrees. "The good news is that we're the most qualified APRIL hunters on earth."

"APRIL knows that too," she says glumly.

But Ben doesn't seem to notice her pessimistic appraisal. He's looking at something on the distant shore. She follows his gaze and sees Xiuying waving and jumping up and down. Next to her, Seymour is sitting in a wheelchair. It's the first time she's seen him since he went into the hospital. He's also waving, his lone skinny arm swinging back and forth enthusiastically. His other arm is missing; the sleeve is pinned up where it used to be.

"Are we succumbing to the singularity?" she asks.

"Like a black hole?" Ben replies, perhaps being intentionally obtuse.

"Like a runaway artificial intelligence. One that supersedes humanity and ushers in the machine age."

"What a sunny thought," he says with a chuckle, "and just when I found somebody who'd marry me."

She glances toward the beaming Xiuying, then back to Ben, who is also smiling. It's nice to find shelter in the calm port of normality. Maybe that's what Ben and Xiuying found with each other. She hugs him, her eyes again filling with tears.

"You are so freakin' lucky," she says, "you don't even know."

His eyes are damp too.

"Our relationship sorta messes up the whole monk thing," he says, clearly pleased and proud, "but I'll do my best not to make her regret it."

The boat bumps against the pier. Emily releases Ben and leaps ashore without waiting for the gangplank. She runs to Seymour and grabs him as he rises from the wheelchair. Maybe she did inherit Audrey's life. And Uncle Frank's. And her father's too. Maybe her remaining days will be difficult and short. But she'll cherish whatever time she has and the people she has to spend it with. And she'll do her best to atone for her mistakes—whenever she realizes that she's made them.

Seymour shudders slightly in her embrace, then wraps his single, slender arm around her.

"Is this where you thought you were headed?" he whispers.

"I've given up knowing where I'm headed," she replies, kissing him. "I'm just here. And that's good enough for now."

# ACKNOWLEDGMENTS

Writing a novel has been a dream and goal for over a decade, but I had no idea how difficult it would be in real life! Luckily, I'm surrounded by loving and supportive people who encourage me even when I'm not seeing any light at the end of the tunnel. That includes my wife, Elizabeth, who had more faith in the project than I did, and my sons, James, Nicholas, and Joseph, who showed surprising forbearance and patience with this crazy quest. I was also greatly aided by my developmental editor, Hannah VanVels Ausbury, who provided mountains of insight, critiques, and targeted praise that guided me toward a superior result. I'm grateful to my Beta readers who were so generous with their feedback, especially Tony, who immediately understood what the book could be; Alicia, who identified large but fixable problems; Jack, who has an ear for sci-fi; Akin, who found lots of bugs; Kevin, who called out both cultural and conceptual mistakes; Joe, who helped me make it more believable; Becky, whose honest encouragement was much appreciated; and Beth who found about a million errors. I'd like to thank my friend Amos, who kept asking me what the book was about, forcing me to finally make it about *something,* and my friend Olivia, who reviewed and helpfully critiqued an early draft. I also owe a great deal to my friend David, who shared his deep expertise and established both the mood and design language for the cover art, as well as graphic designer Matt Davies, who started with David's vision and expanded it into a magnificent finished product. Finally, I would like to thank Shaun, Rachel, Daniela, and the entire team at the Book Whisperer for getting this ball across the line!

Scott Olson

# ABOUT THE AUTHOR

 My work as an early leader in the Amazon Alexa project brought me close to the growing field of machine learning. I became certain that computers would mimic human intelligence to an astonishing degree, and though AI in fiction is a well-treaded territory, I found myself wanting to talk about technology that was closer to reality than the omnipotent Skynet. I imagined an imperfect, alien intelligence that wouldn't have predictable motives or airtight reasoning. That's what I saw in Amazon's nascent electronic brain, and that's what makes realistic AI so ripe for storytelling.

 facebook.com/scottolsonauth
amazon.com/stores/author/B0CCSV7FHN/about